ELV

Nick Nielsen does not live in East London although that is the address he normally gives when cornered. This is his first novel. After an interesting and occasionally successful working life as a semi-professional arm wrestler, he has now settled down to a career at the informal end of the alcohol distillation business. His friends describe him as generously proportioned and possibly fictitious.

S0-AAZ-681

Voyager

NICK NIELSEN

ELV

HarperCollins*Publishers*

Voyager
An Imprint of HarperCollins*Publishers*
77–85 Fulham Palace Road,
Hammersmith, London W6 8JB

The *Voyager* World Wide Web site address is
http://www.harpercollins.co.uk/voyager

A Paperback Original 1998
1 3 5 7 9 8 6 4 2

Copyright © Nick Nielsen 1998

The Author asserts the moral right to
be identified as the author of this work

A catalogue record for this book
is available from the British Library

ISBN 0 00 649888 4

This novel is entirely a work of fiction.
The names, characters and incidents portrayed in it
are the work of the author's imagination. Any resemblance to
actual persons, living or dead, events or localities is
entirely coincidental.

Set in Meridien

Printed and bound in Great Britain by
Caledonian International Book Manufacturing Ltd, Glasgow

All rights reserved. No part of this publication may be
reproduced, stored in a retrieval system, or transmitted,
in any form or by any means, electronic, mechanical,
photocopying, recording or otherwise, without the prior
permission of the publishers.

This book is sold subject to the condition that it shall not,
by way of trade or otherwise, be lent, re-sold, hired out or
otherwise circulated without the publisher's prior consent
in any form of binding or cover other than that in which it
is published and without a similar condition including this
condition being imposed on the subsequent purchaser.

ELV

ONE

From the point of view of an albatross there wasn't all that much to see in London that night. The albatross is renowned for its excellent night vision and its ability to fly silently but this one hadn't eaten for a whole day and the silence was broken by continual gurglings from its stomach. It might as well have been shouting out, 'Hey little snacks, stay under cover – there's a flying digestive system up here just longing to break you down into your component parts' for all the good it was doing. It was a young and somewhat incompetent albatross which had failed to listen carefully to its parents and day-dreamed its way through several important parts of its plummeting lessons, particularly the bit about last-minute deployment of dive brakes, so it was nursing a series of bruises, strained feathers and a crumpled beak that no longer seemed to open and close quite as smoothly as it should.

It wended its slow way over the roof-tops, hooting occasionally, tilting its blunt head from side to side to search the grass below with its big side-by-side eyes. It hadn't had an elephant since dawn yesterday and that had only been a little one.

London lay asleep between its two great rivers. It is, as everyone knows, a long, thin city tapering to a point where the rivers, now gleaming metallic in the moonlight, meet and pour into the bay. There was plenty of grass to search because London was a spread-out, unhurried city with lots of space between its buildings for parks and gardens, and the albatross decided to climb a bit higher as the rumbling from its belly was getting worse by the minute. From up here, the city was laid out below in a neat, right-angled grid of streets, and off to the west down Old Holborn and across Piccadilly Square the moonlight caught the metal mesh of the safety nets rigged along the river. The albatross looked at them. Had it been a lot more intelligent it might have wondered why they were still up when the wind warning had been cancelled. It might even have considered whether this meant another unexpected gale was on its way but instead it merely dismissed them as inedible, lifted its tail to crap and banked back towards the south.

Down in the government district, just beyond the Ministry of Knowledge, it saw a cluster of dandelions twitch and it circled round, watching intently. Yes, the flowers twitched again and the bird, dreaming of a nice plump elephant, folded its wings to drop down out of the sky. As plummets go, it was far from ideal. A certain sloppiness in wing-tip tuck-in started the albatross spinning as it fell and, forgetting what little it had been taught, it stuck out one leg in panic. This only made things worse. In the ideal, ten out of ten, grade A plus plummet, the claws are the only things that touch the ground just as the outstretched wings slow the bird to a halt. This one was a grade D double minus. The first part of the bird's anatomy to hit the ground was its bottom, closely followed by the back of its head. To be precise (and by pure accident) it wasn't the ground that its bottom hit so much as its intended prey which, seeing the flying accident approaching, had been completely unable to decide which way to run. The albatross sat up, checked to see it still had both wings and, feeling something squirming underneath it, turned round hopefully for a quick nip. There was a flash, an electrical crackle and it was left sprawling once more on its back with a beakful of plastic, squawking indignantly.

Its cries, borne on the wind, reached the sleeping ears of Trafalgar Hurlock in his new flat close by. Trafalgar was a good-looking young man of twenty-one and the same wind ruffled his dark curly hair on the pillow. His toes, sticking out of the end of his too-short bed, twitched as he stirred slightly and then went back into a deep dream. This was fine because he was meant to be getting plenty of sleep ready for his first day in his new job. The cries also reached the sleeping ears of Corrugated Rodney in his chair inside the Ministry of Knowledge. This was not at all fine because he was the Ministry night watchman and while he slept, terrible things were happening on the next floor down.

It was the year 95 SEGS and it was a time of plenty. The world was a peaceful place united under a world government which had only two real problems, the mice and the flies. However being a typical government, it was far more concerned with a totally different problem, namely how to get itself re-elected in the coming world general election. It hadn't done anything particularly wrong during the previous five years, in fact it hadn't done anything much at all. The trouble was that no one except the politicians cared anything at all about politics. In a world in which there was no starvation, no poverty, remarkably little illness and no unemployment, it didn't really seem to matter very much who was in charge (except to those who were). The two main parties were the World Democratic Party and the Democratic World Party and the opinion polls were currently running with the 'Don't Knows' at 99.9 per cent because even when someone was able to answer the question, 'Who are you planning to vote for?', the pollsters could rarely

9

remember the answer for long enough to put it down. The point one per cent who did know usually turned out to be members of the government who insisted on writing the answers down themselves on the pollsters' clipboards. On election day, voters tended to wander into the polling stations, stare for a while at their voting cards then start doodling pictures in the boxes instead of putting a cross. Most of them didn't even get as far as the polling stations. At the previous election in the year 90 SEGS, the counters had only been able to find eighty-three correctly filled-in voting slips in the whole world though there were another million which would have looked quite nice if they'd been carefully framed.

Previous centuries in mankind's long history had been marked by struggles against adversity, magnificent gallantry, ferocious wars or daring exploration. Out of this had come great art, scientific achievement, the advancement of knowledge and superb literature. This century, the first one since the Sleep, had instead been marked by a gentle, bumbling level of jovial incompetence interrupted only by the occasional moment of stark terror when a fly showed up or the wind rose. The result was that the greatest literary achievement of the previous ninety-five years was held to be a verse by the poet WEE WEE GOINGS (who wrote only in capital letters) which went:

> STARTLE, STARTLE LITTLE TWINK,
> OH DEAR, I'VE RUN OUT OF INK

and even then, some critics accused him of copying an earlier work he'd found in the databases.

In olden times there had been a saying 'All work and no play makes Jack a dull boy.' It also made Jack an accidental participant in one of the poorest bits of rhyming in the entire history of rhymes but in any case it had been completely forgotten by the year 95 SEGS. A more accurate and up-to-date version might have gone 'All play and no work makes Jack a bit of a dork,' though that wouldn't have rated much higher in the rhyming scheme of things.

The albatross's night-time adventure was marked only by a small crater in a lawn and one or two singed transistors when the TV alarm woke Trafalgar Hurlock from a delightful dream in which everything had been going wonderfully. The news soon put that right.

'Good morning Londoners,' said the newsreader, 'I'm Parallax Doubtful and this is the eight o'clock news brought to you by Metro Television sponsored by Magnaburst, the ground-to-air missile that makes houseflies wish they'd never come near you.' There was a brief, tuneless advertising jingle that forced Trafalgar out of bed and into the kitchen where he switched on the kettle, then he wandered back in to watch the TV again.

'Dominating this morning's news is last night's tragedy in Utopia. Three hundred people are missing in a blowaway on the outskirts of the capital city, Eldorado. We go over now to the Metro Network correspondent in Utopia, Cromwell Lamb.'

The picture cut to a well-tailored woman standing leaning into a blustery wind, lashed by a safety line to a strong section of railing.

'It was just after dark when the alarm system failed here in the northern suburbs of Eldorado,' she said in that specially important tone reporters used to imply that if they weren't there, the story probably wouldn't be bothering to happen. 'The crowd leaving the Rasputin Cinema had no idea that outside a force five wind was blowing, gusting to force six. They were unprepared for

11

the deadly danger that lay in wait for them when they reached the open street. Was this tragedy the fault of the emergency services? I put that question to the chief of the local Windguard . . .'

The kettle boiled and Trafalgar went in to make the coffee. When he came back, the news item was ending.

'. . . and so far, with dawn breaking over a grieving Utopia, all that's been found of them is their hats.'

They cut back to Parallax Doubtful in the studio who was pretending to read something vital. He looked up at the camera.

'A cultural disaster right here in London this morning. Overnight, alert security guards at the Ministry of Knowledge discovered tell-tale signs of a mouse attack.'

Trafalgar stiffened, his coffee forgotten. This was his Ministry – the place where he was about to start his new career, right over the street from his apartment block. It was, had he known, also a terrible fib. There had been absolutely nothing the slightest bit alert about the conduct of Corrugated Rodney, the security guard in question, who had only woken up to the mice's activities when one of them connected the end of his nose to a table lamp on its way back from the scene of the attack.

Doubtful continued, 'We understand that another page has gone from one of only three surviving books in the whole of England. Minister of Knowledge Bluto O'Barron was quickly on the scene, and a few minutes ago he held a news conference.'

The picture showed a short pompous man in formal clothes, surrounded by the media. Trafalgar studied the screen closely. This man was his new boss.

'I took personal control as soon as I heard the news,' the Minister was saying. 'Under my command, a detailed programme of damage limitation has gone into effect.'

'What's been attacked, Minister?' asked a reporter breathlessly.

'One whole page and the bottom quarter of a second page from the Mavis Greer text. We have it recorded in the electronic datastores of course but the original paper version is irreplaceable. I am able to tell you however that I have already taken decisive action. Some time ago, anticipating further events of this type, I set in motion a top-secret programme to deal with the problem at source.'

There was a chorus of 'What programme?' and 'Tell us more.'

'All in due course,' said O'Barron. 'You will have to be patient, but I can tell you this. Only the World Democratic Party is capable of decisive leadership of this sort and . . .'

'But isn't your party the Democratic World Party, Minister?'

'What did I just say?' said O'Barron, looking annoyed. 'Well, whatever.'

'Now,' said Parallax Doubtful, when they cut back to the studio again, 'here with the background on the Mavis Greer text and the significance of this attack is our heritage correspondent, D.K. Mussolini.'

'The Mavis Greer text is a priceless piece of world heritage,' said D.K.'s voice over close-ups of the familiar, brightly illustrated pages. 'One of only eight original paper books left in the entire world, it was first damaged in the year 64 SEGS shortly after being retrieved from a pre-Sleep vault. Since then it has been locked away in high security conditions at the Ministry to protect it against further attacks but last night it seems the mice discovered a new way in through the air conditioning system which normally protects it and the other volumes.'

D.K. Mussolini himself appeared on the screen – a

typical TV reporter, fashionably short with blow-dried hair and a manly, high-pitched voice. 'I understand from conservation staff that the page destroyed last night was page nineteen, the second page of the so-called "finger food" section of the book. If that is so, then it is a severe loss. Mavis Greer's book *The Ricicles are Twicicle as Nicicle Guide to Easter Party Catering* contained much to interest scholars about the mysteries of pre-Sleep life. Page nineteen was thought by some to hold the clue to the true identity of the ricicle. Now we may never know. Parallax?'

'Thanks, D.K.,' said Parallax. 'Sport now and last night saw England take an unexpected gold medal in the field events at the O'Limpic Games. Despite the sweltering heat in Ireland this year, Heinrïch Dumas set a new record of seven feet three inches in the standing start vertical jump.'

Trafalgar watched the recording with close attention. Dumas bent his knees and sprang upwards with extraordinary grace. Trafalgar had shown promise at school in the vertical jump but he'd never managed to beat his own height.

'Fly patrols found an egg cluster six miles due west of London last night. It was successfully destroyed. There were no reports of fly activity in the area during the night,' said Doubtful, then he gave the camera a knowing smile. 'And, finally, wacky explorer Thorm Severdahl has failed again in his efforts to establish what happened to all the Gullivers. Severdahl believes he can find out the secret of their disappearance by putting to sea in the same type of vessel they used. For months now, he and his crew have laboured to produce a sea-going craft following instructions they have found in ancient datastore records. Yesterday they put it to the test but they didn't get far. Their twin-hulled vessel broke up on launching.'

A short sequence of pictures showed a number of men swimming for their lives amid terrifying waves while large white lumps of the boat's hull dissolved rapidly around them.

Doubtful came back on with a poorly suppressed grin. 'The catameringue, as old records call it, was constructed in the traditional way from sugar and egg white. Severdahl still insists that the Gullivers sailed off in the direction of modern Mordor in the Traffic Islands. He says he's going to try again, this time using sugar *cubes*.' He paused and lifted a sardonic eyebrow. 'Well, I guess the world needs a few weirdos. That's all from us. Next news in one hour's time at seven o'clock.'

Trafalgar switched off rather violently, annoyed at the newsreader's sneering tone. He had a lot of respect for Severdahl. There weren't many other people really interested in history these days, that is history beyond the basic level you got in school. In fact you could almost say there weren't any. Trafalgar had gone to university, like every other student, to have a good time, hoping to come out reasonably well qualified in practical drinking, lead guitar and applied shopping. Practical drinking tended to be a messy business and it was when he first tried to put his clothes through the washing machine that he first stumbled over history as a subject. Unable to find out where to put the soap or how to open the door, he'd typed 'washing machine' into the datastores looking for instructions. The instructions were there but, as so often happened, they weren't as useful as they might have been.

'To open the door,' the message on the screen said, 'open the door. Put the soap in the soap container. To locate the soap container, look for the container into which you have just put the soap. That is the soap container.'

He thumped the keyboard in irritation and it skipped

to the next entry which was 'Washington, George' and he read it out of idle interest.

'George Washington,' it said, 'became Emperor of India following the assassination of Julius Caesar. He showed his intelligence as a child when he refused to lie under his father's cherry tree while it was being chopped down.'

Until that moment Trafalgar, like almost everyone else alive at that time, had lived entirely in the present. Now he had seen a little, unexpected glimpse of the past and it fascinated him. His interest in history was born at that moment. It nearly died again the next day when the dean of his college, baffled by his request to transfer at once to the history faculty, tried to find it on a map of the university and utterly failed. A week later, Trafalgar was shown the way to a small wooden shed. Over the door hung an unconvincing sign whose paint was still wet saying DEPARTMENT OF HISTORICAL STUDIES. Inside was a datastore terminal, a chair and, for some reason that was never satisfactorily explained, an exercise bicycle. Here, Trafalgar was left entirely to himself for the next three years. When, at the end of that time, he showed up for his examination, he turned the paper over to find there was only one question.

It said, 'Write about anything you like.'

He was asked to mark it himself and after long consideration he awarded himself a first-class honours degree with distinction which was enough to get him a job in the new Ministry of Knowledge.

The Ministry had been established in 90 SEGS for no particularly good reason except that there seemed to be a lot of information in the pre-Sleep datastores and someone thought it would be a good idea if they started to sort it all out. For the previous ninety years, ever since Wake-Up Day, very few people had really bothered to look deeply into the datastores. They'd only concerned

16

themselves with the really vital information like how to defreeze the pizzas. Quite a few years passed before they got bored with all twenty-eight varieties of frozen food on offer and it was only then that anyone started delving deeper into the electronic records but there was such a mass of it that so far they had barely scratched the surface.

From today, delving into those records was to be Trafalgar's new job so he dressed neatly, took a deep breath and headed for the Ministry.

Bluto O'Barron, the Minister of Knowledge, was half-way through a difficult cabinet meeting in his large office on the first floor.

The cabinet in which the world government met was made of rather nice mahogany with cabriole legs and curly brass handles. Every cabinet member had one and it contained the TV screen which linked them up through the outernet to each other's offices spread across the globe. As there were more than five hundred cabinet ministers, it didn't make communications all that much easier as they hated waiting for their turn to speak which could easily take a couple of hours to arrive, if it arrived at all. The President was speaking. The President controlled everybody else's microphones so she could go on speaking as long as she wanted. That was one of the good things about being President, as well as the big house and the short working hours.

'I need hardly remind you all,' she said, 'of the priority facing us at this crucial juncture in our party's history. If we don't win the coming election then we will lose it. I have no wish to see the World Democratic Party . . .' there was a faint whisper from somewhere out of range of the camera '. . . the Democratic World Party consigned to the dustbin of history. We must therefore focus on the KEY ISSUES, the issues that will make people come out and vote for us. Fear, ladies and gentlemen, fear is the key and what is it that people are afraid OF? Wind and flies. If we deal effectively with those two then we will have won the hearts and minds of the voters and the Democratic . . . er, the World . . . the Party will sweep to glorious victory once more. So,' she said, scowling into the camera, 'I want IDEAS and I want them NOW.'

Bluto O'Barron had been passing his time as he listened to the President wondering what in the world he was going to do to dig himself out of the hole he'd created for himself during his TV interview about the mouse attack on the Mavis Greer text. He had no secret plan for dealing with the mice. He'd made it up on the spot because he couldn't think of anything else to say. Now though, in a blinding flash, he had his big idea.

Trafalgar, whose future life was to be entirely changed by the idea O'Barron was in the middle of having, was in the middle of a further life-changing experience of his own. He'd spent the first hour of his new job filling in all the standard forms.

Date of Birth: 1.3.74.
Address: Flat 301, Appendicitis Court, London.
Father's name: Jasmine.
Mother's name: Hepplewhite.
Favourite colour: Blue.
Height:

He'd been guilty of a tiny little fib about his height due entirely to vanity. He was really six foot six, but he'd written down six foot five and a half to make it sound better. What happened to him soon afterwards was a direct consequence of his misfortune in being too tall. Tall people soon learnt to walk short to avoid all the heightist comments. After doing the forms he was sent to meet his new department head, Mr Lemmon, and it was as he was hunching along a corridor, moving with his usual awkward, curved shuffle, that he failed to notice a mouse trap on the floor in front of him. He stepped right on the shiny paper bait and, feet shooting wildly out from under him, ricocheted off a drinking fountain to career head first and hopelessly off-balance straight towards a pair of double glass doors. He stuck both hands out desperately but just before he reached the doors, they opened and a girl appeared directly in front of him. He came to a sudden, cushioned stop with his hands clutching two parts of her anatomy that a nicely brought up young man such as himself would never have considered clutching without first being formally introduced. However, he barely had time to let go before she swung round, seized him in a powerful grip by one leg and the front of his shirt and, with scarcely a pause, threw him straight out of the nearest open window.

Trafalgar landed on his back with a loud shriek in the flowerbed outside. Curious faces peered out of windows at him as he lay there gasping, trying to get his breath back. He lifted his head and to his horror he saw the girl run out of the front entrance and rush towards him. He tried to heave himself up and she reached out to grab him again. Writhing out of her grasp, he scrambled to his feet and began to run.

'Stop,' she shouted, 'come back here.'

No fear, he thought and fled. He turned his head and saw her pelting after him. He might have kept ahead of her, though he hadn't really got his breath back but she launched herself at his ankles in a flying tackle and brought him down headlong into an ornamental pond. He rose, soaked and slimy, out of the water, waving his arms to keep her away, stepped backwards and fell over again.

'Stay there,' she said crossly. 'I was only trying to apologise.'

He blinked at her, as she stood there frowning at him with her short blonde hair and bright blue eyes, and realised that she was incredibly beautiful. The next thing he realised was that he was looking straight into her eyes, not downwards like he usually had to. This was not just a completely gorgeous girl, it was a completely gorgeous girl of not far off his own height. His voice didn't seem to be working properly.

'Um,' he said decisively.

'I'm Anya,' she said, holding out her hand and he managed to stop himself flinching. 'Don't let me hear you call me Tits. Ever.'

'Ur?' he said.

'That's what they call me around the place when they think I can't hear them. I can't think why.'

Trafalgar could, but it seemed a bad moment to tell her so he just grinned weakly.

'Wuh,' he said firmly.

She looked at him curiously. 'Stand tall, big boy,' she said, walking off, and coming from her it didn't sound like an insult for once.

He arrived in Mr Lemmon's office, dripping wet and trailing pond weed. Lemmon raised an eyebrow.

'Do you regard this as the proper way to call on your superior, Hurlock?' he demanded.

'No, Mr Lemmon. I . . . er . . . I was chased by . . . that is I had a little accident with a fish pond and I . . . er . . .'

'Go and clean yourself up, then get to work. Your desk is down there at the end of the room.'

It was complete bliss to see Anya working away at another desk. It was complete misery ten minutes later when he heard her called to Lemmon's office and saw her, on her return, pack up her desk and vanish out of his life.

'Who?' they said when he asked about her. 'Anya? Oh, you mean Tits, the great big girl.'

It was the usual heightist nonsense but he gritted his teeth.

'Where is she?'

'Don't know. Got drafted. Some hush-hush job. Good thing too. More space for the rest of us.'

Gone. His reason for existence. Vanished as if she had never been.

Lemmon had set him to work on the dullest of jobs, a thorough investigation of the Bible as preserved electronically. The next few days crawled by. There was of course not one single original paper version in existence and everyone agreed that the electronic text in the datastores was a bit hard to follow. There were two schools of thought on this. The fundamentalists insisted that every word of it was accurate and literally true and if anyone couldn't understand it then that was their fault. The rest thought that part of the datastore must have been struck by lightning.

The first book, Genesis, was fairly straightforward – detailed instructions on how you could make a paper aeroplane in seven days, followed by ten ideas for creative things you could do with an apple. Exodus was a long list of incomprehensible dates and times like 'BA001. Heathrow 0915. JFK 2105,' which filled eight hundred pages. The book of Numbers was worse. No one he knew had ever managed to read the whole of Numbers. It started, '20,305, 8.6, 104, 92.8% . . .' and just went on for chapter after chapter in the same way. The New Testament was more interesting because in that came the first references to Gullivers, and Trafalgar was very interested in Gullivers. He had concentrated on the history of the

Gullivers right through his time at university because the disappearance of the Gullivers was the single greatest mystery of the post-Sleep era.

As the datastores told it, when the world had gone to Sleep there had been two races cohabiting on the planet – the people and the Gullivers. The Gospel of Saint Jonathan the Swift and the Epistle of the Apostle Ipustle to the Opestles contained fragments of the story of the old days – certainly enough to confirm that the Gullivers were man-like in shape but enormously larger. There could be no question as to their existence, indeed you only had to use your eyes because they had left just a few of their structures and artefacts behind them. Trafalgar's Uncle Doris had a swimming pool made out of an extremely rare Gulliver lavatory bowl complete with an exquisite plastic clip on the rim containing the remains of some exotic substance smelling faintly of lavender.

The fact remained, however, that when everybody woke up from the Sleep there was absolutely no sign of any of the Gullivers. They had simply disappeared. Trafalgar had spent a great deal of effort cross-referencing everything he could find in the files. There hadn't been very much, just some scholarly disagreement over basic issues like the real present-day location of the land Saint Jonathan knew as Lilliput. Some insisted it was simply an archaic name for England, others placed it in Africa in some far-off time when that continent wasn't the frozen haven of penguins it had since become.

If only the libraries still existed, Trafalgar thought regretfully but then he reflected, in the old words, that it was no use crying in the deep blue sea.

Distracted by thoughts of Anya and bored stiff by what he'd been set to do, he pressed the wrong key on his keyboard and brought up entirely the wrong file on to the screen. He found himself looking, to his utter amazement, at an image of something he'd never seen before. It was a great tower, soaring to a single spike. On the front at the top was a white circle with numbers around it but what was astonishing was the text underneath it which said, 'Big Ben, the famous London landmark. The name refers to the bell that strikes the hours though it is commonly misused for the clock-tower itself.'

Now Trafalgar was very used to seeing Big Ben; indeed he could see it out of his window just by craning his head to the right and it didn't look the slightest bit like this. As for the description, that made no sense either. Clock-tower? That wasn't a clock. Clocks had neat numbers all in a row that changed every minute. Was there a mistake? It said quite clearly 'the famous London landmark'.

He left it on the screen while he went for a cup of coffee to think about it. He had to show this to someone. It was clearly an error of some sort and the datastores were supposedly foolproof. They were never wrong, that was what you were taught as soon as you got to school. It was one of life's certainties, something that everyone knew to be true. If any sort of mistake had crept into the datastores then that was a very serious matter. This was one for his supervisor. His mind made up, he tapped on his supervisor's door. Lemmon wasn't at all pleased to be interrupted.

'Sorry, Mr Lemmon,' Trafalgar said diffidently, 'there's something I think you ought to look at.'

'Can't you see I'm busy?'

Trafalgar looked hard at the desk, which was bare and the computer screen which was off. He had been brought up to be truthful.

'No,' he said.

'This had better not be a waste of time,' Lemmon said menacingly and got to his feet.

Inside the hollow walls, a small horde of mice had gathered, tails linked to savour the moment. A message from the senior mouse passed across their shared consciousness.

'Remember! The secret of good comedy is timing.'

The senior mouse wore a battered army helmet in matt black with a white skull and crossbones on the front. It waited until it heard the two men leave the office then it gave a single command, 'Go!' and the horde scattered to echoes of tinny giggling.

Trafalgar couldn't believe what he saw happening when he got back to his terminal though afterwards there were times when he wondered whether he had been hallucinating. On the screen, something was changing. In the bowels of the supposedly untouchable datastore, mischief was definitely afoot. As he looked, letters in the text were blinking out of existence before his eyes, being replaced one by one. For a second he could see them changing then, just as Lemmon came up beside him, the evidence was gone, the process came to an end and the new words steadied.

'The Statue of Little Berty, the famous New York landmark,' it now said. 'The name refers to the bull that stroked the horse though it is commonly misused for the cockerel itself.'

'Well?' snapped Lemmon as he peered at it. 'What's this about?'

Trafalgar looked at the screen but no words came.

Lemmon read it himself. 'Ah,' he said. 'Interesting. An image from the lost city of New York. And some people still insist it was a mythical place. But you really didn't have to get me all the way down here just to show me that. A simple report is the proper procedure. You've interrupted valuable work.' His eyes challenged Trafalgar to disagree.

24

'Er,' Trafalgar began, 'that wasn't really what I wanted to show you.'

'What then?'

'That's not what it said before.'

Lemmon squinted at him dangerously. 'What did it say?'

Trafalgar told him and Lemmon's look took on a manic edge. 'Air too thin up there, is it?' he said nastily. 'A touch of vertigo perhaps. It's time you came down to earth.'

Three heightist jokes in one go. Trafalgar controlled himself searching for a reply that wouldn't get him fired.

'Forget about it,' said Lemmon. 'It can't change, it's a CD-ROM. You do know what that means, don't you?'

'Completely Determined Really Opinionated Memory,' Trafalgar quoted quickly.

'That's right. That means it makes up its mind then it sticks to it, Hurlock. It took years of painstaking work for the old ones to put this lot together. You're not going to tell me it can suddenly *change*, just like that.'

He looked again at the screen. 'You'd better get on to this,' he said, 'this cock and bull stuff, not to mention the horse. It's obviously some historical reference we don't know about. See what you can find out and no more flights of fancy.'

Trafalgar looked back at the screen and before his eyes, the word 'cockerel' blinked out and was replaced by 'crocodile'.

'Look,' he said in excitement, 'there it goes again,' but when he turned back, Lemmon was already halfway down the corridor.

He thought he could hear the faintest sound of mocking laughter.

TWO

He saw the mouse only an hour later, out of the corner of his eye. There was a tiny blur of colour down on the floor and it was definitely moving. He turned his head very, very slowly. Something was creeping furtively around the corner of a filing cabinet. The filing cabinet was an indescribably dull colour of the sort designed to depress the spirits of any office worker who came to work in an unsuitably joyful mood. The mouse was a broadly similar colour and it might have got away without being seen but for its hat.

The hat in question was an orange party hat set at a jaunty angle and that was a dead giveaway. Mice could never resist wearing silly hats.

Trafalgar watched the mouse like an albatross, then inched his hand out towards the brick that stood on every desk for just such an emergency. He turned his head carefully, slowly swivelling his eyes as far to the left as they'd go until he seemed to be looking through the ghost of his nose. He could see it still, creeping slowly along. Definitely a mouse. His fingers closed over the brick.

Trafalgar was the kindest and gentlest of men and he'd been brought up by his parents in the belief that he should do nothing to harm any of the world's small selection of species so he used up precious seconds looking all round the target area just in case there should be any ants or spiders in the line of fire. When he was satisfied that the coast was clear, he took careful aim at the mouse and hurled the brick with all the force he could bring to

26

bear straight at it. The mouse had excellent peripheral vision. It saw the movement and it was too quick for him. Rearing up, it swerved while the hurtling brick was in mid-air, spinning round in its own length just in time to dodge the impact as the brick crashed into the floorboards. Then it raced off, screaming with laughter, into the darkness behind the filing cabinet as people at the nearby desks, startled by the noise, leapt to their feet.

Trafalgar shook his head, looking at the damage he'd just inflicted on the Ministry's floorboards. They were high quality balsa wood, as hard as nails, but the brick had left a nasty gouge across two of them and it had all been for nothing. He knew better than to go after the mouse. There'd be a fresh hole somewhere in there and it would be well away by now. He looked at the trap behind the cabinet. The bait was top-quality stuff – a large, inviting piece of genuine, book-specification paper but it was completely untouched.

The bloody mice were getting too clever by half.

He bent down to inspect the dent. Light from the window burst across the floor as the sun came out from behind a cloud and he saw that he hadn't after all missed completely because the remains of the mouse's tail lay next to the mark in the floorboards. He picked up the limp, stringy thing by one end and inspected it. It was smooth to the touch, thin and dull-coloured, ragged at the end where it had been torn from the mouse's body. He looked closely at that part where the tiny, ripped strands of copper wire shone inside the insulation. Three-amp, two-core insulated micro-flex. Standard stuff though the bigger mice sometimes had a plug fitted on the end.

The rules were clear. All sightings to be reported immediately, so he went to the intercom and began pressing buttons.

'Pest Control? Trafalgar Hurlock here. Room 16, Floor 3. I've had a mouse.'

'You don't say,' said the voice at the other end with an inflection that said it could barely be bothered and was only doing this job until the talent scouts caught up with its new phone number. 'A mouse? Fancy that. Whatever next? I do declare. What colour?'

'Mousy. How many other colours do they come in?'

'Hat?'

'Orange, crepe paper.'

'Two button or three button?'

'Two.'

'Means of locomotion?'

'Eh?'

'How was it moving?'

'It had legs but it was using its ball.'

'Tail?'

'Well, not any more.'

'Was it laughing?'

'Of course it was laughing. They're always laughing.'

'We'll send the team.' The voice implied maybe, if it could be bothered, if all the other fascinating matters jostling for its attention didn't condemn this tedious exchange to oblivion but Trafalgar knew that was only for his benefit. Mice were taken very, very seriously and especially by the Ministry, especially after last night's raid.

That was borne out five minutes later when the alarms started sounding.

'Attention, all staff. The Ministry is being closed for emergency fumigation. All staff are to leave now. Please collect work assignments before departure for completion at home until further notice.'

Lemmon was waiting to hand Trafalgar his assignment in person and that was when Trafalgar began to suspect

28

that his information about the tampering with the data-base had gone down very badly indeed.

Back in his flat on the third floor of Appendicitis Court, Trafalgar picked up a fresh slate and sighed. He hated slates but standard operating procedure under mouse quarantine was that you kept your screen switched off and used a slate because the mice couldn't eat it. Plasti-sheets would have been quite safe, Trafalgar thought, but rules were rules and nobody was taking chances. The quarantine area stretched in a wide circle round the Ministry and his flat was well inside it. He scratched away and the sound set his teeth on edge. He also hated the job Lemmon had handed him. It felt very like a punishment.

'A stitch in time,' he wrote, 'saves closing the stable door after the horse has bolted.'

This was like being back at school. 'Analyse the follow-ing traditional sayings,' his assignment from Lemmon had said. 'Produce rational explanations and, Hurlock, *try* to keep your mind on the job in hand.'

He looked at what he'd written.

'A stitch in time . . .'

The scratching of the slate pencil set his teeth on edge. 'The meaning of this saying is generally accepted,' he added, 'and is thought to show that some of our ancestors before the Sleep weren't very honest. It is generally taken to mean that if you can fake the right physical symptoms at the right moment you'll probably get away with not doing the job on hand. In this case pretending to have a cramp in your side prevents you having to undertake a task made hazardous by the possible sudden return to their place of shelter of large, over-excited animals.'

He turned his head to look out of the window as doubt nagged at him. How many times in a lifetime would you *need* a saying like that? Was that really the sort of thing

29

they used to say to each other before the Sleep? Sayings today were much more to the point, 'Fly's coming, I'm running,' for example, or 'Force five, you'll survive, force six, shelter quick.' Okay, you could argue with the rhyme but the sense was clear enough.

Granted it was a time of plenty but it was also a time of high winds.

Mice apart, he was quite glad to be working at home, not at the Ministry. It gave him a chance to let his thoughts roam freely without anyone looking over his shoulder or laughing derisively at his ideas. He turned to the next one in the long list headed 'Ancient sayings'. There was a note across the bottom from his supervisor. 'Brief explanations by tomorrow please and DON'T get distracted.'

A rolling stone spoils the broth.

He looked at the familiar words. 'While this is usually taken to mean,' he wrote, 'that unsuitable activities such as cooking and skittles should be kept apart, in Holland a version of this saying is regarded as an ancient safety instruction warning against building your kitchen in an avalanche danger area.' They had a lot of avalanches in the mountains of Holland, he knew, so you could say it made a limited sort of sense.

So far, so good but the one after it was tricky. 'Too many cooks gather no moss.' Nowhere in the data banks was there any evidence that moss had ever featured in pre-Sleep cookery. The Mavis Greer ricicles text, with all its deep but obscure insights into the lifestyles of their pre-Sleep ancestors, made no mention of it, though, because the precise ingredients of the ricicle itself remained a mystery, it was just possible it could have contained an element of moss.

The surviving fragments of text of the fabled *Microwave Low-Fat Snacks for Video Watchers* which had perished in a mouse attack in the year Trafalgar was born also failed to mention the culinary relevance of moss. Across the other side of the Mediterranean in Antarctica, they still had three books, preserved in a tungsten-steel security vault, but they were all about dieting.

Trafalgar was starting to develop a private theory, one that would probably get him laughed to scorn if he dared mention it. He was beginning to think he didn't trust everything in the computer datastores.

Most of the major things, the geography and history, were presumably all right or people would have found out by now. It stood to reason, he reckoned, that the old-timers would have gone to great pains to protect all that properly during the Sleep but since the Big Ben incident he was starting to suspect that there just might have been something odd going on around the edges.

After all, the mice must have a *reason* for their behaviour.

There was nothing a mouse liked doing more than creeping up to a computer and sticking its tail into the disk connections. That was definitely the easiest time to catch them. They'd just be sitting there, shaking with helpless laughter, and you could pick them up with your bare hands. If it wasn't so annoying it would be quite funny really.

If only the books hadn't gone, it would be so easy to check his theory.

It occurred to Trafalgar that perhaps the job he'd been given wasn't as boring as it looked. Perhaps here, in something as simple as these old sayings, there might lie a little part of the proof. He looked at the long list with fresh interest, reached for another slate and began to scratch furiously.

He worked his way down the list. A fool and his money make light work. A friend in need doesn't make a summer. Don't cross your chickens before they're hatched. Two swallows are soon parted. Many hands make nine. What were they, these sayings? Were they the deep insights of an ancient and wise people or were they, as he was starting to think, the sort of thing that would get you fired from the Guild of Cracker Motto Writers for wilful lack of attention to detail. A revolutionary idea struck him. He was deep in thought and well into his tenth slate half an hour later when the doorbell rang.

He opened the door to see the short, immaculately dressed figure of his boss peering at him.

'Oh. Mr Lemmon. What a surprise.'

Lemmon swished past him into the room, turned round and looked up at him commandingly. Trafalgar already found him underbearing and rude. Polite people didn't do that to you, didn't call attention to the excessive height that was, after all, nothing more than a cruel trick played on you by your genetic inheritance.

'Came to see what you were getting up to,' he barked. 'Out of sight, idle hands, eh?'

'Ah, well, it's funny you should say that, Mr Lemmon, I think I've . . . um . . . got something interesting.'

Face to face and feeling at a big disadvantage, Trafalgar tried to bend his knees without making it too obvious.

Lemmon gave him a suspicious look. 'What is it this time?'

'Do sit down, please.'

Lemmon made an ostentatious show of arranging his clothes carefully as he sat in the chair with much rustling and gathering in. When he'd finished, he looked up at Trafalgar.

'Well? Go on.'

'It's these sayings. You know most of them don't make much sense?'

'That's why you're working on them, Hurlock. If they made sense you wouldn't have to, would you?'

'Well, what I did was, I split some of them up and joined up different halves with . . .'

'You split them up? You're meant to be explaining them, not destroying them. Research, Hurlock, rational, reasoned research is about finding meanings for things. Research isn't cutting things up. That's known as making paper chains, Hurlock, not research.'

'Yes, I know, Mr Lemmon, but you see, I'm starting to think somehow they've got muddled up. If you sort of stop them halfway and join them up differently, they seem to work a lot better. I mean, look, I got all kinds of new sayings which make far more sense.'

'I hope you're not going to waste my time.' The words didn't bode well but Lemmon was now watching him with an intent expression.

'Well, here's two I've sort of reassembled. "Don't count your chickens on a busy street." I suppose that comes under the heading of elementary safety really. Then there's "Two swallows spoil the broth."'

'Meaning?'

'I suppose it means you shouldn't drink your soup too quickly because you'll burn your mouth and you won't appreciate it.'

Trafalgar felt very nervous inside. He suddenly wished devoutly that he'd just done what his boss had said, asked no questions and stuck to the job in hand.

There was a long silence in which Lemmon stared at him hard then he said something very surprising.

'Well, now, Trafalgar,' he said with an altogether different tone, 'how do you think something like that might have happened?'

It felt as if a Rottweiler had stopped in mid-attack to offer him a toffee. Trafalgar? Lemmon never used first names. At work they said it was because he hated his own first name, that he thought people would laugh at him because it was cissy, almost girlish. He kept it very quiet but everyone knew that the G stood for 'Genghis' though Lemmon was inclined to pretend it was something macho like 'Gardenia'.

Trafalgar knew all about macho names. His parents had clearly hoped he'd be a hero when they named him. They'd told him the story enough times, Lord Horatio Trafalgar with the two tin legs, who'd refused to interrupt his game of bowls before flying off in his Spitfire to drop the Trojan Horse on Waterloo Station, bringing the Wars of the Roses to a sudden end. It was a story that had echoed, unchanged, down the ages from before the Sleep, a story you could still be proud of.

Lemmon was looking at him searchingly.

'I don't know for sure . . .'

'But you have an idea?'

'I just have this suspicion.'

'Go on.'

'I suspect the mice might have messed up a lot more than we think.'

There. It was out. He hadn't meant to say it. It wouldn't be 'Trafalgar' now, it would be straight back to 'Hurlock' with an added snarl and no chance of promotion. Regretting he'd ever opened his mouth, he knew Lemmon wouldn't let him forget it for a long time.

'That's very interesting, Traff,' said Lemmon with a strange smile.

Traff? Not even his real friends called him Traff. In fact nobody had ever called him Traff before. If this went on, Lemmon would be calling him 'T' next and then what? He found he didn't much like being called 'Traff'. He looked at his boss uncomprehendingly, then blinked as an expression of horror came over Lemmon's face.

A faint, far-off buzz could just be heard.

The hairs on the back of Trafalgar's neck stood to attention. The buzz got rapidly louder. Lemmon stood up uncertainly, with a questioning look.

Sirens began to howl across the river. Slow, very slow, Trafalgar thought. This one must have caught the listeners napping. The sound galvanised him into action. He grabbed his helmet from the peg where it always hung in readiness, pushed the gas mask over his face and headed for the balcony.

Housefly alert.

He remembered Lemmon. 'Shtdwwwnderblldng,' he said.

'What?'

Traff took the gas mask off again. 'The shelter's downstairs under the building,' he said.

Lemmon didn't need a second hint.

Housefly.

The most frightening word in the language. The word mothers used to terrify their children into good behaviour when all else failed. The word that had prompted a million nightmares.

Housefly.

Stupid name really, he thought, not even accurate. Was it possible that the flies had ever been the size of a house? It seemed absurd to suggest they could ever have been so small. These days they were more the size of a cathedral or a fairly large factory even. No houses got anywhere near that size.

Out on the balcony, he tore the covers off the gun. All around his neighbours were coming out too, looking out across the wide expanse of the River Thames to where puffs of white vapour already dotted the sky. The drone was louder and suddenly he could see it, an ominous speck growing gradually bigger – a blackish blob now growing into a dark lump. Not just a dark lump but a dark lump coming straight towards him.

He gulped. Houseflies were the least manoeuvrable creatures alive in the world today. Two thousand tons travelling at fifty miles an hour didn't make for agility. If a fly was heading for you, it was time to move house before the fly did it for you. Still, orders were clear. Only shoot when it's over open parkland or the river. You didn't want to be underneath one of *these* babies when it came down. Prepared by regular drill, he primed the gun, checked the Flit shells in the magazine, seeing his neighbours to each side going through the same routine.

It was at times like this that he worried about the orders. It was all very well, trying to bring it down in the river, but what if they only damaged it? He'd seen the result when an out-of-control housefly nosedived into a building and it wasn't pretty. Trafalgar gritted his teeth.

They weren't meant to get this far. Someone in the outer defences had really slipped up. It was six months since he'd seen one this close. There'd be another search-and-destroy mission when this was all over, looking for a new hatching of fly eggs, but there was a lot of country-side out there and finding all the egg clutches, even though they could reach fifty feet across, was like looking for a needle in a camel.

Nearly close enough. Wait until you see the blacks of their eyes, that was what the instructors said. The buzz was making his windows rattle in sympathy. The fly reached the river and a fusillade of shells burst around it from the far shore. A missile exploded in a big yellow puff just behind it. Trying to stop his hands shaking, Trafalgar set the range, sighted carefully and squeezed the trigger. The guns on either side of him started firing at the same moment and more clouds of vapour burst all round the huge, vibrating insect.

This fly was a tough one, or it had learnt to hold its breath. It kept going through it all. Halfway across the river, then three quarters. Trafalgar stopped firing. Let it go, he thought, they can try again when it gets to the park or if they don't get it there, the guns can bring it down in the other river. At least it doesn't look like it's planning to land.

But for Chrysler things would have been fine. Chrysler lived on the floor below Trafalgar and he'd only turned sixteen a couple of weeks earlier so this was the first time he'd been allowed to man the family gun. He'd done the gunnery instruction course but Chrysler was a wild lad and he'd spent most of the time fancying the girl at the desk next to him. He'd listened to all the exciting bits like how to shoot the gun but he hadn't paid too much attention when they came to the boring bits about precautions and regulations. Now the excitement got the better of him and he couldn't resist giving it one last burst. You could have called it a good shot so long as by 'good' you meant 'catastrophic' and 'suicidal'.

He hit it smack on the mouth, if that's how you can describe something that looks more like a garbage compacter. Chrysler gave a yell of triumph as the drone of its wings stopped abruptly, then realised nobody else was yelling.

The silence all around him was the sort of silence you get when the pilot of your airliner announces in a cheery, isn't-this-fun sort of voice that one of the wings has fallen off.

For a moment, the only sound was the swish of the fly's passage through the air and the gurgling ululations of its flabby body. Then a single voice seemed to rise from all the balconies where anxious eyes were calculating its trajectory: 'Oh noooooooooooo.'

Trafalgar watched, horrified, as it dipped sharply, rolled over on its back and started to fall.

It could have been worse, just. The building it hit was the Ministry of Knowledge, right where Trafalgar had been working so it was just as well that it was completely empty, waiting for fumigation. There was a tremendous crash as the fly knocked the parapet and half the roof into the street and ricocheted off at a crazy angle. The impact brought it briefly back to life so that, wings beating wildly in a final paroxysm, it shot up in the air, streaked down the Thames towards the open water before plunging down to spit itself with a liquid crunch on one of the spikes of Big Ben's crown, where it came to rest like a giant sausage on a cocktail stick.

Trafalgar stared up at the far-off shape, the real Big Ben, not the strange structure he had glimpsed so briefly in the datastore records. Until that moment, he'd never seen any real use in keeping the vast old pre-Sleep monument even though it was one of the very few architectural survivals from the old days. All it gave you was a crick in the neck, but for once it had served a purpose though the Clean-Up Squad were going to have a pretty hard job getting the remains of the fly down off it. He looked at the mess in the street below where a crowd was gathering, pulling lumps of masonry out of the way to clear a route for the emergency services.

I'd better go and help them, he thought. It was one of the few times when tall men had a place, when there was hard physical work to do. It did just a little to make up for all those other moments when people would mutter nasty things at him in the street.

Trafalgar was probably the tallest man between the Thames and the other river, and in the year 95 SEGS small was beautiful.

THREE

Even before his recent experiences in the datastores, Trafalgar had often wondered about the huge monument that was now sickeningly crowned by an oozing mass of fly carcass impaled on its highest spike.

Big Ben.

Big was definitely on the way to being the right adjective. Gargantuan would have been even better but, for the purposes of alliteration, big would suffice.

Ben was the problem.

You might have supposed that something called Ben would look vaguely like a man. Ben, along with Steve, Rose, Halogen and Parsnip, was among the most common of men's names. The datastores were full of famous Bens of the ancient days like Ben Evolent, the good King of Wenceslas, and Ben Krobber the bandit.

The fact remained however that this particular Ben, viewed through powerful binoculars, didn't look very much like a man at all. Indeed, unless human physiology had changed radically since the pre-Sleep times, it had to be said that the face and certain features in the general area of the chest looked much more like a woman. Unless the datastores really weren't reliable . . . He pushed that thought aside in alarm. If that was the case, then nothing could ever be regarded as certain again. The activities of the mice were generally regarded as not much more than a bit of a nuisance but perhaps they really should be taken more seriously and Lemmon hadn't dismissed him out of hand when he'd suggested it.

He could see drips from the carcass trickling down Big Ben's forehead. Maybe the mice just ate some of the letters, he thought. That wouldn't be quite so bad. Maybe the object out there on the island was originally called Big Brenda. That was a reassuring thought, a thought that swept away his doubts and meant this was after all the same old familiar London with its same old statue of a giant green metal woman holding up a torch. It didn't really matter whether she was called Ben or Brenda. He forced his mind away from it. This wasn't the time for thought, it was time for action; the street was filled with rubble and it was clear there was work to be done first. He would have liked to have a shower to get rid of the clinging sickly smell of the fly-spray shells but, looking down at the devastation, duty called.

A voice hailed him when he got down there and Lemmon came up out of the shelter to join him. Dust hung in the air and stuck to their clothes as they crossed the street, picking their way between lumps of twisted wreckage to the damaged Ministry.

'A good day to be out of the office,' said Lemmon.

Trafalgar nodded, looked up and froze. Way up above, on the jagged edge of the shattered roof, a huge slab of stonework was swaying outwards. He knew instantly what it was, the great shield found on all public buildings, carved with an enigmatic message.

Lemmon was walking on, oblivious. Trafalgar was rooted to the spot. High above his head, the stone toppled off the ledge and gravity gleefully took over full responsibility for its immediate future.

Trafalgar found his voice but it came with the wrong words attached.

'The ratio stone . . .' he croaked.

Lemmon stopped, turned round and looked at him,

annoyed. 'This is no time for another of your strange theories,' he said. 'What about it?'

'It's coming down.'

'You mean in a metaphorical sense that . . .'

Trafalgar's shoulder hit him in the stomach in a flying tackle that sent both of them sprawling onto the pavement as the stone hit the road behind them with a thunderous crash and split into fragments.

'Not totally metaphorical, no,' said Trafalgar as he helped his boss to his feet and dusted him down.

Lemmon gaped at the pile of masonry then pulled himself together.

'We need to talk,' he said, 'as soon as you get through here. I'll be back.'

Trust the bosses, Trafalgar thought, always off on an urgent appointment as soon as there's work to be done. Emergency vehicles from the Fly Clean-Up Squad were coming from all directions, their grey lights flashing and their sirens howling. He was elbowed in the ribs by an old woman.

'Get out of my way, you great big waste of space.'

Time to earn some goodwill for the big guys, he thought to himself and took hold of a large lump of fractured masonry. The inscription on the ratio stone, '1:0.15', was now a shattered collection of mathematical bric-a-brac, blocking the road.

He toiled away with the Clean-Up Squad for an hour and a half until the street was clear then, filthy, exhausted and with visions of a hot bath, he went home. He opened the door, hung his helmet on the hook, unzipped his jacket and found himself looking at five pairs of eyes.

'Sorry to impose on you, Hurlock,' said Lemmon, who was standing by the window, 'but this had to be discreet.'

'Let the boy take a shower,' said a familiar voice from

41

his most comfortable armchair – a voice Trafalgar had last heard being interviewed on the television. With a shock, Trafalgar recognised the face of the Minister, Bluto O'Barron himself.

'Yeah, in fact order him to,' said the sharp-faced woman to his right, sniffing ostentatiously.

He looked at them as if hypnotised, opened his mouth quite pointlessly a number of times then bolted into the bathroom. Locking the door behind him, he tried to pull himself together. Out there, sitting in his chairs with Lemmon and O'Barron as if they owned the place were Saccharine Fernandez, the President's Special Adviser, said to be the second most powerful woman on the planet, and two others who, though he couldn't put names to their faces, had the same unmistakeable aura of people who knew which of their profiles looked best on camera and never had to wash their own socks. All these people in *his* flat and he hadn't even tidied up for at least a week – in fact he was almost sure he'd left his unfinished breakfast on the sofa. Fried egg. He hoped Saccharine Fernandez wasn't sitting in it, then just a little tiny bit of him hoped she was, but only for a second.

In a daze, he stripped off his filthy clothes and dropped them down the laundry chute, then washed off the grime and the fly spray as fast as he could under the steaming water. Feeling clean again brought back some of his self-confidence. It was his flat, damn it, so what right did they have to make him feel awkward? It was when he reached for a towel and discovered, with dismay, only an empty hook that part of his self-confidence remembered an urgent appointment somewhere in the next street and scuttled off under the door.

The hook was empty because he hadn't brought a towel in with him. He stood there dripping in acute embarrassment, then flapped his arms around and tried jumping up and down to shake off the water. It didn't do much good. He tried blowing hard at his arms, pretending to be a hot air dryer, but that just chased the drops of water round to the other side where he couldn't reach them. The only answer he could think of was to get into his clothes still soaking wet and hope they wouldn't notice.

A fine chance, he thought. There they were, five of the sharpest-dressed people you could hope to meet in a month of Wednesdays, O'Barron in a hand-tailored pink ballet tutu that made Lemmon's own tutu look like he'd knocked it up himself. Trafalgar preferred casual clothes. He hated having to wear a tutu, though the historian in him knew from the records that way back before the Sleep the tutu had always been the standard power-dressing garb of the ruling classes, called after Desmond Tutu, a Prime Minister of Memphis from the golden age of the legendary King Elvis. The court of King Elvis was still regarded as the inspiration for all that was best in fashion as well as in music. O'Barron's tutu had an irritatingly correct violet pinstripe in the petticoats. Saccharine Fernandez was dressed in the female equivalent, a perfectly tailored and *very* expensive Mickey Mouse suit with real velvet ears, though possibly with a touch of added fried egg, and in a minute he would have to walk into their midst in clothes through which the bath water would be trying to make a better acquaintance with the outside world.

That only seemed like a huge problem for the next ten seconds or so, then it paled into complete insignificance when it dawned on him that it barely counted as a problem at all.

It was, in fact, a problem he would really enjoy having.

Damp clothes would be nice. Dirty clothes would be pretty good too. A handkerchief would be better than nothing. In the pressure of the moment, he hadn't just forgotten his towel, he'd also forgotten to bring any clean clothes into the bathroom with him.

Mere dismay turned to the feeling a plughole has as the water gurgles out. Because no other solution presented itself, he lifted the lid of the laundry chute in case his dirty clothes had found a way of temporarily overcoming logic and kind of hanging around for him in his time of need. There was nothing but the usual dark tunnel leading down to his far-away bin in the basement laundry room, four floors below.

I could just climb down it, he thought, put my clothes on then come in through the door of the flat again and hope they don't notice anything odd. He put one leg into the hole. Even by itself it was a tight fit.

Trafalgar moaned. There was no satisfactory way out. He could stick his head round the door and ask them for help but with the Minister there? Not to mention Saccharine Fernandez. It was unthinkable. They'd have to open his cupboard to find clothes and, since the sink had filled up, that was where he'd been keeping the washing up. In an agony of uncertainty, drips and goose pimples, he decided to count slowly to a hundred and hope for an idea.

He didn't get one. He got something much better. Against all odds and rational probability, he got a miracle and he still had seventy-one left over because it arrived just as he got to twenty-nine.

As miracles go, it was not entirely a comfortable experience. Rather, it was the kind of event that has you phoning the emergency services and checking the fine print of your house insurance. It was loud, dramatic and smelly. As his mouth opened to mumble a forlorn 'thirty', there was a sharp crackling noise and he looked round in alarm. The bathroom filled with a pungent odour of electrical scorching with a slightly organic overtone, as if someone had tipped a goldfish bowl into the back of a television, complete with the goldfish. Wisps of thin blue smoke appeared in the air. Trafalgar stared at them aghast. His bathroom appeared to be on fire which, for a room lined entirely with soaking wet ceramic tiles, seemed to be the sort of disaster you would have to work very hard to achieve as well as one that ran counter to most of the known laws of physics. It was getting difficult to see through the smoke and breathing wasn't a very attractive option either.

Deciding that, whether he liked it or not, it was now definitely time to call for assistance, Trafalgar opened his mouth. He closed it again. 'Help, my bathroom's on fire and I've got no clothes' wasn't normally the way you addressed yourself to a government minister. It might be better, he decided on balance, just to die and hope they all got bored and went away when he didn't reappear.

The smoke writhed, then solved the breathing problem for him by seeming to draw together in one place. There was the thumping noise of a giant umbrella opening in a high wind and the wisps solidified into a figure.

Trafalgar jumped behind the shower curtain and gaped round the edge at it, rendered speechless by shock. Someone was standing in his bathroom, someone wearing military clothing and a protective helmet which covered its face. Someone, moreover, who had definitely not come in through the door.

'Standing' was a misleading description. The figure was behaving like a mime artist doing the usual man-being-blown-about-by-a-force-five number, bending sideways and staggering to keep his footing with one arm flailing around for balance.

All of this would have added up at least to a phenomenon. What turned it into a miracle was that the other arm was quite still and, folded over it, hung a pile of clothes and a towel.

'Quick, take these,' it shouted in a voice muffled by the helmet, holding the clothes out and lurching towards Trafalgar on scrabbling feet. It bounced violently sideways and dropped the clothes on the floor. Trafalgar opened and closed his mouth but nothing came out.

'Look, try not to argue,' the apparition bellowed. 'I haven't got all day. You're jolly lucky I was able to come.'

It lurched again, even more violently, and took a series of ungainly hops to the right, battling against some invisible force.

'Bloody howl-round. I must fix it. Plays havoc with the horizontal hold,' it grunted. 'Watch out for . . .' but then it lost the struggle, cannoned into the bathroom wall and dispersed back into tendrils of smoke with a loud bang, an electric flash and a renewed smell of scorching.

There was a clamour of voices outside. 'Hurlock! Are you all right in there?' called O'Barron. 'What's going on?'

His voice came back to him, weakly. 'It was only a . . . er, just a . . . I'll be straight out, sir.'

'Is there anything wrong?' Someone rattled the doorknob. 'What was that noise? There's a funny smell.'

What could he say? Honesty was second nature to him but there were times, he suddenly found, when it might be the policy most guaranteed to lead to a nice quiet bed somewhere with attentive nurses and a lot of tablets.

'Just a short circuit, I think.'

'What? What's short circuited?'

Searching for inspiration, his eye fell on the shelf by the basin. 'My er . . . my electric toothbrush,' he improvised desperately. 'I'll be with you in a sec.'

He pulled on the clothes quickly, his mind still reeling. They weren't his clothes but they fitted perfectly, then

46

he unlocked the door. They were all clustered round, gazing suspiciously into the bathroom past him and sniffing the still-pungent air.

'Were you yelling at someone in there?' said Saccharine Fernandez.

'Just singing,' he said, trying to smile.

'Singing? You must really dislike that song.'

O'Barron, still looking puzzled, motioned them all to sit down.

'Mr Hurlock. Trafalgar, I should say. You must be wondering why I've taken up my valuable time in coming to see you. We've come because of some things you've been saying to Genghis here just lately.'

Lemmon was trying not to look concerned at the embarrassing confirmation of his first name and failing in the attempt.

'Oh, my goodness,' said Trafalgar, deeply concerned and still trying to get a grip on himself. 'I should have kept my mouth shut, sir. It was just a silly idea of mine.' All these important people coming here specially just because he'd been going on about his daft theories. It was dreadful.

But O'Barron waved his hand to stop him. 'Far from it.' He stood up and began to pace up and down. 'What you said wasn't completely new to some of the more intelligent among us but I'm sure I don't have to tell you it takes us into a very sensitive area.'

All the others stared hard at him and nodded. Trafalgar gulped.

'Yes, of course, sir.'

'Good boy. I don't have to spell it out to you, do I?'

'No, no, sir, no.'

'You understand what I'm saying?'

Trafalgar nodded vigorously.

'So what am I saying?'

'You said, "You understand what I'm saying?" sir.'

'No, before that.'

'Er, I think it was "Good boy. I don't have to spell it out to you, do I?" sir.' O'Barron's manner began to display some slight signs of agitation.

'Have you got the faintest idea what I'm talking about, Hurlock?'

'No, sir. I don't think you've told me yet.'

'All right, all right.' O'Barron went on pacing around the room. As he walked behind the sofa there was a slightly squishy crunch and he stopped to look down. That's where the fried egg went, thought Trafalgar. The Minister wiped his shoe on the carpet then swung round on him.

'I have myself proposed to the President and personally initiated a bold and, though I say it myself, far-sighted plan to deal simultaneously with the main problems facing mankind today.'

'Oh, good,' said Trafalgar.

O'Barron looked at him as if this was not as full a response as he would have liked. 'What would you say those problems are, Hurlock?'

'Er . . .' said Trafalgar incisively. 'Um . . .'

They all stared at him, waiting. 'Wind?' he said hopefully.

'We can't do anything about wind,' said O'Barron dismissively. 'It's a force of nature. It's been blowing people away since the dawn of mankind, since Adam and Yvonne themselves. What else?'

Feeling panic rising, Trafalgar looked out of the window and saw Big Ben with its horrid topping. 'House-flies, Minister,' he blurted out.

'Yes,' said O'Barron, 'and you know the legend of the Lord of the Flies?'

This was a lost text, now existing in only fragmentary

and scrambled form which said that before the Sleep, flies had been small creatures, not over a yard long, but that during the Sleep a giant pig had given them the secret of growth so that since then they had become larger and larger with every passing year.

'Isn't that just a kids' story, Minister?' asked Trafalgar weakly.

'You're the historian,' said O'Barron. 'Have you found any reference in the databases to flies being a problem before the Sleep?'

'Well, I haven't really looked at all the . . .'

'There you are,' said O'Barron decisively. 'What's more to the point is that we now have conclusive scientific evidence that the flies are still getting larger year by year. Extrapolating backwards, our scientific teams have concluded that in pre-Sleep times the flies were indeed no more than a yard long. Do you realise what this means?'

'That they used to be smaller?'

'That we have to do something about them, Hurlock. If we don't they will go on getting bigger.' He swung round on Trafalgar who jumped. 'We need to get our hands on early housefly DNA so that our genetic engineers can compare it with what we have now and come up with a solution.'

'What genetic engineers are those, Minister?'

O'Barron waved a dismissive hand. 'Don't you worry. We'll train some. Anyway the datastores say this DNA stuff is pretty vital. It stands for "Do Not Adjust", you know.'

Beyond the window, the fly on Big Ben was dribbling oceans of DNA down the statue's skirts.

'That is not all, Hurlock, and this is where my plan takes on a remarkably subtle shade. We will kill two birds with one shot. You have told Lemmon here of your suspicions about the datastores.'

49

'Yes, Minister, but I didn't really . . .'

O'Barron held up his hand to cut Trafalgar off. 'We think you may be right. There are some signs that unless we take drastic action the mice may start to affect some of their contents. What do you know about the invention of the computer?'

Trafalgar groped back into his memory, relieved to be able to answer. 'Well, only what everybody knows, I suppose, Minister. It was way back before the Sleep. The inventor was P.C. Apple.'

'P.C. standing for?'

'Politically Correct, sir.'

'That's right. Common enough first names these days but unusual at the time it would seem. There's not much anyone knows about him for sure except he was killed when he fell out of the windows at a place called Dos.'

O'Barron looked grave. 'I'm about to tell you a secret,' he said, 'a state secret of the highest importance. First though, you must agree to join my special team. It's a team that's all my own idea and we're still one short. From what I hear, you may be that one and that's why I have honoured you with a personal visit. We need people who think the way you do, people who aren't afraid to use their brains. People who can think laterally and think fast. Once you're in, there's no going back. Are you in?'

Bemused and with his mind still partly full of what had just happened in the bathroom, Trafalgar nodded agreement.

'Okay,' said O'Barron. 'It's like this. We have reason to believe from records recently discovered that Apple didn't really die after the windows business. He switched identities, went on inventing under an alias – Isambard Brunel MacIntosh. He called himself IBM for short. Any idea what he did next?'

'No, sir.'

' 'Course you haven't. How could you?' O'Barron's face darkened. 'We now think that he invented ... the mouse.'

'Oh!' It was an involuntary gasp. Trafalgar was wrestling with this new and bewildering information, P.C. Apple, such a complete hero that in modern folklore he'd been immortalised as Floppy Diskmas, the rosy-cheeked favourite of children everywhere, with his fat tummy, his grey robes and his blue beard, getting stuck in your laundry chute as he came to take away your unwanted toys on Halloween Night. P.C. Apple responsible for the invention of the mouse, that ultimate pest of pests?

O'Barron was watching his reaction. 'Yes, it *is* a shock, isn't it? Apple, that great man, turned out to be rotten to the core.'

Saccharine Fernandez butted in. 'The Minister here has recently suggested to the President's Council that, although so far they've done only insignificant damage, the mice have to be stopped. If they're allowed to continue with their activities, they may pose a real threat far beyond anything we suspected so far.'

'Beyond even the destruction of the books?' Trafalgar suggested hesitantly.

'Way beyond.'

The books should have been part of the Sleeptime arrangements. When Trafalgar's great grandparents had woken with all the others, ninety-five years earlier, the libraries and the computer datastores were meant to be waiting for them to remind them of all they had forgotten during their long doze. Sleep does tend to drive things out of your mind and five hundred years' sleep drives everything out of your mind. Trafalgar's great grandmother had been renowned for the staying power of her guilty conscience and after five hundred years asleep, she

51

was the only one of the whole population to remember anything at all from before. What she remembered was that she had forgotten to take back her library books. At ten pence a day per book with compound interest that would have cost her over eight hundred thousand pounds but she was as honest as her great grandson and, although she couldn't remember exactly what a book *was*, she knew she had to face the music. She couldn't find anything that might have been a book and when she went to the library to make a clean breast of it she couldn't find a library either. She found instead a large building with rows and rows of empty shelves and just the odd fragment of the more indigestible book spines left behind as a cat might leave the less choice bits of a mouse.

It was the same everywhere. Only the best-protected books had survived the Sleep and most of those soon went the way of the rest when careless people, not realising their value or the danger they were in, left doors open.

It was all a question of cellulose. Mice had a passion for cellulose that was almost beyond belief. Let them anywhere near a book and it was gone in no time flat. Cellulose was their stock in trade, the substance from which they made new mice. If it is true that you are what you eat then the mice had become libraries though it made a lot more sense to say that the libraries had become mice.

It didn't occur to anyone for a long time that the mice might also have a vested interest in getting rid of the information contained in the books.

Saccharine went on with her revelation. 'You've spotted it, or we wouldn't be here talking like this. Just lately, the mice have started to corrupt electronic information.

We don't know why they're doing it but we believe they're attracted in some way by the current in the wires. It's clearly random and mindless. They couldn't possibly *intend* to scramble the records but it's also clear that unless we act now, there is a chance that key data could be corrupted in the future.'

'Oh, but surely,' said Trafalgar, 'surely it already has been? If they've mixed up the old sayings, they must have been doing that sort of thing ever since the Sleep.'

There was a pregnant silence and he realised he had overstepped the mark. This was not an acceptable thought.

'Mr Hurlock,' said Saccharine with artificial sweetness, 'you cannot surely think this possibility would not have occurred to us? The best brains in the world have been working on this for months now and we're quite sure the datastores are largely intact. We've cross-checked them. Last month we completed a thorough survey. We tested two thousand key factual points against the datastores here in London, as well as in Buenos Aires, Narnia, Eldorado, Tokyo and the Emerald City. They all agreed on all counts, so unless you believe that the mice are organised enough to communicate over huge distances to synchronise their input, then let me assure you, the databanks are completely safe.'

She gave a tinkling laugh at the absurdity of the idea and looked around her colleagues with a satisfied smirk.

'Could I ask . . . Could I just ask what *sort* of facts you checked?' said Trafalgar, greatly daring.

'Obvious stuff,' she snapped, irritated that he wasn't prepared to accept her word. 'Basic facts across all the main subjects – history, geography, space exploration.'

'I only ask because I'm interested in history, you understand. I just wondered what exactly they were.'

Saccharine Fernandez clearly didn't have the faintest idea. One of the other men stepped in.

'Two examples, Hurlock. They all agreed that Batman commanded the American forces at the Charge of the Light Brigade and that the first moon landing was made by Neil Diamond in Stephenson's Rocket.'

'Oh, that's all right then,' said Trafalgar and everyone else nodded with the satisfied air of having proved their point beyond any shadow of a doubt. Trafalgar thought of the Big Ben caption that had changed before his eyes. It didn't just imply deliberate interference, it also implied that those doing the interfering were rational. However Saccharine Fernandez had made a strong point; if information was being changed, it was inconceivable that the mice could have the sort of international communication system that would allow them to make the same changes in every one of the world's datastores at the same time.

He couldn't see behind the skirting board, where the mouse in the orange hat, a new piece of flex clipped on in place of its missing tail, giggled quietly to itself and dialled up the Tokyo coordination centre on its internal modem.

'I don't need to tell you, Hurlock,' said O'Barron, 'an election's coming up. At times like these, voters expect bold solutions. Today's housefly incident could have been tragic. As it is, it will hold up the work of the Ministry for weeks while we repair the damage. I'm sure I don't have to tell you the problems involved in tracking down each of their breeding sites and the damned things are getting bigger all the time. It's evolution gone mad, I'm afraid.'

The story of evolution was taught at school. It was invented by Charles Brown on his travels with his beagle Snoopy when they arrived in Darwin and he was hit on the head by a fossilised apple, causing him to fall into a bath shouting 'Eureka', for reasons that had never been satisfactorily explained.

'I have therefore come up with a plan of action that cuts right to the heart of this problem and will enable us to deal with both problems at their source, allowing us to sweep to victory in the er . . . that is, allowing us to perform a significant service to the world's population. This team will discover why the flies started growing and also how to stop the mice breeding.'

Breeding was what the mice did in their little factories with all the cellulose moulds and printed circuit production lines. You'd sometimes find the factories in the back of an undisturbed cupboard or under the floorboards and then you got Pest Control there as fast as you possibly could.

O'Barron stood up, looked out of the window at the damaged building opposite, then turned back to Trafalgar.

'We've put together a special team to tackle the problem. We feel a historian with the ability to think laterally would be a useful addition to it. Its purposes are top secret for the moment until we're ready to announce it. We're calling it the Evolution Limitation Volunteers, the ELV.'

'Can I have a little time to think about it, Minister?'

'No, certainly not. You know too much already.'

'But, Minister, you said they were volunteers.'

'That's right,' said O'Barron with a rather unpleasant grin, 'and you're going to volunteer for the trip.'

'A trip? Where are we going?'

'It's not *where*, it's *when*. You're going back in time to before the Sleep to sort out this evolution thing once and for all.'

FOUR

Trafalgar was left with a great deal to think about after they'd gone. Time travel indeed. Of course, he knew of the work of the great pre-Sleep inventor Professor H.G. Wells, whose authoritative reference book on chrono-navigation, *The Time Machine*, had unfortunately failed to survive. Every child had studied the heroes of chrono-navigation in school under Lost Technologies, names such as Spielberg, Kirk and De Lorean. What had shocked him was O'Barron's response when he had protested.

'But Minister,' he'd said, 'scientists have tried for years, haven't they? I mean there isn't enough information left, is there?'

O'Barron had stared at him intently. 'Wasn't, not isn't. Now you're on the team, I can tell you. You will have access to datastore records that very few people even suspect exist.' He had turned round and walked behind the sofa again, then he'd stopped abruptly and peered at the ground with a look of disgust before going on.

'Last year we made a very exciting discovery. During routine demolition work on a fly-blown building, one of the Clean-Up Squads accidentally broke through into an ancient chamber and discovered five whole pages from Wells's great book. Some of it disintegrated on examination but we recovered more than half of it. It speaks quite plainly of the machine in which Wells travelled back. That's where you will start.' He had frowned, then wiped his shoe on Trafalgar's curtain.

When his visitors had left, with the sudden air of people

who couldn't think why they would have bothered to stay for quite so long, Trafalgar had felt more or less the way a carpet might feel after hosting a party for over-weight gourmets with poor hand/mouth coordination. Above all, his brain seemed unable to get to grips with the apparition in the bathroom. Granted someone some-where might have invented a dematerialising robot butler with thought-reading capabilities and a good stock of gents' casual clothing but why had they decided to try it out on him? He knew you shouldn't look at a gift horse before you came to it but it had him stumped, not to mention the fact that it had taken him two hours and a whole bottle of heavy-duty abrasive cleaner to get the scorch marks off his tiles.

The ELV headquarters building was down by the point at which the other river met the Thames and poured into the great bay where Big Ben stood on its island – the long strip that was London sandwiched between them. People had recently started giving the second river capital letters, the Other River, or even the River Other as if they felt sorry that it didn't have a real name of its own. The datastores only ever talked about one river in London but the other river was just as big as the Thames so capital letters seemed only fair.

It was an unremarkable office block, but by the entrance was a shining brass plate with the initials ELV on it. In a subtle attempt to preserve secrecy and mislead the public it said underneath EXTREMELY LARGE VEG-ETABLES but as the public insisted on strolling past saying things like, 'Oh look, there's the time machine place' at the tops of their voices, the ruse didn't seem to be work-ing as well as it might. Inside the guarded entrance was the real sign, EVOLUTION LIMITATION VOLUNTEERS, and their motto 'There's no time like the past.' Next to that was the etched head of H.G. Wells, instantly recognisable by his flowing beard and his remarkable pointed hat with the two curved horns sticking out of it. At the Ministry of Knowledge, opinion had been divided as to the purpose of the horns. Some thought they were electrical terminals, designed to produce a tremendous arc across their points which might have been an important contributor to chrononavigation. Others believed they were simply a fashion accessory, possibly a rare example of the horns of the Dilemma, a now-extinct mountain goat which, according to the datastores, died out because it could never decide whether to go up or down the mountain and usually starved to death where it was.

Trafalgar went inside and was shown into a large laboratory full of busy people. They were all tall which was the second thing he noticed after he'd seen Anya standing at the far end – a bonus far beyond his expectations. What more could he possibly have hoped for? It seemed that she saw him for a moment as she turned to go out through a door and he was almost sure she smiled. His tonsils quivered and locked solid.

A young man of about his own age came over, holding out his hand.

'I'm Stilton Cheesemaker. Call me Stilts,' he said, smiling.

Trafalgar gulped and tore his eyes away from the doorway through which she had disappeared.

'Trafalgar Hurlock.'

Trafalgar stood six foot six in his socks and, to minimise heightist criticism, he wore the thinnest possible socks but Stilts was at least two inches taller still and didn't seem particularly bothered by it. He followed where Stilts led, looking around the busy room with interest. In a cage in the middle of the nearest table sat a placid rabbit. Pointing at it was a ramshackle construction of lenses, electrical terminals and circuit boards. A very thin man with enormous and rather pointed ears was adjusting it.

'Experiment number one,' said Stilts. 'Puckeridge here has been working on it for a month now.'

'What's it supposed to do?' Trafalgar asked politely.

'It's going to send the rabbit into the future,' Puckeridge said.

'How far?'

'As far as we like.'

'Will it work?'

'I'll show you. How far ahead would you like it to go?'

'What about . . . er . . . let's say a fortnight.'

'No problem.' Puckeridge turned a knob and flicked a switch. A large silver ball covered in tiny mirrors began to revolve, sending coloured reflections zooming round the walls and the ceiling.

'There you are,' he said. 'It *is* working.'

Trafalgar looked closely at the rabbit which was eating a carrot in a fairly normal way.

'Are you sure?' he said.

Puckeridge looked a little defensive. 'It's just working a bit slowly at the moment,' he said. 'I haven't got it completely finished yet. You'll see. You can't just expect it to whizz off. It gets there in the end but it takes a little while.'

'How long?'

'Well, it depends how far ahead it's got to go.'

'For a fortnight?'

'A fortnight? Well, you know, about . . . um . . . let's say a week, give or take a bit.'

'Puckeridge,' said Stilts in a warning voice.

'Well, all right, two weeks then, but I haven't got the music right yet.'

They turned away to the next experiment but they'd only gone three steps when Puckeridge shouted after them, 'Look, look! See? It's worked.'

They turned back and where the rabbit had been there was only an empty cage. Trafalgar gasped. Stilts simply raised his eyebrows and pointed at Puckeridge's right sleeve.

'No, no, no,' said Puckeridge and held it out for them to see.

Stilts moved his finger a fraction and pointed silently at the other one.

'Nothing there,' said Puckeridge with an attempt at a convincing smile, though they could see that some bulky object was wobbling around inside it and there were distinct chewing noises. He looked down as if surprised as a whiskery nose poked out of his cuff. 'Good heavens,' he said. 'There you are. Two weeks into the future and it's already come back again, just like that. Absolutely fantastic.'

'Come on,' said Stilts. 'You can't deal with him when he's in that mood.'

All around the room, people were doing incomprehensible things often involving startled animals. A worried-looking woman walked past them wearing a copy of H.G. Wells's helmet with a trailing cable connecting her to the mains. A warning buzzer sounded.

'Whoops,' said Stilts, 'stand clear.'

Everyone who was close to her got out of the way. Five seconds later there was a series of lurid flashes as thick sparks crackled between the horns and her eyebrows stood on end. Each time it happened, she screamed, looked round, then checked her watch with a resigned expression.

'Is *any* of this working?' Trafalgar asked.

'Oh, well, er, you know, the early bird never boils.'

'In other words, no.'

'That's where you come in. I'm just a computer whizz. You and the other datastore research people need to give us scientists a bit more of a steer. You're joining Tits and Rumpole, I think.'

'Tits? You mean Anya?'

'Sorry, mustn't repeat these sizeist jokes. There's no sizeism round here.'

Trafalgar's heart leapt. He was going to be working with Anya. Maybe even in the same room. He could feel his voice box starting to seize up.

'Who's Rumpole?' he said to cover himself.

'Grumpy old bastard, I'm afraid. I shouldn't say so. He's a cousin of mine, but I wish you the best of luck with him.'

They came to a cubicle where an elderly man sat hunched over a workbench mumbling. He had a bald top to his head fringed by a wild halo of white hair.

'Meet Trafalgar, our newest recruit,' Stilts said loudly. The man waved a hand in the sort of floppy-wristed way that said, 'I don't really want to say hello because I'm very busy, but I suppose I must and what I'd really like you to do is take the hint and go right away.'

The hand fell to his side, exhausted by the length of the message it had just delivered and Stilts said, 'This is Aspirin.'

The old man stopped what he was doing, looked doubtful for a second then shook his head decisively and said in an irritated voice, 'No, that's quite wrong.'

Stilts chuckled. 'Demerara?' he suggested.

'No.'

'Parsley?'

'Don't be absurd.'

Trafalgar looked harder at the object on the bench. It was a large hourglass with a nozzle fitted to one end. The nozzle went to a vacuum cleaner. The old man switched the machine on and the sand in the bottom half of the glass was sucked up into the top.

61

'See?' he said. 'Promising, don't you think?'

He tried to switch it off again but it was a very old machine and something inside chose to stay switched on. It went on sucking. All the sand vanished out of the hourglass into the cleaner bag. The man gave a dreadful shriek and hammered at the switch with his fist but the motor continued to whine. A sudden dead silence had fallen on the rest of the room and everyone was watching. He picked up the vacuum cleaner and slammed it down on the floor. There was a ping as the switch flew into the air on the end of a long spring and the motor finally stopped. Trafalgar looked around him. Everyone was absolutely still, watching the scene.

The old man was clutching his head.

'I've ruined everything,' he wailed. 'I've destroyed the entire space-time continuum.' He clutched at Trafalgar with sudden wild hope in his eyes. 'Perhaps not. Perhaps I've done it. Do you feel different? Has everything stopped? Is time moving backwards? What do you . . .' His voice tailed off and a small, sticky sound like a toffee-coated sob emerged heavily from his mouth. His eyes had shifted to a point beyond Trafalgar's shoulder and Trafalgar turned to see what he was looking at. One person and one person only was moving in the whole of that frozen room. Puckeridge was walking backwards along the aisle from his bench.

'Look,' the old man yelled. 'Look. Success at last.'

Stilts turned to look too.

'Do stop mucking about, Puckeridge,' he called. 'He's quite excitable enough already.'

They left the old man trying to get all his sand back from the innards of the vacuum cleaner bag.

'What *is* his name?' Trafalgar asked.

'Haven't a clue. He can never remember. He said it was Aspirin yesterday but it changes every day. Last week it was Camomile for two days in a row but that was a record. He gets cross if you press him, says he's got far too many things to think about without having to bother his head with things like that.'

'Stilts?'

'Yes?'

'These experiments . . .'

'What about them?'

'They're completely daft.'

Stilts didn't answer.

'Well, aren't they?'

'Shush.'

'What do you mean, shush?'

'I mean don't even *think* that. If O'Barron started to suspect something like that then we'd all be in trouble.'

'You agree then?'

Stilts gibbered slightly. 'You come up with something better. That's what you're here for. We're just trying out ideas from the history research team. We've got to do *something*. Reinventing the time machine is not easy. Rome may have been built in a day, but they had the Jolly Green Giant to do it and even he couldn't get the roof on the Parthenon.'

This was of course simply another piece of corrupted history. They didn't have the Jolly Green Giant. In fact they had a flying wolf with an anti-gravity sledge to help them, but that comes later.

Stilts led him out of the laboratory into an office, lined with computer monitors. Two other people were hard at work. Trafalgar's heart skipped a small beat when he saw that one of them was Anya. The other was a middle-aged, pugnacious-looking man who turned to glare at them.

'Shut that door. Can't you see I'm busy? How can I work when I'm constantly interrupted? Keep the noise down for heaven's sake.'

He turned back to his keyboard and Stilts whispered to Trafalgar, 'You're in luck, he's in a good mood today. He can be awful.

'This is Trafalgar Hurlock,' he said loudly. 'He's come to work with you.'

Anya arched an eyebrow at Trafalgar and reduced his available vocabulary to a fraction of its usual size.

'I'm glad you've dried out,' she said.

'Nnnngh,' said Trafalgar.

'A talkative one, a bloody talkative one. That's all we need,' muttered Rumpole.

Trafalgar sat down as quietly as he could, wondering what he was meant to do, but there was a message waiting for him when he logged on.

'Attention, Hurlock,' it said. 'Welcome. You have high-level access. Immediate tasks: 1) Search all historical records for chrononavigational references. 2) Do everything else necessary. B. O'B.'

Trafalgar was already starting to recognise O'Barron's style. Instruction 2) was clearly intended to allow him to take full credit for anything Trafalgar might turn up.

The excerpts from the Wells book told him nothing new. He read them several times then turned with a sigh to what looked like a long and fruitless wander through the vast, confusing electronic corridors of the datastores. After an hour or two of research he tapped in the words 'De Lorean' and to his surprise, the screen filled with moving pictures. They were poor quality and all too brief but he had no doubt as to what they showed. The De Lorean was undoubtedly a car and he knew all about cars from his pre-Sleep history course at university. Cars were a bizarre idea dating from the days of the surplus, when there was too much of everything to go round and they had to find ways to get rid of it all. The history books said that cars were machines specially constructed to dis-

pose of enormous quantities of several different sub-
stances all at the same time. Large rings of rubber would
be attached to their rollers, driven rapidly round and
round by an engine that consumed fossil fuel. True, no
one was quite sure what fossil fuel was and every attempt
to grind up fossils had resulted in piles of an inert grey
powder that resisted all attempts to light it. However,
surviving video clips showed the engines grinding the
rollers against abrasive tarmac surfaces to wear the rubber
down and spread it evenly into the environment, a process aided by the machines moving along the tarmac
strips as they performed the grinding.

Ministry of Knowledge experts concluded that rubber,
perhaps in liquid form, came pouring out of its source in
such vast quantities that such methods simply had to be
adopted to keep it at bay. The De Lorean was clearly one
of the many devices used in this way, though this one
was covered with all kinds of extra machinery which
presumably gave it its chrononavigational capability.
Trafalgar was nearly stumped. There was very little of
the original material to go on in the brief undamaged
sections of the pre-Sleep recording and nothing that gave
enough detail to help. There was however a datafile
attached to the pictures and he called it up on the screen.

'De Lorean,' it said. 'Pre-Sleep time machine invented
by Doctor Spielberg and his assistant Einstein. Fragmentary video indicates it travelled successfully in time, once
it had achieved a velocity of 88 miles per hour.'

Trafalgar was finding it very hard to keep his mind on
the job because every time he turned his head he could
see Anya's perfect profile out of the corner of his eye but
he did his best. After a long inspection of the De Lorean
material, he turned to Einstein. There was a short entry
in the datastores on Einstein's theory of relatives which
didn't seem to help very much. If relatives announced

they were coming to stay, said Einstein, you should move away as fast as possible but *not* faster than the speed of light because then you wouldn't be able to see where you were going. His expression, $E = mc^2$, referred to the extreme example of the emergency (E) created when both your mother-in-law (m) and her second cousin (c^2) decided to visit at the same time.

It was only half past three, well before the usual finishing time, when buzzers sounded throughout the building and the speakers broadcast a warning.

'Wind alert. All personnel are advised force seven winds are due imminently. All personnel to leave the building immediately.'

'Bloody wind,' snorted Rumpole. 'Typical.'

'I don't understand,' said Trafalgar. 'Why do we have to leave?'

''Course you don't understand,' said Rumpole, 'you young 'uns never do, do you?'

Trafalgar decided to ignore him. 'Isn't there a tunnel?'

'Would they be telling us to leave the building if there was?'

Anya took pity on him. 'It's being repaired.'

'Very slowly if you ask me,' grumbled Rumpole.

'We have to go above ground for the first two hundred yards,' she said. 'That's why they're giving us lots of warning. We'd better get a move on.'

'Wuh . . . wuh.'

She left.

'Stop stammering and get your helmet on,' said Rumpole.

'I didn't bring one.'

'You can get one from the store. Third on the left in the basement.'

If it hadn't been his first day, or perhaps if Anya's voice didn't have quite such a capacity for scrambling his brain,

Trafalgar wouldn't have got lost. Second on the right? Fifth on the left? Left and right produced rather a distracting image in connection with Anya. He found the store after searching for a long time, chose himself a helmet and realised as soon as he went out through the front door that he had left it very late indeed. The wind was rising fast.

He could see the last person scuttling down into the tunnel entrance at the far end of the street and he set out to follow them. That, at least, was his intention but halfway there a great gust of wind slammed him in the chest and drove him backwards on sliding feet in the direction he'd come. He grabbed a lamppost and hung on tightly until the gust passed. His mistake was in letting go when the wind dropped. Two seconds later, when he'd gone only a few feet towards safety, it came back with its big brother and before he could grab at any handhold, he was off the ground.

Blowaway.

He'd been warned about it all his life, he'd been taught all the drills but it had never happened to him before. He got himself into the feetal position, just as the books showed, clasping his feet with both hands, curled up in a ball with his head tucked in tightly. He bounced off something uncomfortably solid, cannoned down on to the road and began to roll very rapidly towards the water.

FIVE

The first thing Trafalgar saw when he dared to open his eyes was some graffiti sprayed on the wall next to ELV headquarters. He had trouble reading it because it was doing cartwheels past him at enormous speed. This seemed an eccentric way for graffiti to be behaving. Logic therefore suggested that the enormous speed and the cartwheels were down to him rather than the wall so he started to panic as that seemed the only logical thing to do. The panic didn't last long however, because another wall, made of very solid concrete, drove it out of his mind along with everything else including consciousness.

He came round in complete blackness with a tight band right around his head, which was hurting a great deal. He was sitting on something uncomfortably lumpy. The words of the graffiti he had seen just before the wall arrived were still spiralling around inside his mind. Their message read, 'Time is nature's way of preventing everything from happening at once.'

Not helpful, he thought, and tried some experimental movement. Most of his limbs complained that they weren't nearly ready for that sort of extreme action but at least they all seemed to work. His vision didn't. He couldn't make out even the vaguest shape of any objects in the darkness and when he felt his face there was only a smooth surface – his nose and eyes seemed to have disappeared. Then his fingers found the peak of his helmet jammed down where his mouth ought to have been by the impact and he pulled it off. The pain felt immediately better but it didn't greatly help with the darkness. A tiny chink of grey light showed high above him but the beam that played down from it met a cloud of dust before it was halfway and decided to go and play somewhere else.

I have fallen through a hole, Trafalgar thought.

Into what?

'Hello?' he called and a whole horde of echo-Trafalgars answered, making him jump. That wasn't a good thing to do because whatever it was he was sitting on now felt very, very lumpy.

It was as quiet as the grave.

He felt carefully around him and his hands touched splintered wood and some hard, smooth, irregular objects. It was only then, accidentally touching his helmet, that he remembered the lantern built in to the top of it. A moment later, he wished he hadn't. It had every right to be as quiet as a grave. Even if it had been extremely noisy it would still have been as quiet as a grave because it *was* a grave.

There was another thing too. It wasn't entirely surprising that he was sitting uncomfortably. The pelvic area of the human skeleton is a wonderful thing, carefully designed to make it comfortable to sit down but that only applies when it's your own pelvis you're sitting on.

He was sitting on somebody else's.

The lantern showed that the pelvis in question was still coupled up to the rest of the skeleton. That would have been startling enough to justify the scream that issued involuntarily from his lips but there was a lot more. The pelvis underneath him was quite large. In fact, and at that moment Trafalgar saw no particular reason for understatement, it was enormous. He was, to be precise, sitting on what had once been the lap of a skeleton which stretched away into the darkness so that the lantern's beam didn't let him see beyond its kneecaps in one direction and the top of its ribcage in the other.

Trafalgar knew instantly what he had found and he knew for certain that his name would go down in history for it, just like Howard Carter finding the legendary tomb of Tooting Common under the Belgian Pyramids.

He, who had studied Gullivers for so long – he, Trafalgar Hurlock, had found a Gulliver.

When that momentous thought sank in, he started to be more excited than frightened and he began to take stock of his surroundings. The Gulliver was lying in the remains of an enormous wooden box. Trafalgar had crashed through the top of it and the rotten wood, which now lay splintered on the ground, had broken his fall. He climbed down on to the floor and paced it out. The skeleton was thirty-eight feet long from the top of its skull to the toes of its enormous feet.

The Gulliver's skull stared at him. It was four feet wide across the eye sockets. He stared back. This was the very first hard evidence of the Gullivers. Legend said they had once been commonplace before the Sleep, coexisting with humans, and then they had gone. They had been incredibly useful because they were so very good indeed at dealing with the problem of the surpluses but when everyone woke up from the Sleep, there was no sign of them. They weren't needed any more because, since the Sleep, the surpluses had certainly never been a problem. It was as if the Gullivers had tiptoed away in the long night, leaving only the normal-sized people behind.

Trafalgar looked at the skeleton's feet and tried to imagine something that size tiptoeing.

He couldn't see as well as he had before. It dawned on him that the light cast by his helmet lantern was a lot weaker than it had been and that if he didn't use what was left of it to find a way out, he might very well be joining the Gulliver skeleton in bony loneliness or even lonely boniness. He decided it was high time to search the chamber for a way out. Steps led up from one corner but they were Gulliver-sized steps, about five feet tall, and when he had struggled up several of them he found the way ahead completely blocked by rubble. Somewhere way up high, the dim grey light beckoned but he guessed the hole in the roof was at least sixty feet above him. Apart from the shattered wood of the coffin his search revealed two other things. One was a small hole by the floor in one corner. It didn't look very inviting when he knelt down to inspect it, appearing to lead steeply down when he was quite sure that up was a much more preferable direction. The other thing was more interesting by far and, though it didn't compare with Tooting Common's golden gloves, for someone in Trafalgar's line of work it was just as exciting.

It was obviously a pre-Sleep artefact, a flat plastic rectangle about two feet high and four feet square, lying on the floor of the chamber next to the splintered remains of the coffin lid. Trafalgar was so thrilled to see it that, for a moment, he completely forgot his predicament. His lantern thoughtfully reminded him of it a second or two later by going out completely.

In the near-darkness, broken only by the faint light from above, he could hear the howl of the rising wind up there beyond the hole in the roof. A small hail of stones and earth fell down around him. It must be hurricane force by now from the sound of it, he thought, wondering how many people had been caught out in the open. In some ways it was lucky he had fallen down the hole because otherwise he'd probably be somewhere way out to sea by now. After all, if he couldn't find a way out he could just wait until the wind dropped then he could shout loudly and go on shouting until someone heard him.

A moment later, the wind did drop but what it dropped wasn't as helpful as he had hoped. It dropped a large tree with about a ton of earth still clinging to its roots straight into the hole Trafalgar had fallen through. The tree stuck in the hole, upright, plugging the gap as if it had always been there and those people who were puzzled by it when they came out of the tunnels didn't like to admit that they weren't sure they'd ever seen it before.

Trafalgar didn't know it was a tree. All he knew was that somebody seemed to have switched off the skylight because he was now in pitch-blackness, just as dark as when the helmet had been jammed over his eyes. He sat down heavily on the plastic case.

There was a burst of organ music.

Trafalgar shot into the air and looked wildly around him. The chamber lit up with coloured light and it took him a moment to see that it was coming from a screen on the flat top surface of the artefact.

A choir began to sing and giant writing in letters six inches high scrolled across the screen. 'The Videowill,' it said, 'a product of the Valhalla Corporation. Guaranteed information storage for five hundred years. Compatible with Windows 132 and Dos version 89.4.'

Dos? Windows? Trafalgar's head reeled. This was indeed the stuff of legends. He stood, staring down at the screen. The writing disappeared from the screen, which then flickered into a fuzzy image of an old man's head. There was a whistling sound.

'Bloody junk,' said the old man's voice and a hand reached out towards the screen. There was a slapping noise and the picture joggled around wildly but the whistling stopped. 'Cheap rubbish,' the voice went on, then cleared its throat and began to sound a little pompous.

'I am Robert Smith,' it said, 'and this is my last will and testament. If you are reading this, you have probably found my bones.'

Trafalgar stared at it. *This* was a Gulliver? *This* was the Gulliver whose bones stretched out behind him? It looked almost normal. A bit thin perhaps but otherwise just like a human, though its name had a wild, alien ring to it. The Gulliver broke off and began to giggle.

'What's the point?' it said. 'There's nothing to leave behind. There's just my reasons, that's all, my reasons for not going to sleep with Bill and Groucho and that moron John and, anyway, who's going to listen to those?'

Trafalgar realised there was something in the background behind Robert Smith's head. There were buildings but what buildings – impossibly tall towering things – but there beyond them in turn was something very familiar, Big Ben – perched on its island out in the bay. They'd used a very strange lens. Big Ben looked tiny compared to the buildings. This was an amazing find. Not only did it prove that Gullivers really existed in pre-Sleep London but also it showed that architecture had been radically different then.

'Whatever,' the voice said wearily. 'I'll tell it anyway. It's the year ... er ... 2112. The last of the old years. Call me old-fashioned but I think this downsizing stinks. Who says it will work? I know the arguments. I should know them, shouldn't I? We're running out of everything. There's not enough to go round. I know – I'm as much to blame as Groucho. I've helped persuade everybody else to downsize but now it comes to the crunch, I don't *want* to be a foot tall. OK, so there'll be enough to go round, two hundred and sixteen times as much thanks to that old cube law. Gravity won't feel so heavy. We should be able to jump like fleas. We'll never be hungry again. I know all that. I appreciate New York was hell the way things were – people killing each other for a crust of bread, no fuel, no anything, but who's to say it will be any better? I've helped build the machines. I've seen everyone climb into the pods. I've waved them goodbye, watched them drift off, said see you in five hundred years.

'Five hundred years? Unbelievable. 2612, that's when everyone's due to wake up. That's the time it'll take them to get everyone and everything down to size. Tiny trees, mini flowers, the lot. 2612. They're not going to call it that though, are they? The year zero SEGS, that's what Groucho says it'll be.

'SEGS? I ask you.

'I just can't be bothered. Now, when it comes to it, I don't want to follow. I want to stay in the *old* New York, the way it's always been.'

It fell silent for a moment and looked thoughtful. So New York *wasn't* mythical, Trafalgar thought, or maybe the Gulliver was just very confused because the pictures showed he was definitely in London.

'I guess it's been lonely working on the stay-behind team. All my friends are down there in the capsules, slowly shrinking, one cell at a time. We'll be finished with the job tomorrow. Bill's just got the wasps and the flies still to do then he and John will go and join them, if John can just keep his mind on the job. Five hundred years of silence. Not a living thing moving anywhere on planet Earth, everything shrinking.'

He looked around as if to make quite sure he was alone. 'They think I've already gone to sleep but I haven't. I'm going to be the last one, the last full-size human still awake anywhere in the world, then I'm going to go down into the old crypt and go my own way, the old-fashioned way. I want to go out as one man not one sixth of a man.'

He broke off again. There was a small scratching noise but Trafalgar, his mind reeling, ignored it. Downsizing? Planet Earth? What in the world was planet Earth?

'I just don't believe it will work,' the face on the screen said. 'All those robot machines, taking everything apart, tearing down Chicago, San Francisco, even the good old Big Apple, rebuilding it all smaller, taking themselves apart? All those tiny people and tiny creatures waking up and just carrying on as if nothing else had changed but with no more shortages? Life doesn't work like that. Things foul up. I don't trust . . .'

The scratching sound got louder for a moment and the screen flickered, then the voice carried on but now it sounded different, squeaky.

'. . . anyone or anything. I'm a potato, my mother was a gooseberry. One and one make yellow. When in danger or in doubt, run in circles, scream and shout.'

On the screen, the man's ears grew longer and longer and his chin was melting. Late, far too late, Trafalgar woke up to what was happening. He rushed round to the back of the box and there, in the dim reflected light of the flickering image, its tail plugged in to an input port was a mouse wearing a fez, heaving with silent laughter. Trafalgar kicked at it wildly and it shot off into the dark fringes of the chamber. There was a foul smell of scorching plastic then a spark from inside the box. The screen went blank and the darkness was only relieved by flickering flames licking out of the input port. The smoke started to make Trafalgar cough. It was as he was groping his way away from the box that the mouse shot under his feet. Stepping on it, he slid wildly across the floor and for the second time that day found himself tumbling out of control, this time straight down the hole in the corner of the chamber.

It was a bumpy ride for the first few yards then it got

smoother and he realised he was inside some sort of large pipe. There was a small trickle of what he sincerely hoped was water in the bottom of it which sped him on its way as it levelled out into a gentle downhill run. Then he came to a junction where it met a larger pipe which had rather more liquid in it and he knew for certain that it wasn't water. He clamped his mouth shut and held his nose. If he ever got out of this, he was going to need a serious bath. Everything, including himself, was flowing rather faster now.

He got his bath almost immediately. He flew out of the end of the pipe in the middle of a torrent of very second-hand water and landed with a splash in the bay where he immediately sank like a stone.

SIX

Humans float even when they are weighed down by a heavy burden of serious doubt, which proves that even the heaviest doubts weigh less than water. Trafalgar surfaced, spluttering but undoubtedly cleaner than he was when he went in the water. Being *on* the surface rather than underneath it was only a slight advantage because the surface seemed very undecided about where it wanted to be. It was heaving up and down, blown by terrifying winds into waves at least thirty feet high, and Trafalgar was heaving up and down with the waves at immense speed. His stomach was also heaving up and down but it seemed to be about half a second behind him.

He could see no immediate prospect of surviving the experience which was at the very least a nuisance as he badly wanted time to consider the immense implications of what he had just learnt.

Trafalgar knew how to swim, but swimming was something you did in swimming pools where the top of the water met the air in a nice, orderly, flat sheet. Swimming in the usual flat sort of way right now would put him fifteen feet under the water in every wave and fifteen feet above it in the troughs. A mathematician might have said that was fine when you took the averages but it was starting to occur to Trafalgar that you couldn't breathe averages. He felt like an aquatic yo-yo and he knew he wouldn't be able to keep it up for very long. Any hope that the Windguard might spot him from their lookout posts along the shore was extremely slim. In this kind of weather they'd be on full alert with nets and ropes around the edge of the water, trying to catch the blow-aways as they shot past but he was already too far away. The solid land at London's tip was dwindling fast as the wind took him out into the bay and even if they could see him, which was not likely, they wouldn't be able to get to him.

In 95 SEGS nobody went to sea except in a hovercraft on a dead calm day.

That was one of the reasons why, a few seconds later, Trafalgar didn't immediately recognise the object that fell into the sea almost next to him with a tremendous splash. He stared at it, beating his way up a wave with flailing arms, as it bobbed up and over the next mountainous lump of sea. It was made out of some sort of wood and was about three times his length. It seemed to be hollow inside and it floated for about half a minute then it sank. He was sorry to see it go. It had taken his mind off his predicament for a little while, but he was puzzled for all that. The wind was now less strong than it had been and it didn't normally blow anything much larger than a human any great distance. This thing could have been a water trough of some sort, or maybe a giant window box or possibly even a mould for a garden pond liner. He looked nervously at the sky, wondering if anything else might be coming in his direction.

Something was.

Something big and brightly coloured was falling straight towards him. He swam as hard as he could to get away from it and it splashed down into the waves twenty feet from him. He trod water again and looked at it cautiously. It was a roughly similar shape to the other one but it wasn't made of wood. It seemed to be some sort of rubbery plastic. The wind caught it and it began to drift away. Trafalgar considered swimming after it on the grounds that it would at least be something to hold on to but then he thought again. The other one had sunk, hadn't it? He used up precious seconds wondering whether to make the effort to chase it and by the time he'd decided that this one didn't look like sinking, it had blown too far away and was heading out in the direction of the open sea.

There was a faint crackling in the air and, from far away, he thought he heard a sob.

It was definitely getting difficult to stay afloat. There was an awful lot of water mixed with the air he was breathing and his arms were growing very tired. He looked up at the sky just in case these falling objects came in threes and discovered they did because the third one was about to land right on top of him. He dived down and a millisecond later it hit the sea with a thump exactly where he had recently been. He surfaced, coughing and spluttering, and there it was right next to him, bobbing around. What's more there was a large message painted along its side.

The message was addressed to him.

'Trafalgar Hurlock,' it said, 'this is a BOAT. It FLOATS. It will SAVE YOUR LIFE. Just get in, right?'

Helped by a wave, he hauled himself over the side and collapsed in the bottom. Another message was taped to the seat next to him. When he had got his breath back he read what it said.

'Don't ask questions. Just do what you're told. I'm getting really fed up with this. Press the green button to start the engine. Steer towards the shore. PTO.'

He turned it over. The message on the other side started 'Make sure you . . .' but after that the water had smeared it into an indecipherable rainbow of ink.

Trafalgar badly needed some thinking time but the

wind was still high, the waves were still sickeningly enormous and this didn't seem the right moment for quiet contemplation. He stood up, pressed the green button and, as the boat instantly shot forward, staggered off balance and fell straight over the side.

As the water closed over his head yet again, he heard another, louder, sob.

It was quite peaceful under the water but oxygen was not readily available and lacking the time to evolve a set of gills, he swam back up to roughly where the surface was for some of the time. The boat was out of sight, so he looked expectantly up at the sky, waiting for the next one. The sky contained only fast-moving clouds and absolutely nothing by way of a fourth boat.

This was a definite setback. He'd very quickly got used to the idea that the sky was raining boats and now it had stopped, he realised he had rather liked it that way. A constant supply of falling boats held out the prospect that some time soon he would manage to get into one and stay in it. He went on treading water and for the first time started to worry about what might be lurking *in* the water. Not having much to do with the sea, people didn't have much to do with fish either these days but schoolboys told stories of the ferocious mackerel that would snap you in half if you fell in. He was sure they were just stories. He hoped they were just stories. He pulled up his legs as far as he could and tried standing on his hands but it didn't really help.

There was another burst of crackling in the air.

It wasn't the only noise. There was a purring, splashy sound and something soared over the crest of a wave a hundred yards away. It was definitely the boat. It's gone right round in a circle, he thought. It's coming back towards me, but will I be able to get into it as it comes by? The boat made matters easier by heading straight towards him and he grabbed at it desperately. For a second he thought he was safe but its sides were smooth and wet and his hands slipped off – then someone else's hand closed round his wrist and yanked him straight out of the water into the boat.

When he opened his eyes there was a fog of smoke everywhere around him and the crackling noise was really loud. A familiar figure in military uniform and a helmet was holding on to the boat's wheel as its body tried to skitter sideways.

'You again,' Trafalgar said.

'I could say the same,' it yelled indistinctly. 'I *told* you, didn't I? I *said* on the instructions, didn't I? I distinctly remember I said, "Make sure you sit down before you start the engine." Can't you read?'

'It . . .'

'Oh, I know, I know. It got smeared. Don't tell me. All I ever have to do is clear up after you. There's just too much to remember. I can't do everything.'

Trafalgar felt slightly affronted by the man's sarcastic tone but it didn't seem polite to let that show when his life had just been saved.

'Who are you?' he said.

'Doesn't matter now,' said the other. 'If you just knew how my head hurts when you do this.'

'Do what?'

'Make a mess of things.' The man got carried away, took one hand off the boat's wheel to gesticulate and was tugged off to one side, feet flailing wildly for a moment before he could pull himself back. He let out another great sob.

'You owe me,' he said. 'Just think, before you say *anything at all* to the wolf, just think about the consequences, OK?'

'What wolf?'

81

'Oh right, what wolf, eh? You'll know. Oh, my head. It's worse when you talk. Now sit down and hold on. I've only got five minutes.'

'What happens in five minutes?'

'I go back again, don't I? It's pre-set. Don't you understand anything at all? Oh no, where are we? 'Course you don't.'

'Please tell me who you are.'

'NOT NOW. Stop asking questions. There's no time.' The figure broke off and began to laugh wildly. 'No time? Get it? Oh, never mind. Might as well talk to myself.' That seemed to set him off again.

Trafalgar sat in cold, wet, silent mystification for the rest of the way. The boat raced across the waves to the shore. Just by the point, the man steered it into the shelter of a little pier so that Trafalgar could jump out onto the rocks. He turned to say something suitably grateful but the other man spoke first.

'If in doubt, keep quiet,' he hissed. 'Least said, soonest mended, OK?'

That wasn't right. 'Don't you mean "Least said, catches the worm"?' Trafalgar asked hesitantly.

'You should know,' said the man, then with what looked like a derisive gesture he turned the boat and roared off into the murk.

The wind had dropped to a tolerable force four and Trafalgar trudged, dripping, up over the rocks towards civilisation. He was met on the way by two very agitated men from the Windguard, one fat and the other fatter, who were racing down with enormous momentum but not a great deal of velocity towards the water.

'What was that?' shouted the fat one, staring past Trafalgar and pointing out into the driving spray.

The man's parting instruction echoed in Trafalgar's head, least said . . .

'What was what?' he said unhelpfully.

'That . . . that thing. On the water.'

He turned to look. It was out of sight.

'I don't see anything,' he said. 'Probably a badger.'

The fatter one looked him up and down. 'You don't get badgers so close inshore. Anyway, how did you get so wet?' he asked suspiciously.

'I slipped.'

'Shouldn't be anywhere down here, not in a wind. You should know that.'

'Research work,' said Trafalgar, just wanting to get home. It was true, after all, even if it hadn't been deliberate. 'Government project.'

'What department are you then?' the fatter one demanded.

'I'm with the ELV.'

It had a salutary effect. They saluted him. They might have pressed the point but a beeper went off and the fatter one looked at his watch.

'Fourses,' he said to the other.

'Already?'

'Yup, come on. Doughnuts.'

'Not doughnuts again please.'

'When were you weighed last?'

'After second breakfast.'

The fatter one looked at the slightly less fat one critically. 'You look a bit marginal to me,' he said. 'Better stuff a few down.'

Trafalgar watched them go waddling off. You had to be at least thirty stone to get into the Windguard. It was dangerous to be in the gale rescue business if you were any lighter. Meals on the hour every hour helped but anyone who failed a sudden weight check would be suspended from duty and lashed to a safety line until they'd bloated up again.

He squelched back towards home thinking hard. Someone was watching over him and this was no robotic butler. The mystery man in the helmet was someone who had extraordinary skills in the surveillance and air-sea rescue business and knew a great deal about him even if he was a bit on the rude side. He shivered and looked behind him. His watch showed it was only an hour since his blowaway. A lot had happened in that time but his brush with drowning and the rescue seemed almost commonplace beside the rest of it. The experience in the underground chamber had shaken everything he had ever been taught.

There were no Gullivers. There never had been. There were just large humans who had gone to sleep and become smaller humans. The datastores were completely wrong about that. All he was certain of now was that he couldn't be certain of anything at all.

Back in his apartment, he changed gratefully into dry clothes and sat down to go on ruminating. He couldn't help thinking about the wolf. What wolf? This man in the helmet who . . .

Crackle. Crackle, crackle. Smoke billowed and the 'whomp' hurt his eardrums as the very man, still wearing the helmet, materialised in front of him.

Trafalgar looked at him in horror and thought of the cleaning.

'In the bathroom,' he yelled. 'Now!'

At least the tiles came up with a bit of hard work. The man ricocheted off the wall and lurched through the doorway, juddering, leaving black, greasy marks where his feet had touched the carpet.

He grabbed the towel rail to steady himself and faced Trafalgar.

'Yes,' he said, 'you're quite right. You've worked it out by yourself, so now I can tell you that I am indeed the future you, come back to . . .' An expression of consternation came over his face and he looked at his watch. 'What time is it?'

'THE FUTURE ME?'

As far as it's possible to look shifty inside an opaque helmet, the figure looked shifty. 'Depends. Go on, tell me the time.'

'Quarter to five.'

'Not quarter to six?'

'No.'

'Damn. Blast. Bloody hell. This is where I screw it all up, isn't it?'

'You're *me*? You're the future *me*?'

'Yes. No. No, I'm not. Well, yes, I am, but you've got to work that out for yourself first. Forget I was ever . . .'

Whomp. He was gone and Trafalgar didn't even think about the two hours extra cleaning he'd left behind. He stood quite still and stared into mid-air.

That's me? he thought. THAT is really ME? I'm going to learn how to time travel? So it *is* possible. It must be. I came back and saved *myself* with the boat, not to mention the clothes. He felt his knees going wobbly and slumped down into a chair. *I* made all that mess, knowing I was going to have to clear it up? Unbelievably selfish. Hang on though, he thought, by the time he made the mess he knew I would already have cleared it up. That made his head ache. An hour passed in much the same sort of fevered speculation then the crackling started again and Trafalgar was not at all surprised when he heard the 'whomp'.

This time no one appeared but a voice called 'In here!'

He opened the bathroom door and the figure was sitting on the edge of the bath, holding on to the towel rail for dear life.

85

'Yes,' it said, 'you're quite right, so now I can reveal that I am indeed the future you, come back to put you on the path to . . .'

'Give it a rest,' said Trafalgar. 'You've already done that bit.'

'Look,' said the other, 'play the game. You can't just mess around with time like that. I made a genuine mistake. You could have done the same. Well, come to think of it, you *did* do the same. I mean you are me after all, so it was all *your* fault.'

'Are you sure you're me?' Trafalgar asked. 'How do I know?'

The other man took off his helmet with one hand, the other one still clinging to the towel rail as his body twitched sideways. It was definitely him. A bit older, a bit more battered and tougher looking as though he'd seen a lot of living in between, but definitely him.

'Look, I've only got five minutes then the pill will wear off.'

'What pill?'

'The headache pill. That's the worst of time travel. You'll find out. Anyway, shut up and listen.'

'That's not very polite.'

'I wouldn't say it to anyone else but there's not much time. I just made a mistake, that's all, and it's set up a little temporal paradox so, please, just play along with it.'

'What happens if I don't?'

'The headaches get worse. They're bad enough anyway. They're twice as bad when I'm anywhere near you, plus there's all the howl-round, then when anything starts getting a bit illogical, they're real killers. A twist in time brings migraine, that's what they say, well – that's what they're going to say.'

'You can't rhyme migraine with time.'

'It's a proverb, not Shakespeare – and don't start giving me that couldn't-care-less look. They're going to be your headaches one day.'

'I wasn't,' said Trafalgar who wanted to ask what a Shakespeare was but didn't quite dare.

'Anyway, just pretend I wasn't here before, all right? This is the moment when you've just realised that I'm you and that therefore you're going to be the one who discovers the secret of time travel and . . .'

'*I'm* going to be the one? You mean I'm going to re-invent the time machine?'

'Well, sort of. Yes. Look, it's not a good idea to start asking a lot of questions about the future. It just makes it all harder to sort out in the end and, believe me, it will be you that has to sort it out. I mean take the bloody wolf for example . . .'

'WHAT wolf? You keep going on about the wolf.'

'Well, it's a good example of why these paradoxes are a really bad idea. Whatever you do when you see the wolf, don't even think about lettuce, OK?'

He rubbed his forehead hard with one hand. 'Oh no. It's wearing off. Stop talking and just listen. I can't do all this for you. You've got to invent the machine.'

'Where do I look? In the datastores, I mean.'

Trafalgar 2 stared at him wildly. 'It's not in the data-stores. Don't you understand? It's never been done.'

'What about the De Lorean?'

'It was just a car, done up for an old movie. Pure fiction. No one's ever time travelled before.'

'So what else is wrong?'

'Everything that matters.'

'H.G. Wells?'

Trafalgar 2 let out a ghastly moan. 'Questions, ques-tions. My head.'

'Where do I start?'

'First principles. Try remembering what you're just about to do next. Ow.'

'That doesn't help.'

A more urgent question struck him. 'Tell me one thing. Do I . . . do we . . . I mean, does Anya . . . will I . . . ?'

'You want it on a plate, don't you? I'm not telling you but if you don't pull your finger out, you won't . . . oooh. Aaaargh.' Trafalgar 2 let go of the towel rail to cradle his head in both hands, slid sideways on juddering feet, crashed into the wall and imploded.

'Oh great,' said Trafalgar into the smoke-filled room. 'Thanks for the help.'

The next morning, eating his breakfast, he tried to decide what to do. Normally, it would be obvious. O'Barron was directly in charge of the ELV project and by rights he should go straight to O'Barron and tell him the whole thing – the Gulliver discovery, the corruption of the data-stores and the coming invention of the time machine. On the other hand, Trafalgar 2 had advised him to keep his mouth shut. He tried to make up his mind for a long time, then he reached for a coin. Heads, he'd tell O'Barron, tails he'd keep it to himself.

He tossed it up high and watched it spin down through the air. It landed, bounced, rolled and came down heads but there was a brief crackling in the air, a flash of something passing across the table and the coin suddenly lurched over on to the other side.

'Hey, cut that out!' he said angrily but there was no one to say it to.

It *was* heads, he thought defiantly. I'll stick to that. As soon as he got to work he made an appointment to see O'Barron.

The Minister heard him out in complete silence.

'This underground chamber,' he said at the end, 'the

chamber where you found the Gulliver skeleton, could you find it again?'

'I don't know, sir. I was in the middle of a blowaway. It must be about two hundred yards from the back door of the building going straight towards the water.'

'We'll check it out.'

'It should be easy to find, sir.'

'Maybe. And all our records are suspect, you say?'

'That's right,' Trafalgar agreed, pleased that the interview was going so smoothly. 'The mice have changed all kinds of things.'

'Now why would they do that?'

'I don't know, sir.'

'And there never has been a time machine?'

'No, sir. It was just a story.'

'Anything else you want to tell me?'

Trafalgar had saved the best for last.

'Well, yes, sir. Apparently, even though there never has been any time travel, I am going to invent a time machine. Quite soon, I think.'

He didn't see O'Barron's hand move to the buzzer, so it came as a complete surprise when four men burst in through the door and took him by the arms.

'Mr Hurlock needs to be in a quiet, safe place until he starts to feel better,' O'Barron told them. 'The secure wing of the state hospital would be best for his own safety, I think. Do see he doesn't do himself any mischief on the way.'

SEVEN

They were very nice at the hospital and allowed him everything he wanted except the one thing he really wanted, which was not to be in the hospital. Writing materials, a datastore terminal and a desk to work at were all provided. The occasional doctor came to ask him questions in irritatingly condescending tones, quite convinced, after reading his file which included a note from the Minister, that he was barking mad.

On the second morning, Trafalgar began to think they might be right.

He'd slept very well. He had no memory at all of having woken up in the night and he was quite sure he had left nothing on the desk before he went to bed, but there in the middle of it was a pile of mouse-proof plasti-sheets and the writing on them was undoubtedly his.

The trouble was the only bit he could understand was the line scrawled across the top. It said, 'Woke up, couldn't get back to sleep. Hit by brilliant idea for chrononavigational interface synthesiser. I'd better make some notes. Do hope I remember it when I wake up in the morning.' What followed was a sheet full of the sort of equations that look like the result of a Scrabble tragedy.

Trafalgar inspected it warily and for a long time. There was no smell of scorching and no signs of dirty marks on the floor or he would have been inclined to suspect interference by Trafalgar 2. He put the sheets carefully away in the drawer and before he went to sleep that night after a long and very dull day, he made quite sure the desk was tidy.

In the morning he was relieved to see it looked exactly the same but the relief only lasted until he opened the drawer and saw there were more sheets of writing inside it than there had been the previous day. The bottom line of a long, long series of calculations was ringed around in red with an exclamation mark next to it. Below it was a complicated diagram of something that could equally well have been the intestinal arrangements of a crested newt or the lubrication mechanism of a mass-transit hover-train.

Underneath the diagram, his handwriting said, 'Right. Cracked it! This WILL WORK. Another wakeful night spent to good effect. Funny that I couldn't remember last night when I woke up. Oh, well, I expect it will be the same again. I've written it all down just in case. Must remember today to ask the nurses for the following.' An eight-page list of electronic components followed. Trafalgar looked at it gloomily and put it back in the drawer. They thought he was crazy enough already without asking for all this.

'I must think I was born yesterday,' he decided.

He woke up suddenly in the middle of the night to a strong smell of bleach and a very faint crackling noise. There was a pain in his big toe.

'Who's there?' he called, though he knew the answer and there was a violent motion in the room. He reached out to switch on the light.

The crackling was now coming from under the bed.

'Come out,' he said. 'I know you're under there.'

Trafalgar 2 looked annoyed when he appeared.

'Why do you *always* have to make things difficult?' he said.

'I knew it was you. It was obvious. Anyway, how

91

come there's no smoke? You're not skidding around.'

Trafalgar 2 pointed at his feet. One of them was bare and a cable was attached to it by a spring clip. That explained the pain in Trafalgar's big toe because the other end was clipped on to it.

'Cures the howl-round,' he said, 'at least until a static charge builds up.'

Trafalgar sniffed the air. 'And the bleach?'

'Just getting rid of some stains.'

'You've been here for the last two nights, haven't you?'

'I might have been.'

'You're trying to get me to think I've invented a time machine, aren't you?'

'You *have* invented it.' Trafalgar 2 pointed to the desk. 'There it is, congratulations. Completely gobsmacked, I was, when I came in and saw that. Clever old thing, I thought.'

'Where?' Trafalgar looked at the desk. There, coupled up to the computer, was a large silver box covered in knobs and dials. 'That's it? *That's* a time machine? I didn't invent it. You did, at least I suppose you did.'

'Exactly. That's what I said. You invented it.'

'Yes, but that's cheating. You can't just pretend ... Ah!' A thought had struck him. 'You mean I, you, we invent it in the future and you've brought it back here.'

'If you like.'

'Wait a minute. What's to stop you coming back here now from *before* you invented it and taking it forwards to give to yourself later on, then just pretending you invented it? Then it would still be here but *nobody* would have invented it.'

Trafalgar 2 winced and began to rub his forehead. 'Stop it. That hurts. You don't know what it's like. Anyway, that's silly.'

Trafalgar looked at him hard. He knew himself well enough to spot the signs when he was being evasive. 'You *did* invent it, didn't you?'

'I haven't really got time for any more questions.'

'Hang on. How come I have this machine here and *you* don't seem to need one at all?'

'Of course I need one. It's not here, that's all. I pre-set the time. Ten-minute visit.' He nodded at the machine on the desk. 'It's that same one, later on.'

'One last time. *Did* you invent it?'

'The tablet's wearing off. Anyway, time's up, I'll be going any second.'

'I want to know. I want an answer. I . . .'

The answer he got was 'whomp' and, as Trafalgar 2 had neglected to take the connecting cable off first, it was coupled with a very uncomfortable yank to his big toe.

He looked at the box on the desk. Underneath was a little, badly printed booklet. It said, 'Instructions for the Chrononavigational Global Positioning System. Please read before use.'

As if I wouldn't, Trafalgar thought. I mean to say, first thing you do when your future double gives you a time machine is you start fiddling with the dials at random, right? I mean, everyone knows *that's* stupid.

He sat down on the bed and began to read.

It said:

1) Read this.
2) Set dials A and B to precise longitude and latitude required.
3) Set dial C to precise date required. Adjust SEGS to AD.
4) If you don't know any of them, type in fullest possible description of destination. Guessing is dangerous.

5) Hold black handle on machine or, if using for
   mass travel, connect to conductive strip
   surrounding all travellers. If using remote setting,
   strap remote transmitter to convenient portion of
   anatomy.
6) Press knob.

NOTE: Internal database has been completely
corrected for factual errors.

KEEP AWAY FROM MICE. Contains small plastic parts.
Not for children under seven years of age without
adult supervision. Only use with 3-amp fuse.

Trafalgar finished reading, rang the bell and thirty-
eight minutes later the ward sister bustled in.

'I need to see Mr O'Barron,' Trafalgar said. 'I've got
something important for him.'

'Mr O'Barron. Let me see now, I don't think I know
the gentleman.'

'The Minister of Knowledge.'

'Oh yes, of course, the Minister. Well, now, I'll just be
seeing to that.'

She pretended to look behind the door and under the
bed. 'No, I'm sorry. I don't think he's here.'

'Look, really, I'm serious. Please go and call the Ministry and say Trafalgar Hurlock has invented a time mach—
er, has done what he said he'd do.'

'I think it's time for your rest,' she said.

'It's half past eight in the morning.'

'A very good time for a rest.'

'I'VE ONLY JUST WOKEN UP.'

'Don't shout at me. It makes me difficult,' she said and
turned on her heel.

'Please. Just phone the Ministry. They'll . . .'

He heard the key turn in the lock.

He wasted an hour fuming and kicking the furniture before it occurred to him that the locked door didn't matter a bit. If Trafalgar 2 was right, then the machine on the table meant he could go anywhere, any time. If he was wrong, then it was just as well to find out now, or that door was going to stay locked for a long time.

He switched on the computer.

The screen came up with a menu.

1) Datastores
2) Word Processor
3) Games
4) Time Travel

He pressed 4.

The machine gave a tinny trumpet fanfare and a rather poor image of a cobweb and a dusty vault came up.

'Enter desired date. All dates in AD. Please add 2,612 to dates expressed in SEGS. Alternatively, enter plus or minus time interval from present. Minimum setting, five minutes.'

He typed in minus five minutes and pressed enter.

There was another fanfare. He hated it already.

'Enter exact geographical coordinates of destination or accurate physical description. Be precise. If obstructed, machine will locate nearest available free space.'

He typed in, 'O'Barron's office. Ministry of Knowledge.'

'Strap remote transmitter to convenient portion of bare skin.'

There was a metal disc attached to a Velcro band. Trafalgar inspected it for signs that this was the remote transmitter but all it said on it was 'Made in Atlantis'. It was always the same with instructions. They invariably missed out the important bits. He hoped for the best,

95

strapped it on to his arm under his sleeve and – taking a deep breath – pressed the large green knob on top of the machine.

His head exploded and the world turned upside down. A strong taste of stale cheese filled his mouth. It was just like being back in the Gulliver's tomb. A metal helmet seemed to be clamped over his head and he couldn't see anything when he opened his eyes. Two hands grabbed his legs and pulled hard. His head popped out of the wastepaper basket into which he had plunged and he collapsed on to an unfamiliar carpet amid a forest of legs. Smoke billowed around him and the crackling seemed to be coming from inside him.

There was a deafening chorus of laughter.

O'Barron's office was full of people, all pointing at him and roaring their heads off. His own head felt like someone had already roared it off. It throbbed with the most acute headache he could ever remember. He tried to speak but something was getting in the way. There was still an extremely strong taste of cheese in his mouth.

O'Barron held up his hand and the laughter stopped.

'Yesterday's lunch,' he said in a helpful tone of voice.

Trafalgar, suddenly aware that he was still in his hospital pyjamas, stared at him uncomprehendingly.

'It's in your mouth. My lunch. From yesterday.' The laughter redoubled. 'It was a cheese sandwich,' O'Barron explained, 'in the waste bin.'

Trafalgar spat the stale sandwich on to the carpet.

'I . . .' he began.

'No time,' said O'Barron. 'Two messages. Come back an hour ago and read this first.' He gave Trafalgar a sheet of paper.

'What do you . . . ?'

The world inverted itself again and he tumbled on to the floor of his hospital room.

But for the fact that he landed on his head again, the headache would have gone. As it was he felt a dull, bruised sensation. He sat perfectly still and pondered on O'Barron's words. The man hadn't seemed surprised at all. What had he meant? Why had all those people laughed at him?

The sheet of paper said 'Check the README file. Tell the computer to miss the wastepaper basket next time.'

Readme files had not changed over the years. They were all the really important instructions that computer software designers forgot to put in the manual and which you only ever read in a state of total fury and desperation after wasting hours trying to make the damned thing work properly. This one was no exception. When he found his way into it through the computer, it contained all the things he really needed to know and what those things showed was that software designers were just as stupid in the future as they had been since disks began. The file said:

1) Default setting for duration of time travel is ONE MINUTE. Reset to higher value if you need to stay longer.
2) Default setting for orientation of arrival is UPSIDE DOWN. Reset to right way up if you prefer.
3) Take strong headache tablets before travelling.
4) Read the README file before operating machine.

Trafalgar dressed properly before he tried again, then swallowed three painkillers, reprogrammed the computer for one hour earlier, reset the rest of the information and pressed the button for a second time. His head exploded all over again but this time the pain was slightly dulled. He arrived the right way up on the carpet in front of O'Barron's desk and, clutching at it, managed to keep his balance. The room was empty. It was, he realised, rather early in the morning for a Minister but, as that thought crossed his mind, the door opened and O'Barron walked in. He looked at Trafalgar in utter astonishment and a little fear.

'Hurlock? How did you get out? How did you get in?'

'I've got a machine. A time machine. Well, it does space too.'

O'Barron still had his hand on the door handle and looked very wary, as if he might make a run for it at any moment.

'Don't worry,' said Trafalgar, 'I'm not mad. Just watch, you'll see. I'll disappear in a couple of minutes, then I'll be back in an hour's time. Have you got a spare plasti-sheet? I've got to give you a note to give to me and you've got to tell me to come back an hour ago; that is now.'

O'Barron continued to look at him as a man might look at a talking horse.

'This is meant to stop me worrying?' he said.

'Yes. You'll see,' said Trafalgar, writing frantically. At least he knew exactly what to write. 'You've got to get me out of the hospital. I've got the machine there. When I come back, I only stay here for a minute so give this to me quickly. Oh by the way, stay away from the waste-paper basket because that's where I'll land and I'd be really obliged if you *wouldn't* invite all those people to come along and laugh at me.'

O'Barron, speechless, took the note and backed away from him. Trafalgar's feet dragged sideways across the carpet leaving black stains behind. He released his grip on the desk, sailed sideways into the wall and, with another loud 'whomp', the machine threw him forward to where he'd started.

'Damn,' he thought, 'I forgot to ask him to get rid of the cheese sandwich.'

EIGHT

O'Barron had many, many faults. He was a power-mad, grasping, greedy, selfish egomaniac but he was no fool. When Trafalgar imploded out of existence before his eyes, leaving only wisps of smoke behind, he quickly checked behind the curtains, under the desk and inside the cupboard, then he took his pulse, pinched himself, inspected his tongue in the mirror and finally came to the only remaining conclusion that Trafalgar was right. He sent his men to get Trafalgar as soon as he'd recovered sufficiently from his astonishment, then he sat back to wait for the promised reappearance and – prompted entirely by Trafalgar's warning and a vague feeling that there might indeed be a good laugh to be had out of it – summoned his senior staff to share the spectacle.

It took over an hour for O'Barron's team to reach the hospital, which was probably as well because, if they'd been there any quicker, they would have got to Trafalgar's room before he'd thought of using the time machine to go to see O'Barron, thereby putting a further wrinkle into the already crumpled framework of space/time/logic as well as increasing his consumption of painkillers. As it was, Trafalgar had barely got his breath back from the second trip before they burst politely in through his door and ushered him outside to a luxuriously upholstered government rickshaw. He clutched the time machine throughout the journey.

'I'm hanging on to it,' he insisted when they tried to

stow it in the luggage compartment. 'The mice mustn't get near it.'

They humoured him.

Word had spread like wildfire round ELV headquarters as O'Barron's staff at the Ministry repeated the story of the wastepaper basket and threw in some gratuitous rudeness about the colour of Trafalgar's pyjamas. The ELV team didn't care a toss about the style of the first time trip. They cared much more about the simple fact that it had taken place and there was a hero's reception waiting for him. Puckeridge slapped him on the back and offered him a glass of champagne which dribbled through a hidden hole all over his shirt. The woman with the electric helmet tore it off with a shriek of relief and jumped up and down on it until it was a flattened mass of metal and electrodes, shouting, 'Free, I'm free.' Rumpole glared at him and barked, 'Well done,' in a furious way, then Trafalgar turned and found himself face to face with Anya.

'Hey, you're not such a twit as you look,' she said and he was framing a witty reply along the lines of, 'If you want to travel, I've got the time,' when she followed her remark with a smile of such potency that his brain melted and turned his thought processes into hot marshmallow. All he could manage in reply was a smile of his own and though she seemed to be saying something to him in a questioning tone, he couldn't quite focus on it. She gave up in the end, shook her head and walked off.

'How did you do it?' asked the old man who might be called Aspirin, or Camomile or something.

'Oh, you know,' said Trafalgar vaguely. 'It sort of suddenly just came to me. In the night, you know.'

'I was nearly there myself, as a matter of fact,' said the old man. 'Just another few days and they would have been calling it the Hereward Richthofen Time Device.'

'Why? Is that your name?' Trafalgar asked.

'Is what my name?'

'Hereward Richthofen.'

'No, I don't think so. What gave you that idea?' He looked at the device with interest. 'Is it sand powered? It is, isn't it? I was so near you see. It's just a question of getting the right coloured sand.'

O'Barron called them all to a special meeting in the afternoon. Trafalgar found himself resenting the way the Minister leapt to his feet to offer Anya the chair next to him. There was an expression on O'Barron's face that was close to being a leer.

When everyone had finished shuffling around, muttering and coughing, O'Barron stood up and did what bosses are best at doing: he took the credit for it.

'You will all know by now,' he said, 'that my plan has succeeded and by careful recruitment of the right people and precise allocation of tasks I have managed to secure the re-invention of the time machine. Trafalgar Hurlock, working within my guidelines, has put the final touches to my plan and he will now fill you in on the details of how it works.'

There was a scatter of applause as Trafalgar stood up.

Did O'Barron say *re*-invention? he was thinking. Didn't he understand what I said? It didn't seem quite the right time to contradict the Minister publicly.

'It's fairly simple,' he said. 'You just type in where you want to go and when you want to be there and press the knob, that's all.'

He sat down, hoping they might not notice that he'd skated over some of the trickier parts of the technical specification. There was a silence while they all looked at him expectantly.

'And . . . ?' said O'Barron.

'And? Oh, and then you get to where you want to be.'

102

He stopped again. They were all still staring at him. 'With a headache,' he added in an effort to be helpful. 'A pretty bad headache actually.'

O'Barron cleared his throat. 'We rather hoped you might tell us *how* it works,' he prompted.

'Ah.' Trafalgar searched for an idea, *any* idea. 'It's a bit difficult to follow really.'

'Don't worry,' said O'Barron, smiling broadly. 'We've got the best brains in the country here. I'm sure they'll understand if you just run through the broad principles. There's a blackboard over there if it would help.'

Trafalgar stood in front of the blackboard completely stumped. Memories of being hauled up before the class in school flooded back. Physics.

'What is the first law of thermodynamics, Hurlock?'

He could never remember. Was it 'Don't pick up a hot plate if you've got cold fingers' or was that the third law? Literature had been just as bad. Getting muddled up between William Schwarzenegger's plays.

'No, no, no, Hurlock – the soliloquy "To pee or not to pee, that's indigestion" is from *Omelette* NOT *King Kong*.'

He'd never been able to understand what people saw in Schwarzenegger anyway. None of it made sense, except maybe *A Midsummer Nightmare on Elm Street*.

The blackboard stared at him unhelpfully and he was uncomfortably aware of all the expectant throat-clearing. With the sudden enormous relief of someone realising the vampire advancing towards him is a vegetarian, Trafalgar remembered the plasti-sheets full of equations which had appeared in his hospital room. He pulled the whole sheaf of them out of his bag and began to scratch away, copying them laboriously and wholesale on to the blackboard with much unpleasant scratching of chalk. Behind him he could sense the dull creaking of several enormous brains working, interspersed with the occasional quiet 'uurp' and 'phwoot' as, carried away by their calculations, they temporarily lost control of several important orifices. The atmosphere inside ELV head-quarters always got a bit fruity when there was a lot of thinking going on.

There was a long silence when he had finished, then the woman who had been wearing the electric helmet and whose hair was scorched in an unusual pattern of concentric circles said, 'You do realise that this equation merely describes the chemical processes involved in making fudge?'

You bastard, Trafalgar said silently to his future equivalent. You were just trying to pull the wool over my eyes.

'No, no,' said a cadaverous man with glasses so thick that they were supported by a small cantilever structure bolted to his nose. 'The constant K is wrong. It's 1.74 for fudge. I believe this variant relates to caramel in its purest form.'

'Caramel? That's absurd. Caramel with a temperature range of six degrees? It's quite obviously fudge.'

'I expect you're both right,' said Trafalgar hastily. 'It's probably fudge *and* caramel – something between the two. I'm sure they're each very important.'

This was greeted by a suspicious silence, then the man with the thick glasses said, 'Oh, all right then, *don't* tell us. I suppose we'll have to take it apart and work it out for ourselves.' He got up and moved towards the machine purposefully.

Trafalgar picked it up. As he did so, he noticed a sticker on the underside that he hadn't seen before. It said, 'Do not undo cover without first making Will. Guarantee invalidated if disturbed. Failure to follow this instruction may lead to global annihilation. Lead-based paint, not to be sucked by small children. Do not drop.'

'I don't think that would be a very good idea,' he said.

The cadaverous man read the sticker and laughed. 'Oh, come off it,' he said. 'You just want to keep it all to yourself.'

He grabbed the machine, pulling it out of Trafalgar's hands and, putting it down on the table, took a screwdriver from his top pocket. As he slotted the screwdriver into the first screw, there was a loud 'whomp', a brief swirl of smoke and he dropped, unconscious, to the ground. For just a micro-second Trafalgar was pretty certain he'd seen Trafalgar 2, dressed in his helmet again, in the middle of an uppercut to the man's chin but the vision was gone so rapidly that he couldn't be quite sure.

The effect was sharp. The rest of the team looked at the warning sticker with new respect and no one made the slightest attempt to get on closer terms with the machine.

'Pick that man up,' said O'Barron, badly shaken. 'There's no time for messing around. The important thing is that we do now have a working model of the O'Barron Temporal Relocator. For the next stage we need to incorporate it into a large enough vehicle to take the whole of the expedition team.'

'What team is that, Minister?' said Anya.

O'Barron gave her a smile which made Trafalgar's fists twitch. He had never been a violent person but what had just happened suggested that one day he might be. He closed his eyes and wished for another instantaneous reappearance by a punch-dispensing Trafalgar 2 but nothing happened.

'A very good question, my dear. The team that's going back in my device,' said O'Barron.

My dear? *My* device? Trafalgar's outrage took two more upward lurches.

'I'll post names of the members of the team later on,'

O'Barron went on smoothly. 'In the meantime, the rest of you can start building the vehicle.'

He looked at the machine on the table as if it might bite.

'You'd better look after this, Hurlock,' he said.

On the way out, Stilts pulled Trafalgar gently to one side and waited until all the rest had gone.

'Come on,' he said, 'tell me. You didn't invent it, did you? You've got no more idea how it works than I have. Where did it really come from?'

Trafalgar decided he could trust Stilts. 'I did. I mean, I will. Well, I think I will.'

'That's not perhaps quite as clear as it might be.'

'Well, I just haven't invented it quite yet, you see? That comes later. I came back and gave it to myself.'

'Ah! And if you don't?'

'I will. I'll have to. It's already happened.'

'But just supposing I killed you, right now. Supposing I pushed you out of the window.'

'This is theoretical, isn't it?' Trafalgar asked, looking nervously at the window.

The window looked back at him impassively. Nothing to do with me, it seemed to be saying. I'll probably just break up into a thousand little bits and let you plunge through to your death if someone pushes you hard enough. Hey, I'm just a window. It's in my nature.

'Well, yes – I suppose it is but answer it anyway.'

'I rather suspect you wouldn't be able to because I'd come back from the future and stop you.'

'You're going to be awfully busy.'

'I know. I've already notched up about nine or ten jobs to do. I think I'd better start writing them down. I don't know what would happen if I forgot some.'

'I expect you'd just have to come back and remind yourself.'

He went back to his office and sat down at the terminal. Rumpole had gone out for a quick shout. It was just him and the gorgeous Anya, looking feline, dangerous and ready for anything. She glanced sideways and smiled at him again in exactly the way he'd always wanted someone to smile at him, a smile that told him *she* knew who the real credit should go to, a smile that told him this was the moment to seize his opportunity and declare his feelings to her so that any competition from the Minister was ruled out before it could get started.

'Look, Trafalgar,' she said, 'I'd quite fancy you if you could manage to say something a bit more interesting than "nnnnwugh" to me.'

His heart gave a great leap and he gazed back at her as his brain put together an elegant little speech to the effect that it was only her amazing beauty that robbed him of all his powers of speech and that his heart was hers for ever to do with whatever she cared. A tiny, wobbly noise that sounded like 'erbl' trickled past his lips and scuttled away into the surrounding air. She looked disappointed, then irritated and finally incredibly pissed off. Trafalgar stared at her in the usual puzzled fashion for a few seconds then the door burst open and Rumpole grumbled in, followed closely by his personal black cloud.

'Bloody stupid door,' he said, kicking it. 'Hate the bloody thing. Hinges, I ask you – dumb idea. Work, work, work.' He looked around. 'Now I suppose I'll have to sit down. Bloody chair. Just sodding well stands there. Chairs? Don't give me chairs. I've had chairs up to here.'

The moment was lost. The other two got on with their work and Trafalgar stared at the extraordinary box. On an impulse, he switched it on and tapped an enquiry into its datastore.

'Big Ben?' he wrote.

The screen flickered and a picture appeared. It was a

picture he'd seen before and the caption was also the one he'd seen before until it had been changed.

'Big Ben,' it said underneath, 'the famous London landmark. The name refers to the bell that strikes the hours though it is commonly misused for the clock-tower itself.'

Trafalgar stared at it, fascinated and horrified in equal measure. Yes, yes, yes, he thought. It was all true. This was the original, correct data. He looked quickly around for mice. Whatever happened, this must not be corrupted. How far, he wondered, did the damage go? He remembered his first meeting with O'Barron and Saccharine Fernandez and the checks by which they had set so much store.

He entered 'Stephenson's Rocket' and looked at the picture that came on the screen with astonishment.

Neil Diamond went to the moon in *that*? It didn't look very aerodynamic. The text said, 'The Rocket. First successful steam-powered locomotive built by George Stephenson. Achieved maximum speed of 29 miles per hour in 1829.'

'Locomotive' meant nothing to him at all but a steam-powered spacecraft was a new idea. Trafalgar did a quick sum. It was nearly one and a half million miles to the moon. At top speed, it would have taken them the best part of six years to get there. There was something wrong here. There weren't any fins, just a tall chimney and lots of wheels. How did they keep the coal from floating off into space?

He went on checking. He tried 'Moon' next and got a completely different account of the first man on the moon. Neil *Armstrong*? Who on earth was he? The spacecraft looked much more convincing. The real poser though was the distance to the moon. According to this machine it was only two hundred and twenty-two thousand miles, not nearly one and a half million, which it should be. Had the moon got further away?

Just in case there was any mistake in the units he looked up 'Mile' and got a big surprise. It was a very short entry.

'Mile,' it said. 'Unit of measurement equal to 1,760 yards, 5,280 feet or approximately 1.6 kilometres.'

Fine. Everybody knew that. But there was one more line.

'One mile is equal to 0.15 old miles.'

That was a very familiar number, 0.15, the number on the ratio stones.

He checked the distance to the moon again. The moon hadn't moved. Two hundred and twenty-two thousand old miles was nearly one and a half million new miles. At 29 old miles an hour, Stephenson's Rocket would have taken only a year to get there. *Only* a year? Trafalgar went into a trance as his mind ranged back to the Gulliver Robert Smith's words on the Videowill. 'I don't want to be a foot tall,' the Gulliver had said and that hadn't made any sense because Trafalgar knew all too well that people weren't a foot tall. So much had happened since then that he hadn't really been able to think it all through but suddenly he understood. In the Sleep everyone *had* been downsized, not just everyone but everything, but they'd downsized the measurements too. It must have been a huge step for mankind to take and it was no wonder the ancients had taken the trouble to put it on every major building. It was just a shame that nobody had the faintest idea what it meant. Everything in the whole world was just under one sixth of its old size. The Videowill was not the testimony of a madman, it was the last words of an original full-size man who had decided to die alone on a sleeping planet rather than join everybody else in the downsizing Sleep.

Not everything was smaller. The houseflies weren't,

for a start, nor were the seas, the continents or the mountains. It explained the waves. Of course, the ancients used to travel the seas in their catameringues. It would have been easy if the waves seemed only a sixth of the size. The winds too. They would only have seemed like gentle breezes in comparison. It was no wonder the old records had no mention of blowaways. He went on checking the datastores right through that afternoon and the more he checked, the more he realised the enormity of the problem they faced. Almost everything was wrong. Late in the day, just before the time came to lock the machine away, he remembered the Gulliver's strange term for the world they lived on and he looked up details of the solar system. That was when he found out he really was on a different planet. So much for Neptune. According to this database, Robert Smith had got it right. They were indeed living on a planet called Earth. That took some getting used to. It was hardly a glamorous name.

At that point, he thought he'd better make a back-up of this priceless record. He tapped the 'Copy' command into the keyboard. The machine hiccuped. A message appeared on the screen. 'Copying ready to proceed,' it said. It was only when it told him how many floppy disks he needed that he gave up the idea.

The list of names went up on the notice board the following morning. It contained good news and bad news.

Trafalgar Hurlock
Stilton Cheesemaker
Anya Ninety-Five

Trafalgar breathed a huge sigh of relief at that point. Stilts and Anya – he could hardly have wished for more. Her surname came as a surprise. He hadn't realised Anya

110

had aristocratic connections. Double-barrelled, no less. He read on.

> Idaho Puckeridge
> Belle Tower
> Sopwith Camel
> Halogen Tinker

He knew Puckeridge of course, but the other three names meant nothing to him at all. The former Aspirin or Camomile or Hereward Richthofen was standing behind Trafalgar as they crowded round the notice board, jostling for a look.

'Is my name on it?' he asked.

'No.'

'How do you know?' said the old man cunningly. Trafalgar ignored him. He had just come to the next name and it looked like bad news.

Enteritis Rumpole

Never mind, thought Trafalgar. At least he'd have Anya more or less to himself, and maybe, with a bit of practice, he might even be able to say something to her. Having Rumpole along would be a minor irritation, it was true, but that minor irritation was quickly overshadowed by what came next on the list.

Bluto O'Barron (Mission Leader)

Unbelievable. The Minister himself was coming. Horrified, Trafalgar wondered if O'Barron was after the glory or after Anya. He didn't mind so much about the first but he certainly minded about the second.

*　　*　　*

The unveiling of the time machine was a big event for the whole of ELV headquarters. It was Anya who actually found the plans from which it was constructed but O'Barron took the credit on the grounds that his instructions to search the databases were entirely responsible. Quite what else the database search team might have done if he hadn't told them to search the databases was unclear. There was a wide choice of different design of time machine in the files, and they could be built in a number of different materials of which wood, steel, gold and leather seemed to be the favourites.

The wooden ones looked easiest to build and also most capable of accommodating a large team, so carpenters had been hammering and sawing non-stop. Trafalgar was very unsure indeed about the whole business. Trafalgar 2 had quite clearly said that the Gullivers had never had time travel, so it was pretty obvious that the mice had been at this stuff too. The real time machine was still securely locked away in the safe. Trafalgar now knew that it contained the only real account of the world's original history and geography in its data banks and that account was hugely valuable. He also knew that if he confronted O'Barron with all of this, he would probably wind up in the same hospital room again and the only way he would ever convince O'Barron of the truth would be to take him back and show him. Their trip should do just that, then one day, maybe, when there was time, he could use the uncorrupted data in the time machine to set the whole store of human knowledge back on its proper feet.

After they'd dealt with the mice of course.

For all that, he did try to talk to O'Barron about one of his doubts.

'Minister? I don't think those drawings are quite right.'

O'Barron always had an important, hurried, oh-what-is-it-now? look about him except when he was gazing at Anya when he had an important, unhurried, I-know-exactly-what-it-is-now look. He gave Trafalgar a burst of the first type.

'And why do you say that?'

'I told you, sir. My information was that there never has been a time machine before.'

'What you're neglecting, Hurlock, is that if *you* could come back from the future and give yourself a time machine then plenty of *other* people could have done the same.'

'But I would have told myself that, sir.'

'Maybe you don't . . . er . . . won't . . . er . . . will not have been knowing about it.'

There didn't seem to be the right sort of verbs for time travel.

'I think I would have, sir.'

O'Barron looked at him in annoyance. 'Well, maybe I myself decided, will decide, er . . . will have decided to come back and *put* the drawings in the datastores.'

There was no arguing with the man and anyway, Trafalgar decided, there wasn't much point. His magic box was going to provide all the working bits. The bigger time machine was just a dummy really, a vehicle they could all fit inside. It didn't really matter what it looked like.

He was in the canteen having lunch when they finished work on it. He was enjoying his lunch, a strawberry pizza with gravy, when the announcement came over the loudspeaker system. The strawberries were just right, fried to curled, tasty perfection so his heart sank at the prospect of leaving it half eaten but the canteen was emptying fast with excited ELV staff hurrying to see the unveiling.

They'd really gone to town on it. The plans had been

followed to perfection. The machine stood balanced on end, brought to life in beautiful, polished wood, brass and steel, soaring a hundred feet into the air. They hadn't just done the bodywork, they'd even copied the machinery inside even though Trafalgar knew perfectly well it was only the mechanisms already inside *his* little box that really mattered. He inspected it. There was plenty of space within for all of them, plus seats and beds on the upper deck and a cargo hold below for all their food and equipment. There was a neat socket in the command chamber where his own time device would fit in, coupled to a computer and a series of wires and amplifiers which, Stilts believed, would spread its effective field right through the whole ship.

O'Barron held up a hand for silence.

'I'm delighted to see the machine has been prepared so quickly. It is a tribute to the organisational skills brought to bear on the problem from the highest level. We will launch our expedition tomorrow morning at a special event. I will be choosing a name for the time ship based on my knowledge of great vessels of the past. In the meantime, I have a surprise for you all. In recognition of the importance of this event, the ELV time team has been redesignated as a military unit and not just any military unit. From now on, you are to be members of the SOS.'

This sent a thrill through the entire audience. The Synchronised Olympic Swimmers were an elite unit, legendary from time immemorial. Under the command of Abraham Lincoln they had rescued the Knights of the Round Table from Mother Teresa's fearful Mongol hordes and driven them all the way back to Berlin just before the Ice Age. These days, it was true, it didn't have a great deal to do, what with a united world government and little need for military action, but some of its exploits against the houseflies had been pretty exciting and it was very good at mock battles. There was definitely a special quality in the uniform of the SOS. Trafalgar fell into an immediate daydream in which his grandson climbed on his knee and said, 'What did you do in the war against the flies, Granddad?'

'I was in the SOS,' he would say quietly.

'No! Really?'

'I was. And Grandma too.' He could just see Anya nodding lovingly at him from her rocking chair across the room. This daydream was getting a little out of hand.

'You and Grandma? Wow! Imagine that. I never knew that.'

Yes indeed, a man could be truly proud to be a member of the SOS.

He snapped back to reality, such as it was, to hear the climax of O'Barron's speech.

'Members of the time team, your uniforms await you. Wear them to glory and let the initials ELV ring down the ages.'

O'Barron threw up his hand in a dramatic gesture and pointed to the time ship. Trumpets sounded from the speakers and a cloud of green choking smoke billowed out around it. Everyone started to cough and within seconds the entire crowd was trying to trample over itself to get through the door as O'Barron's voice behind them wailed despairingly.

'CARBON DIOXIDE, I said. Can't you get *anything* right?'

Later, when the gas had cleared, they were finally able to put on their new uniforms, unisex green tunics with the proud green beret with its hanging floppy point. Trafalgar was delighted to get out of his skirt and put it on. Skirts were so draughty.

NINE

The time machine sat inside O'Barron's triple-locked high-security safe, guarded by laser movement-detection systems, infra-red intrusion beams, floor-mounted vibration-sensitive pads and a large brick balanced carefully on top of the door. Trafalgar slept securely in his bed, his keys clutched in his hand, knowing that only two people on the planet had the means to get inside the safe and that even in his wildest nightmares there couldn't possibly be any conceivable threat to the safety of the precious data contained in it.

His nightmares weren't quite wild enough.

Trafalgar turned over in bed and dreamed of Anya. Even in his dreams, he couldn't find anything to say to her. The city around him was almost completely asleep. On its southern edge, the head of the Windguard night shift was grumbling over the quality of the 3 AM steam pudding.

'No good, these light, fluffy jobs,' said the sergeant. 'I like them done the way my mum used to make them. Good solid ones. Eight eggs, ten pounds of flour, two scoops of cement, that's the way to do it. And as for the custard, where's the lumps, eh? What's the good if you can't walk across it with dry boots? This lot's all runny.'

High up in his observation tower the night watchman, ear trumpet in place, scanned the horizon every two minutes, listening for the far-off faint buzz of any night-flying houseflies.

In a flat overlooking the other river, a tired mother read *Snow White and the Temple of Doom* to her wakeful baby for the hundredth time. That was about it in terms of meaningful activity.

Except in O'Barron's office.

In O'Barron's office, a key was carefully inserted into the lock of the safe and its door was swung open. The brick wobbled and fell, producing an unpleasant squashing noise and a brief, truncated scream.

Blissfully unaware that anything was wrong, Trafalgar turned over again in his bed and started to snore gently.

In O'Barron's office, a connector lead was pushed into the back of the time machine and a computer monitor came on with a low electronic hum. The time machine began to display the contents of its database.

What it showed was completely absurd.

'England,' it said, 'an island off the northern coast of France, joined to Scotland and Wales.'

O'Barron rubbed his toe. He'd forgotten about the brick. He went on tapping away at the keyboard. *Everyone* knew Scotland was next to Peru and as for Wales – well, you couldn't join a country to a wale. The wale would never keep still long enough. He was very glad, knowing Hurlock's peculiar theories, that he'd bothered to check. True, Hurlock had come up with the goods on the time machine – apparently. Privately, O'Barron had convinced himself that the entire credit for the invention really did belong to his own masterly overview. Hurlock *was* eccentric though. All that nonsense about finding a cave with a Gulliver's bones in it. They'd searched the whole area in detail. All they'd found was solid ground with no trace of an entrance. Oh, and a tree, but the search team hadn't thought of reporting that.

All told, it meant Hurlock was very unreliable.

O'Barron had consulted Saccharine Fernandez.

'I don't trust him,' Fernandez had said. 'He smokes in the shower and as for his singing . . .'

They agreed it was ridiculous to suggest that the mice had got at *everything*, not just ridiculous but probably dangerous. A few things maybe, but not everything. It would turn civilisation upside down. There was no knowing how people would react to that sort of rumour. They might stop believing anything at all. They might even stop believing politicians. Granted, there seemed to be a bit of a muddle here and there, and some minor things seemed to have been rearranged. Of course, there was undoubtedly an urgent need to go back and sort out P.C. Apple *before* he dreamed up the mice but what O'Barron was finding in the time machine's datastore was just ludicrous. He gave an amazed chuckle at the latest piece of nonsense. Mars? The nearest planet? The nearest planet was Snickers. To confirm his view, the stupid machine claimed Neptune was uninhabitable. Uninhabitable? I mean to say, he thought, here I am living on it.

It was just as well he had found out before Trafalgar used the garbled information to carry them off to heaven knows where. He started to perform the standard check list, looking up the key points of well-known, universally agreed history.

'Batman,' said the datastore. 'Fictitious crime-buster, known alternatively as the "caped crusader". Comic-book secret identity of rich socialite Bruce Wayne, living in Gotham City.'

Oh really! Completely absurd. Fictitious indeed. No mention of the Charge of the Light Brigade at all and what rich socialite would ever think of living in Gotham City. It was widely regarded as a cultural backwater. What rubbish this was.

After an hour's work, O'Barron had come to the conclusion that every single fact stored in the database of this machine was absolutely, completely, dangerously, absurdly wrong. The only question remaining was what on earth he should do about it. There wasn't much time and he could just imagine how obstinate Hurlock would be if he tried to argue it all out with him, point by point. As it was, they just couldn't trust it and he knew that, very soon, they would be relying on the machine's data-stores for every aspect of their travel to wherever and whenever. He shuddered at the thought.

Better, he decided, to sort it out as quickly and quietly as possible. The decision made, he took a cable from his drawer, connected the time machine to the main computer system and began to wipe all the information inside it, replacing it with the tried and tested facts in the international datastore. For a moment he thought he heard shrill electronic laughter from somewhere under his floorboards but it must have been a trick of the wind.

The opening bars of the country's best-known tune burst out across the square outside ELV headquarters, the musicians blowing lustily into their violins and working the slides for all they were worth. Trafalgar always felt self-conscious singing the national anthem but this was a special occasion and, for once, he gave it all he had, keenly aware of Anya's soaring treble next to him. Five hundred voices rose into the morning air as one.

'Half a pound of tuppenny rice, half a pound of treacle. Mix it up and make it nice. Pop goes the weasel . . .'

Trafalgar had never been in the presence of so many important people before. The President, all her ministers, the press. This was the day the ELV project finally went officially public. The six ELV members of the time team, dressed slightly self-consciously in their new uniforms stood together, their three travelling companions next to them. The nine of them had met for the first time that morning. Belle Tower, Sopwith Camel and Halogen Tinker were from the Environment Ministry and they had arrived dressed in ordinary civilian clothes. Their minister, Clint Canute, who'd come to see them off, realised she'd been upstaged as soon as she set eyes on the team's SOS tunics.

'Ah,' she said to O'Barron. 'Forgot something. Back in a couple of ticks,' and she ushered her three out of the door.

It was an hour before they reappeared which defined a new exchange rate for the tick at one tick equals thirty minutes. The change in their style of dress was the only noticeable difference.

'Oh right, so now they're suddenly Red Berets,' Stilts hissed to Trafalgar as they came back in through the door. 'Is that pathetic or what?'

It was hardly the fault of the three team members who were now looking very self-conscious indeed in their blue tunics. The red berets flopped over their left ears as they were meant to but there all resemblance to members of that other legendary special forces unit ended. Belle Tower had a round, podgy body and a matching face. Sopwith Camel looked as if he might have an athletic body inside his clothes. The trouble was his own body seemed to be in there too. It was difficult to know what to make of Halogen Tinker because *his* body seemed to have more than the usual number of elbows and knees and his brain was equally loosely connected. Halfway through any sentence, he would become so distracted by some passing thought that he would trail off and never quite get to the end of it.

'Red Berets! Paras, indeed,' snorted Stilts, sarcastically. 'They've got as much to do with the parrotshoot regiment as I have. I'll bet they've never shot a parrot in their lives.'

Everything was ready. The storage compartments of the time ship were loaded with food, drink, spare parts and clean underwear. The climax of the ceremony was to be the moment when O'Barron broke the traditional bottle of shampoo over the ship to name it. Then the members of the team would file in through the door, strap themselves into their seats and push the button. There'd been a bit of an argument about this. The public relations department of the Ministry of Knowledge – or Anonymous McWhirter as he would have been known to friends if he'd recognised such a concept as friendliness – had been very insistent about it. Several people, at different times in his life, had tried to explain what friends were but he'd never been able to see what possible use they could be and a career in public relations had come naturally.

'You can't just come straight back,' he'd said. 'I know you don't *need* to be away for any length of time but, I mean, what's it going to look like if you all get in the thing, then get straight out again and say "Hello, we're back"? I mean it's not exactly spectacular, is it? It's not exactly Christine Columbus discovering Disneyland, is it? It's hardly your actual "One small step for man, one giantburger with extra pickle please."'

He'd cast his eyes to heaven. 'You've got to ham it up a bit. Come back five minutes later, no, I tell you what – we'll *tell* them you're due back in five minutes but you *really* take ten minutes, then everyone should get totally worked up with unbearable tension when you're late. We'll have lots of dry ice and fireworks and stuff too.'

There was a long silence while they all looked at him. Stilts was the first to speak.

'We're going on the most amazingly dangerous and uncertain mission in the entire history of the planet and you say it needs fireworks and dry ice?'

The man who had briefly been thought to be Hereward Richthofen looked at Stilts in alarm. 'You're going on a dangerous mission? Dear me! Where to?'

O'Barron took it upon himself to make the final speech and the self-importance oozed out of his mouth in great indigestible gobbets.

He must have put in the midnight hours going through the quotations in the datastores because he'd borrowed shamelessly from Schwarzenegger.

'Friends,' he began, 'snowmen and countrymen, buy me a beer. As the bard went on to say: in the town where I was born lived an owl and a pussycat who sailed to sea. Today, nine brave souls . . .' here Trafalgar did a quick count and realised O'Barron was including himself '. . . are indeed sailing to see – sailing off into the unknown to see what they can do to help us out of our present predicament, to help us to a better world in which you are safe from houseflies for ever. In doing so, we shall take our inspiration from the past, from the wise rulers of the golden ages before the Sleep, from gentle Attila, from kind King Adolf and perhaps above all from the great empire of Graceland and the King of Kings, Elvis himself. I intend to pay him a state visit and return to this, our own age, bearing with me the wisdom of those glorious days.' And materially helping my chances of being the next President, he thought to himself. 'This expedition is taking place because a bold decision has been made by myself and other members of your government – the sort of decision, I might say, that only the World Democratic Party . . .'

It looked as though he might have a lot more to say in a similar vein but rude fate intervened. Rude fate, or Roodfeit as he would have spelt it if he could write, was the name of a housefly. Houseflies are not known for their imagination and almost all of them are called Roodfeit which means 'Buzz'. This is only a minor irritation as they have very little gossip worth passing on to each other so the occasional confusion over exactly who they're gossiping about doesn't matter much.

An ululating wail cut rudely into O'Barron's speech.

Housefly sirens.

He stopped talking and looked up at the sky. Four hundred and ninety-nine other heads followed his gaze. A black speck was growing rapidly bigger.

If O'Barron had wanted proof that the expedition's aims were vital, he could not have asked for better; however, right then he would happily have done without it. Forgetting the microphone was live, he mumbled the sort of invitation that ministers are not expected to make in public. No one was in a mood to accept.

'Housefly raid,' boomed a voice on the loudspeaker. 'Track plotted in this direction. Take cover.'

'I name this vessel the TS *Titanic*, a proud and successful name from the past,' he said hurriedly. 'May God bless her and . . .'

His voice trailed off. None of the guests was listening. Nearly five hundred people were trying to get through a single door at the same time, the door that led to the fly raid shelter. The time team who were lined up behind O'Barron on the platform looked at the squirming, undignified mass of punching, kicking VIPs and, as one, decided not to follow.

'Um,' said O'Barron, 'where was I? Oh yes. Naming the ship.' He sounded as if he was trying to keep his voice steady. He swung the bottle hard against the time ship. The top flew off and, being plastic, the bottle bounced back again, dribbling luminous pink shampoo down the front of O'Barron's clothes. They all looked up at the sky again. Trafalgar held up a finger, lined up so the oncoming fly seemed to be balanced on the end of it. He didn't have to move his finger. The fly just got bigger and bigger. No question. It was on a collision course.

They looked at O'Barron. He looked at the fly. The fly looked dangerous. O'Barron looked speechless.

Trafalgar broke the deadlock. 'The machine,' he said, 'into the machine.'

'No,' said O'Barron in a squeaky voice. 'Squashed. We'll be squashed. We're going to die. Run. Hide.'

'We can escape,' Trafalgar said urgently. 'We can take the machine somewhere else.'

'B . . . b . . . b . . . but . . .' Trafalgar pushed him in through the door and the others followed. The first mass launch of the TS *Titanic* called for unhurried, calm, precise care. The rising drone from outside called for panicky, dithering frenzy. He dithered. The screen waited for his instructions. They faced each other, equally blank. The screen's cursor blinked. Trafalgar cursed and blinked.

'Strap yourselves in,' he shouted, hoping for inspiration. He saw Stilts was in the seat next to him. 'Where shall we go?' he said.

The drone outside was rising rapidly in pitch. Something huge was blocking the light out of the windows.

The speech was still fresh in their minds. 'King Adolf's time,' Stilts said, then, plucking inspiration from thin air that wasn't going to stay thin for very long if the fly had its way, 'Omaha Beach.'

There was no time to think. Trafalgar punched it in with trembling fingers, looked at it for a split second, wondering whether this was wise and as a huge roar of tumbling masonry erupted outside, he pressed the button.

Woodwork shrieked as the machine wrenched itself out of the here and now into the there and then. The *Titanic* was well built as wooden boxes go but the tug of the machine at its middle sent it banana-shaped. There was a long, long moment when Trafalgar felt he was being stretched out to twice his normal length, then the air turned into iridescent blue treacle and some invisible origami expert seemed to be trying to fold him up into a paper chrysanthemum. His head exploded into the very worst headache of his entire life. There was a chorus of groans from everyone around him that told him he was not alone.

Then they arrived.

Omaha Beach, the datastores said, was the best place for a summer holiday in the entire history of the world. Young post-Sleep Neptunians, barred from sea-bathing most of the time by the waves, had yearned and drooled over the images of it. Miles of golden sand, the warmest, calmest, bluest water there ever was and you could *swim* in it. There were no waves at all and under the benevolent influence of the jolly, mustachioed King Adolf even the ice cream was free.

The view out of the *Titanic*'s windows showed there was certainly sand. The time ship had come to rest stuck firmly in it at a slight angle. Sand was the only good thing about the place and it wasn't all that good because instead of sitting there in undulating heaps in a normal, predictable, sandy sort of way, it was unaccountably mushrooming up into the sky all around them and, every time it did, there was a violent bang and a cloud of smoke. Because the air was full of flying, noisy sand it was some time before they could see what else Omaha Beach had to offer. Then there was a sudden lull in the deafening series of eruptions and they caught a quick glimpse of the rest of the beach. They all wished they hadn't.

'I should have known it would be bloody crowded,' said Rumpole. 'I bet they've taken all the best places *and* I didn't bring any swimming trunks.'

'They're not in trunks, they're all dressed up,' said Belle Tower.

'They're all Gullivers,' said Stilts.

'They've all got guns,' said Sopwith Camel.

'They're all coming towards us,' said O'Barron.

Wave after wave of enormous men, thirty to forty feet tall, helmets on their heads, guns in their hands, were sprinting up the beach, shooting in their direction, and on the other side more giant men were shooting back. On the sea were large floating *things*. Trafalgar recognised them as boats but they were far bigger than the ones with which he had recently been pelted. They all seemed to be shooting too and their guns were very big indeed. As a location for a holiday or a quiet test flight, it was not entirely without drawbacks.

'Shall we go somewhere else?' suggested Puckeridge diffidently.

'Good plan,' said O'Barron firmly. 'Hurlock. Somewhere else. Now.'

Afterwards, the soldiers of 'B' company all swore to the same story. They'd been pinned down by enemy machine-gun fire, stopping them advancing up the beach, when a large wooden object appeared from absolutely nowhere, embedded itself in the sand for about thirty seconds then disappeared equally abruptly. It gave them just the cover they needed to rush the machine-gun post so they were very grateful but they wished people wouldn't laugh at them whenever they tried to describe the object in question. After all, without that break, the whole course of the D-Day invasion might have been different.

What happened next was largely due to Trafalgar's splitting headache. Failing completely in its attempt to

126

unravel the gibberish he was typing on the screen, hampered as he was by trembling fingers, blurred vision and utter terror, the machine chose its emergency default setting, thirty miles further away and roughly six months further on – a setting designed around the principle that if that doesn't get you out of trouble then you'll still be in trouble.

It was a minor eccentricity typical of default settings that it chose a point not only thirty miles away but also ten thousand feet up in the air, and here we're talking ten thousand *old* feet, the sort of feet that are a foot long. It was simply a very unfortunate coincidence, if you believe in that sort of thing, that another solid object was trying its best to occupy that same piece of airspace at the same moment. The other object was a Norseman aircraft of the US Air Force which failed to survive the encounter but that wasn't as disastrous as it might have been because it was already in the middle of crashing even before it collided with the *Titanic*.

127

TEN

The entire one-hundred-foot length of the *Titanic* juddered, bent and twanged in ways that large wooden structures simply shouldn't do, especially when they're ten thousand feet up in the air and their crew's immediate future depends entirely on them continuing to be a structure rather than a random collection of separate splinters. A screw shot past Trafalgar's ear and he found himself looking through a new window that hadn't been there a moment before. It had jagged edges and a very cold wind was blowing through it. He could see the ground a long, long way below through thin layers of grey cloud. There was a deathly silence throughout the ship but it was the sort of silence that promised to be rapidly replaced by lots of screaming and shouting as soon as the people who were being silent succeeded in remembering how to make a loud noise.

It occurred to Trafalgar that there was something odd about the wind. In his experience, winds generally blew from side to side but this one, as far as he could tell by sticking his hand out of the ragged hole in front of him, was blowing upwards. The clouds were whizzing up past him, which confirmed it. He was about to share this interesting observation on high-altitude meteorology with his colleagues when a possible explanation struck him and he squinted down at the ground. It was definitely still a long way below but last time he'd looked it had been a long, long way below. If this kept up it was soon going to be just below and then not below at all. Above even.

It further occurred to him that although the *Titanic* had the means to move itself to somewhere else, it didn't seem to be fitted with any means of staying there once it arrived if all there was underneath it to hold it up was air. A couple of very large rocket motors, he felt, would have been a thoroughly worthwhile addition to the blueprints.

Anya was looking at him with a doubtful expression on her face.

'Are we all right now?' she asked.

'No,' he said, taking care to keep his voice calm. 'As a matter of fact we're falling like a stone and I'm afraid we're all going to die.'

Oh goody, he thought, I've actually managed to say something to her at last. What a wonderful start. Now perhaps I can tell her what I feel about her and maybe, if she feels the same way, we can spend the rest of our lives together. Then he thought about what he'd just said which seemed to imply that he ought to get a move on because the rest of their lives looked likely to total about a minute and a half. At least they both managed to scream together.

One day, he promised himself as he stabbed at the keyboard, one day I'm going to do this calmly and carefully. Not today.

'Time?' it asked.

'Now,' he typed.

'Place?'

'Ground level,' he typed, 'somewhere quiet,' and pressed the button.

There was a thump and showers of sand spurted in through the holes in the woodwork. The temperature rose sharply. The grey skies had gone and sunlight flooded in. Trafalgar let out a long breath, hugely relieved. Anya gave him an uncertain smile. The rest of the team unbuckled their seat belts with dazed expressions and looked around them.

'Are we at the beach now?' asked Belle in a voice that wobbled in time with her chin.

Trafalgar looked out through the nearest hole. There was sand as far as the eye could see, which was quite a long way. Perhaps it was second time lucky and this really was Omaha Beach. It was certainly nice and quiet, not to mention hot – in fact, very hot.

'YES,' Puckeridge shouted. 'There it is! There's the sea. Oh, it's beautiful. Heavenly. Let's go for a swim!'

Trafalgar turned to look in the direction he was pointing. More sand.

'Only joking,' said Puckeridge feebly.

'Shut up, Puckeridge,' said O'Barron whose bossiness rose effortlessly to the surface every time his cowardice left it the space to do so. 'And that's an order.'

One of the ingredients for the seaside was certainly in place. There was plenty of side. All it lacked was sea. But at least they were no longer in any danger of free-falling themselves into sawdust and strawberry jam.

'Not bad, Trafalgar,' said Anya quietly. 'There's hope for you yet.'

It's nothing, his brain tried to say. I did it for you.

His mouth said, 'Abullab . . . b . . . bb . . .'

Damn, said his brain and stalked off crossly.

'Right,' said O'Barron incisively. 'Time to get organised. Hurlock, I want you to . . .'

That was as far as he got. He was interrupted by a tremendous sepulchral groan that echoed out from the cargo hold below their feet.

'. . . to, er . . . to go down and see what that was.'

'Me?'

'Yes, you, and as I'm the captain of this ship, I think from now on, I must insist that you all call me sir.'

'But he's the pilot,' said Puckeridge. 'Hadn't someone else better go, sir?'

O'Barron looked annoyed. 'All right. You go then.'

'I didn't mean me,' said Puckeridge quickly. 'I haven't finished ... er ...' he looked around '... undoing my seat belt, sir.'

'I suppose I'd better bloody well go,' grumbled Rumpole, 'if nobody else will. I'll probably get eaten alive, shouldn't wonder.'

Heroism was a previously unsuspected quality in Rumpole and they were all impressed as they watched him clamber down the ladder into the cargo hold. There was a short, tense wait. Trafalgar found himself thinking of the scene from *Goldilocks and the Three Aliens* where the teddy bear bursts out of Goldilocks' stomach. He wondered if the others were too. It had always made him cry as a child.

Rumpole's head reappeared. He looked thoughtful and almost cheerful as if life had at last managed to live up to his lowest expectations.

'Is everything all right?' O'Barron asked.

'Not what you'd normally mean by all right,' said Rumpole. 'There's a bit more in the cargo hold than there used to be.'

'What?'

'Well, I'm no expert, sir, but as it's about forty feet long and has arms and legs, I'd say it was probably a Gulliver.'

'How many arms and legs?'

'Two, sir,' said Rumpole curtly.

'TWO?' squeaked O'Barron, taking a step backwards. 'Only TWO? That's not a Gulliver. That's a horrible one-legged, one-armed alien thing.'

'Two of each,' said Rumpole wearily, 'you idi ... er, sir.'

Trafalgar noticed that Rumpole seemed to get away with a high level of disrespect for their leader. He wondered if a terrible temper might not be rather worth cultivating.

'What's it doing there?' said O'Barron in alarm. 'How did it get in?'

'I would have asked it but I think it's unconscious.'

There was another echoing groan from below. 'Or at least it *was*.'

Stilts, Puckeridge, Trafalgar and Rumpole descended as quietly as possible into the cargo hold. It was full, very full, because lying squashed up on top of all the crates and boxes was a giant. It was built to the same proportions as the skeleton in the vault but this one was rather better upholstered and more nearly approaching full working order, though it had obviously just been through a somewhat damaging experience. It was dressed in a green military tunic, all ripped and blackened, and a bent pair of glasses, each lens the size of a soup plate, sat askew on its nose. Rumpole, who clearly thoroughly enjoyed danger, climbed up on the boxes and stared into its face with Trafalgar just behind him.

One of its eyes opened.

They watched nervously as it moved its head and blinked at them. Its enormous mouth opened and it spoke in a deep rumble.

'Goddam,' it said. 'What hit me? Did we crash?'

It focused on Rumpole and Trafalgar, who was poised ready to run for the ladder.

'Gotta lay off the hooch,' it said. 'You're not here. Not possibly.'

Rumpole once more rose magnificently to the occasion. 'Excuse me, sir, or madam perhaps.'

The Gulliver growled menacingly.

'Sir then,' Rumpole said hastily. 'Are you by any chance a Gulliver?'

'You speak American?' said the Gulliver in tones of amazement. 'Little green men, speaking *American*?'

'Well, no, actually, I don't, I'm afraid,' said Rumpole apologetically. 'Wish I'd learnt it, but I didn't. Dead language, you see? Not much left of it, anyway I could never handle all those clever brushstrokes. Only Latin, I'm afraid, that's all I speak. Only language there is these days. No one speaks American.'

'You speak it pretty damn well for someone who never learnt it.'

'Sorry?'

'Ah, never mind. What did you say again?'

'I asked if you were a Gulliver,' Rumpole repeated politely.

'Gulliver? Hell, no, I'm er . . . Glenn Miller, that's me. I'm a band leader. Maybe you heard of me?'

'A Glemmiller,' Stilts hissed to Trafalgar. 'He says he's a Glemmiller. What's a Glemmiller?'

'I don't know.'

'I'll go and check it out in the datastores.'

'No, sorry,' said Rumpole to the Gulliver, 'I can't say I have.'

'That proves I'm dreaming. I'm only the most famous band leader in the goddam world,' snapped the Glemmiller. 'It's coming to something when even your own hallucinations never heard of you.' He groped in his pocket and brought out a battered silver flask. Working awkwardly, forced into a sideways crouch by the confines of the cargo hold, he unscrewed the cap and a pungent smell filled the ship.

'Don't mind if I have a coupla swigs of reality juice, do you, boys?' he asked. 'Only I seem to have jarred my brain a little.' He tried to move his leg and the side of the *Titanic* creaked in protest.

'Can you get me out of here before my limbs all drop off?' he said.

That was a horrible idea. Trafalgar hadn't realised such a thing could happen to a Gulliver, because whatever this one said, that was undoubtedly what he was. He didn't want to watch his arms and legs falling off so he helped open the cargo bay door as quickly as possible and the Glemmiller, with much cursing and contorting, levered himself out on to the sand. Trafalgar and the others stood in the open doorway and looked up at him in awe. He was not far short of half the height of the *Titanic*. How did he get in? Trafalgar wondered. The *Titanic* must have materialised around him. That was an unexpected hazard of time travel.

The Glemmiller took another big swig from the flask and jumped up and down to flex his legs. The ground shook and Rumpole fell over.

'Hey, cut that out,' he said.

Whatever was in the flask, it seemed to help. The Glemmiller could look straight at them now without the haunted expression he'd worn at first.

'Are you guys from the moon or something?' he asked.

'No, no, nothing like that,' said Rumpole reassuringly. 'Don't worry. We come from right here on good old Neptune.'

'Neptune? Oh sure, I see.' The Glemmiller looked up and down at the *Titanic*. 'And what the hell's this?'

'This? Oh, it's the *Titanic*. It's our time machine.'

'Time machine?' laughed the Gulliver, gazing at it. '*Titanic*? There I am crashing down into the English Channel in a burning plane and I get rescued by a giant grandfather clock?' He stuck his head down and peered inside. 'It's even got a pendulum.'

'What's a grandfather clock?' asked Trafalgar, thinking, I knew there was something wrong with those plans.

'It's a machine for telling time.'

'Not a time machine?'

'You call it what you want. I call it a grandfather clock.' He took another long pull at the flask. 'I remember,' he said. 'I've seen the movies. This is where I have to say, "Take me to your leader," isn't it?'

Trafalgar looked back doubtfully at the ladder up to the top deck.

'I think we might have to bring him to you,' he said. 'You'll never fit up there.'

This proved harder than they expected. O'Barron was not at all keen to go down to see the Glemmiller.

'Tell him I'm very busy,' he insisted from inside a cupboard.

'What shall we say you're doing, sir?'

'Secret documents. That sort of thing.'

Stilts gave the handle a gentle tug and the cupboard door swung open. O'Barron was sitting on the floor, sucking his thumb.

'Right-o,' he said, jumping up, 'I've finished now.'

He came reluctantly down the ladder followed by the rest of them. Stilts stayed behind.

'What do I say?' O'Barron hissed.

'Try "I come from your future,"' suggested Rumpole.

O'Barron cleared his throat. 'Hello, I come from your future,' he said in a voice that was only slightly squeaky.

The Glemmiller regarded him morosely. 'If you're the future, I'm going to go right on living in the past,' he said. 'How far in the goddam future?'

'We come to you from the year 95 SEGS,' said O'Barron grandly.

The Glemmiller grinned wolfishly. 'The year 95 what? Sounds like fun.'

Trafalgar felt perhaps it was time to explain to everyone what he'd learnt from the time machine and the Videowill.

'Ninety-five SEGS,' he said. 'You have to add 2,612 so that makes it the year 2707 in your time.'

His words were greeted by astonished looks from all around him.

'By the way,' he added, 'what *is* your time?'

'Nineteen forty-four and that's quite a big enough number as far as *I'm* concerned.'

Trafalgar looked at the Glemmiller and realised it was a heaven-sent opportunity to prove his point.

'Do I take it from your reaction,' he asked politely, 'that there aren't any people our size in this time of yours?'

'Damn right.'

O'Barron interrupted in an astonished voice, 'What? None at all?'

'None.'

'Maybe you just didn't notice?'

'Oh, come on now.'

'And if you don't mind me asking,' Trafalgar continued, 'do you happen to know who commanded the American forces at the Charge of the Light Brigade?'

'American forces? That was some limey battle. I don't know. Balaclava? Cardigan? Something like that?'

O'Barron snorted and hissed into Trafalgar's ear, 'He's raving, Hurlock. He'll be saying it was trousers or shirt or something next.'

'Not Batman?' Trafalgar said.

'Batman. Who the hell's Batman?'

He seemed suddenly to have had enough of this and, turning his head, he looked all around him.

'This isn't France,' he said. 'Where's my plane gone? This is a goddam desert. What is this, the Sahara?'

'Oh no,' said Rumpole firmly. 'The Sahara's frozen. This couldn't possibly be the Sahara.'

The Gulliver sat down on the sand and took his head in his hands, then after several more gulps at the flask, he pulled a long metal flute out of his inside pocket and began to play.

Someone tugged urgently at Trafalgar's sleeve. He turned. It was Stilts and his face was grim. He held his finger to his lips and handed Trafalgar a sheet of paper. It was a printout from the datastores and it said:

GLENN MILLER: BAND LEADER.

That much was true then. Trafalgar read on. 'Leader of the most bloodthirsty band of pirates who ever lived. Went missing with his ship the *Mary Celeste* during the War of Jenkins' Ear. Also invented sliced yoghurt.'

Ah.

'Nice tune,' he said carefully to the Glennmiller.

'One of mine,' said the Glennmiller. 'You must have heard it? "In the mood". Everyone's humming it.'

Rumpole couldn't let that go. ' "In the mood"?' he said indignantly. 'Don't be bloody silly. I know that song, everyone does. It's "Sing a song of sixpence".'

This man is six times our size and a possible killer, Trafalgar thought to himself desperately, and Rumpole's doubting his word. He tried to distract him.

'I could never get the words to fit, could you?' he said. 'Too many syllables or not enough notes or something.'

Miller didn't act like a pirate. He smiled, drank a bit more and tootled a jaunty and completely unfamiliar little tune on the flute.

'Now that's "Pop goes the weasel",' he said, then he put the flute down.

'Pity we haven't any sliced yoghurt,' said Trafalgar

slowly and loudly, just to test the water. 'I do like sliced yoghurt.'

The Glennmiller looked baffled. 'What's yoghurt?' he said. 'Does it go with whisky?'

A horrible thought flashed through Trafalgar's mind. The datastore. Surely, after all the care he'd taken, the mice couldn't have got at it? Maybe the Glennmiller hadn't *yet* invented sliced yoghurt. That would explain it, or at least he devoutly hoped it would.

O'Barron nudged Rumpole and whispered, 'See, I told you. He *is* mad. We'll have to watch him.'

The Glennmiller pulled a sad face.

'Guys,' he said, 'I'm sorry to do this but in a minute or two I'm just going to have to stop imagining you and get going. I gotta be in Paris by tonight. Okay?'

'Er, yes – fine,' said Trafalgar, feeling the best course was still to agree with everything he said. 'Any time that suits you. We're ready, aren't we?'

He looked at the others for confirmation. The rest of the team had been creeping cautiously, one by one, nearer the doors of the cargo hold and now they were all standing there watching. O'Barron was peeking out from behind a particularly large box.

'Ready for what?' asked Rumpole.

'Ready to . . . well, ready to stop being imagined.'

'How can you be ready to stop being imagined?' Rumpole objected. 'Either you're imaginary, in which case you can't be ready for anything, or you're not, in which case nobody can stop imagining you.'

'Just go along with it,' Stilts hissed.

'Right,' said the Glennmiller with a hiccup. 'I'll count down from ten and then I'll do it. I'll er . . . I'll just stop.' He looked at them.

'Sorry,' he added.

'Well, that *is* stupid,' said Rumpole, crossly. 'There's

138

no point at all in being sorry, is there? I mean if we're imaginary, there's no call to be sorry and if . . .'

Stilts handed him the datastore printout. He broke off to read it and blinked twice. 'And like I was saying, if you want to apologise, you go right ahead, that's fine by me.'

'Ten,' said the Glennmiller, 'nine, eight, seven, six . . .'

'Hang on,' said Rumpole, 'that's not right.'

'What's not right?'

'The numbers. You got them wrong.'

'No, I didn't.'

'Yes, you did. You said, "ten, nine, eight, seven." I heard you.'

The Gulliver nodded.

Trafalgar hacked Rumpole surreptitiously on the back of the shin. Rumpole swore and fell over, then remembered what he'd just read.

'Sorry,' he said, 'my mistake.'

Just as well, Trafalgar thought. If the Glennmiller wanted to count like that, did it really matter? They all knew it was really ten, nine, seven, eight, but, hey, if the Gulliver wanted to do it differently, well then let possible bloodthirsty pirates be possible bloodthirsty pirates, that's what he'd always said – at least since he'd read the piece of paper. Surely the *numbers* couldn't be wrong? Could they?

'Whatever,' said the Glennmiller. 'Where was I? Um, six . . . five . . . four . . . three . . . two . . . one.'

He said 'one' without any great air of expectation and when nothing happened, he took another long drink.

'OK, you've gone,' he said.

The datastore note had done the rounds by now and there was a chorus of 'Yes', 'Right you are', 'Gone – that's us all right', and (from Puckeridge) 'Byeeee, byeeee, byeeee', dwindling in strength.

'You're still here,' said the Glennmiller flatly.

'No. Well, yes,' said Trafalgar. 'Sorry about that.'

'And this is a desert. At least there aren't any icebergs.'

'No,' said Stilts carefully, 'I don't think there are.'

'Icebergs,' said the Glennmiller as if it were terribly funny. '*Titanic*. See?'

'Oh, yes, er . . . right.'

It seemed to have got hotter still. They could hardly look at the sand for the glare of the sun on it.

'I suppose we're all going to die,' said the Glennmiller gloomily.

'Well, no,' said Trafalgar as if it were obvious. 'We could always go somewhere else.'

'Have I missed something?' said the Glennmiller. 'Go somewhere? How?'

'In this,' said Trafalgar patting the side of the *Titanic*.

'This? This is a clock. I can't get to Paris in a clock. I gotta be in Paris tonight.'

'No problem,' said Trafalgar. 'It'll get you there.'

'Oh yeah?' the Glennmiller said and looked ruefully at his ripped clothes. 'What a mess,' he said. 'I can't show up like this. Gotta look smart. Some chance.'

'We could fix those,' said Stilts. 'We've got needles and material and stuff like that.' He held out his sleeve against the Glennmiller's. 'Same colour, see?'

'Terrific. Let's do it.'

There was a large box in the hold marked 'Green cloth and computer spares'. They opened it. There wasn't any green cloth inside or computer spares. Instead there was the former Hereward Richthofen, fast asleep. When they woke him up he was unabashed.

'Yes, I threw out the cloth,' he said. 'I had to. There wasn't space for me.'

'But you weren't meant to be on the mission,' said O'Barron.

'My name was on the list.'

'No, it wasn't.'

'How do you know?'

'Because I wrote the list.'

'Well, it wasn't *not* on it.'

'Yes, it wasn't.'

'What's my name then?'

As people usually did, O'Barron gave up. The only fabric left on board was a large box of multi-coloured signal flags. No one knew what any of them meant, nor could they imagine who they might be signalling to, so it was an easy decision. The Glennmiller wasn't at all happy about the strange motley hue of his battledress but the contents of the flask seemed to be stopping him worrying too much.

It was now getting very hot indeed with the sun climbing higher in the sky, and the varnish on the outside of the *Titanic* was starting to soften. While the rest of the team stitched and stitched and the Glennmiller, sitting on the shady side of the *Titanic* in his underwear, tootled tunes on his flute with his long, sensitive fingers, Trafalgar inspected the ship for damage. There were small bits of metal jammed in dents and gouges all over it and lots of holes. He had no way of recognising them as bits of aeroplane but he couldn't see anything to suggest the *Titanic* wouldn't go on working.

That was because he couldn't see inside the computer where a tiny little hyper-chip, seventeenth from the left and forty-first from the top on the motherboard, had been cracked in two by the impact with the falling aircraft. The chip was only one thousandth of a millimetre long so even if he'd spotted it, he wouldn't have seen anything. Come to that, if someone had told him it controlled the computer's time-base corrector, it wouldn't have meant much to him.

That would have been his mistake.

If the Glennmiller had been sober, it might have made a difference too because when he was dressed again – everyone insisting his new multi-coloured look was very fetching – Trafalgar typed the details on to the screen and queried them with him. It had taken ages and a great deal of effort to get him back into the cargo hold but the ever-hotter sun made them all keen to squeeze him in and, after much sweaty effort, he was jammed uncomfortably inside. Trafalgar had to shout down through the hatchway to him.

'Paris, Argentina, right?'

'Paris, France.'

Trafalgar looked at the list of places and couldn't see that one.

The Glennmiller groaned. 'Goddam Never Never Land,' he growled.

Trafalgar brightened. 'Got it,' he said.

'I should think so too.'

Trafalgar had found it right at the bottom of the list. 'Paris, Never Never Land,' it said.

'Strap in,' he called and pushed the button.

The state of the datastores would, by itself, have made the band leader's chances of arriving where he wanted to be fairly slim. There is an old computer expression known as 'Gigo' for 'Garbage In, Garbage Out'. What went into the computer's damaged motherboard was undoubtedly garbage. What came out, minced up by the cracked hyper-chip, was mega-garbage.

Considering that state of affairs, Germany was quite a good near-miss for France. The year 1284 however was not quite such a near match for 1944 but an error of 660 years was a lot better than it might have been. It wasn't immediately obvious that they'd made a mistake at all when they opened the hatch to see they'd landed in a grassy meadow by a rutted country lane.

'Where's Paris?' said the Glennmiller truculently as he crawled out of the hold, stumbling around in the grass.

They looked out at a giant's landscape, the final private proof for Trafalgar that he was right about the down-sizing. The desert had looked pretty normal. Sand has the ability to go on looking like sand even when it's six times the size. This didn't look normal at all.

'What's happening?' yelled O'Barron. 'Everything's HUGE. What the hell have you done now, Hurlock?'

A butterfly flew into the hold and he dived behind a crate for cover.

'Hey, wait a minute,' said Trafalgar. 'I know what that is. It's a Blue Admiral. It's quite harmless.'

'Harmless? It's a foot across,' yelled O'Barron.

Any idea they had of climbing out for a look round was quickly abandoned when they saw the ground. There were rats everywhere, huge rats almost as big as them.

'Let's get out of here,' Stilts said.

'There's a signpost behind you,' Puckeridge called to the Glennmiller.

'The hell with it,' shouted the band leader and they all put their hands over their ears in pain at the noise. 'Who needs a signpost? I'll find Paris, I'll smell it out.'

He took a last pull at his flask, hurled it over a hedge and shambled off down the lane, kicking rats out of his way and weaving from side to side as he played his pipe with his long fingers. The summer sun caught the bright colours of his pied tunic.

'Thank goodness he's gone,' said O'Barron.

Trafalgar, who wasn't at all sure they were in the right place, lifted the binoculars and looked at the signpost.

'It doesn't say anything about Paris,' he said doubtfully.

'What does it say?'

'Hamelin, two leagues,' he said.

'Oh dear,' said Stilts. 'I hope he likes it in Hamelin.'

ELEVEN

A cracked hyper-chip will go on functioning in an erratic fashion for exactly thirty-five seconds. After that, the tiny current arcing across the crack will cause it to fail utterly and if the chip in question is the time-base corrector of a chrononavigational device then that will lead to totally unpredictable consequences. Unfortunately, in those circumstances, although it is still strictly true to say it will go on functioning for thirty-five seconds, those seconds may all happen at once or may decide to leave extremely long gaps in between themselves so that eventual failure could take anything from no time at all to several thousand years. In the extreme case, when the crack happens to occur as the chrononavigational device is moving through time in a backwards direction, failure may occur long before the device was ever invented, let alone built. Because this is the way it usually happens, accidents with time machines tend to occur when you're reversing without looking where you're going.

That is why the maker's guarantee on every hyper-chip has forty-eight pages of small print which boils down to 'don't call us and we certainly won't call you.'

The time machine had come to Trafalgar with no instruction manual so he knew nothing of this.

Inside the *Titanic*, there was a row of sorts going on. It was the sort of row you have to have if the person you are rowing with is not only your boss but a government minister with a very high idea of his own self-importance. It doesn't unfortunately make much difference if the government of which he's a minister isn't going to come to power for another 1,418 years. The row was, therefore, oblique and expressed in roundabout terms which, on Trafalgar's side, didn't sound anything like as rude as he would have liked to be.

He was staring at the monitor screen, which showed a picture of something that looked a little like the *Titanic* except for the point on top and the fact it had four round faces instead of just one. Where the caption had once started 'Big Ben, the famous London landmark . . .' it now said:

'The Statue of Little Berty, the famous New York landmark. The name refers to the bull that stroked the horse though it is commonly misused for the crocodile.'

Despair.

It was incontrovertible proof that this once perfect datastore had now been completely corrupted.

When? How?

'We're in trouble, I'm afraid, sir,' Trafalgar said to O'Barron.

'TROUBLE!' yelled O'Barron. 'Oh no. Where? Where are they? Stop them. Don't let them get me. Don't . . .'

'No, no,' said Trafalgar in exasperation. 'Not that sort of trouble. Your safe.'

'Oh, thank goodness for that,' said O'Barron. 'Are you sure?'

'No, I mean your *safe*. The safe in your office. It wasn't. Safe, I mean. The mice must have got at it.'

'Impossible,' said O'Barron who was perfectly well aware that the mice had had nothing to do with it.

Stilts bent over the keyboard. 'We can soon check,' he said. He typed, 'Query authority for last data change.'

'No need for that sort of thing,' said O'Barron too late.

'Memory totally replaced 2.45 AM 21/7/95,' said the screen, 'authority B. O'Barron.'

145

'*You* changed it?' said Trafalgar incredulously. 'You completely changed the entire datastore, the only uncorrupted datastore in the entire world and filled it up with this . . . this drivel.' He remembered himself. 'Sir,' he added.

'Had to be done,' said O'Barron defensively. 'Most insecure as it was. Full of nonsense. No choice. You wouldn't understand. Executive decision. Tough call. Buck stops here. Lonely at the top. Yours not to reason why. Etcetera.'

'Etcetera? Did you say etcetera . . . sir?'

'Well, you know, more of the same sort of thing.' O'Barron looked frankly uncomfortable.

'I think it's time everyone heard the true state of affairs,' said Trafalgar and he gave them a brief summary of everything he had discovered about the downsizing and the widespread corruption of the databases by the mice. There were some dazed looks on their faces when he finished but the evidence was undeniable in the form of the huge butterfly, perched on a box, fanning its wings so hard that their hair was being blown in their eyes. In the silence at the end, Trafalgar turned back to O'Barron.

'Do you understand what you've done . . . sir?'

'Look, stop leaving that gap before you say sir, it's very disrespectful.'

'We are now stranded here, heaven knows where and heaven knows when, entirely at the mercy of a datastore which contains any number of mistakes and you expect me to say sir just like I normally would . . . sir?'

'Yes, I do.'

'Well, I won't.'

'Well, answer me this, Hurlock,' demanded O'Barron aggressively. He had rapidly decided that attack was the best form of defence. 'If you knew this stuff was so important, did you take elementary precautions?'

Trafalgar was startled by the shift in O'Barron's approach.

'What do you mean?'

'I mean, once you had established the importance of this allegedly unique, allegedly uncorrupted database, did you follow the proper procedure as laid down in the Ministry of Knowledge Basic Training Manual and make a *copy* of it, Hurlock?'

'Well, as a matter of fact, I did try to but I didn't have enough floppy disks.'

'That's a pathetic excuse. You could easily have gone and got some more. It would have been a simple enough matter to go down to the stores. Have you put this entire expedition in jeopardy through *laziness*, Hurlock?'

'It did need rather a lot, you see. I didn't think the department budget would stand it, sir.'

'Absurd. How many did you need?'

'Er, let's see. I had thirty-eight . . .'

'And?'

'It said I needed another one billion eight hundred and thirty-eight million two hundred and sixty-five thousand seven hundred and thirty-two.'

'Oh. Well, you should have used your initiative.'

'I did. I used my initiative and gave up the idea . . . sir.'

'STOP THAT!' O'Barron paced about the deck. 'It's very simple,' he said. 'We've got to go back to just before I changed the datastore and stop me. Not of course that I accept that I didn't do it in the best interests of everyone and not that I believe *any* of Hurlock's wild suggestions.'

'But how can we?' said Stilts. 'It's too late for that or too early or something.'

'There's no rush,' said O'Barron. 'We can think this all out calmly and logically and decide what to do. It is absurd to suggest that Hurlock's ludicrous version of the datastores is in any way more reliable than mine. We must analyse the position carefully. There's all the time in the world.'

This wasn't entirely accurate. They'd left Halogen Tinker on guard as a watchman which wasn't perhaps the best of choices. His head appeared at the hatchway.

'I say,' he said pleasantly, 'there's, er, three of those, you know . . .'

'What?' snapped O'Barron.

'Is it time for tea yet, I haven't had er . . .'

'Three?'

'Yes, three great big . . . Oh, what a nice butterfly!'

'Three great big what?'

Puckeridge had gone to a window. He turned. 'Horses,' he said. 'Two hundred yards away. As tall as the ship and there's metal men on top of them with bloody great spears and machine guns.'

Stilts looked at him sternly. 'Is that true?'

'Yes,' Puckeridge said. 'Well, all except the machine guns.'

'Spears?' yelled O'Barron. 'Time to get out of here. Enter this, Hurlock.' His eyes whirled. 'Somewhere nobody can argue about. The time of King Elvis, all right?' He stared objectionably at Trafalgar. 'Any problem with that?'

'We don't *know* any more, don't you understand? Maybe even *he* wasn't the way he's described . . . sir.'

'King Elvis? You're joking. The Blue Suede Crown? The Golden Discs? The Royal Hunt of the Hound Dogs? The Heartbreak Hotel Palace on the summit of Jailhouse Rock? The Kingdom of Graceland? The most famous national anthems in the history of music? Are you seriously suggesting someone made all that up? Come on, pull yourself together, Hurlock. There's no time to lose, man, do it NOW. That's an order.'

148

Certainly the noises of clopping, clanking, snuffling, farting and mystified, guttural shouting were getting louder by the second. Trafalgar turned to the keyboard with a heavy heart and as his fingers touched the keys, he suddenly knew what he had to do. He had to prove to O'Barron once and for all that the datastores were wrong and he realised the Glennmiller had given him the means to do it – that or die in the attempt.

He typed the details on to the screen.

Puckeridge rushed up the ladder. 'Hurry up,' he called, 'I think they're about to charge.'

O'Barron looked at his watch. 'That's ridiculous,' he said. 'We've hardly been here any time at all. How much do they want?'

'Er, no, that's not precisely what I meant.'

The hoofbeats outside were definitely accelerating. Trafalgar shot a quick look through his hole to see the point of a very long sharp spear coming rapidly nearer, backed up by several tons of fast-moving horse.

'Hang on,' he shouted and pressed the button.

The horseman was startled to see the object he was about to impale blink abruptly out of existence, throwing him off balance so that he somersaulted off his horse, inadvertently pole-vaulting on his lance into the lower branches of a tree which, being unable to support three hundredweight of armour plate plus its bratwurst-fed inhabitant, dropped him on his head on the ground.

'Rats,' he said with feeling, which was a subject on which, being a Hamelin town guard, he was quite an expert.

The *Titanic* did not arrive in King Elvis's kingdom. It landed instead, as Trafalgar had intended it should, on the creaking and rather smelly deck of a two-masted ship

149

lying becalmed in the middle of the ocean. It was a calculated risk on his part. If he was right, then the ship would have nothing whatsoever to do with bloodthirsty pirates. The Glennmiller hadn't seemed to him to be the bloodthirsty sort and it was a wonderful opportunity for demonstrating to O'Barron once and for all that they shouldn't believe *anything* they read in the datastores. The crew would answer their questions and O'Barron would *have* to listen.

If he was wrong, on the other hand, then they would be fish food unless they could use the element of surprise to run away very quickly indeed. He had an emergency destination already programmed in though it wasn't perhaps as specific as he might have liked.

'Somewhere else,' it said. 'Somewhere safe, flat, quiet, not too cool and not too hot.' He didn't know what the machine would make of that but it was better than nothing.

The element of surprise was a little stronger than he expected. The crew of the ship were a superstitious lot and the First Mate had been whiling away the off-duty watches telling them ghost stories of the sea and chuckling at the result. He'd made it worse by creeping through the 'tween decks at night moaning, so when – right in the middle of the second dog watch with not a breath of wind – a large grandfather clock that had definitely not been there a few moments before suddenly materialised in the middle of the quarter-deck, surprise was a very mild term indeed for the emotion that seized them. The whole crew had been lying listlessly on the deck trying to find patches of shade so every one of them was on hand to see what happened. They were all, even the First Mate, staring at the *Titanic* in horrified silence when, a few seconds later, a door in the clock opened and a small horde of tiny green-clad figures emerged clutching their heads and groaning horribly. It was, therefore, completely understandable that the entire crew, led by the First Mate, should immediately hurl themselves over the side of the ship and start swimming away for all they were worth.

Trafalgar, wishing his headache would go away, did his best – shouting after them as loudly as he could manage, 'Stop. Come back. We bring greetings from the Glennmiller. We mean you no harm. We just want to ask you some questions.'

It only made them swim harder. They had no idea what a Glennmiller was but it didn't sound very nice.

'Just where the hell are we, Hurlock?' demanded O'Barron. 'What is this *thing*?'

'It's a ship, sir.'

'What ship?'

'The *Mary Celeste*.'

'The *Mary Celeste*? The pirate ship? You disobeyed my orders and landed us on a *pirate* ship? Have you taken leave of your senses?'

'Well, as you can see, it's hardly that, is it? I mean they weren't the fiercest bunch of pirates you ever saw, were they? They've all run away – well, swum away. Anyway where are the cannons and the cutlasses and all that? Where's the skull and crossbones . . . sir?'

O'Barron's complexion was turning puce. 'That was a forty-seven-word sentence, Hurlock. It deserves more than one "sir" in it, don't you think?'

'Sir, yes, sir. Sir, sorry, sir.'

'DON'T BE SARCASTIC.'

'I am just trying to prove to you once and for all that the datastores are wrong and we simply cannot go on trusting them. YOUR datastore says this is a bloodthirsty pirate ship. It is, therefore, absolutely and completely wrong.'

'You're MAD, Hurlock. You'll be the death of us trying to prove these daft ideas of yours.'

There was a sudden gust of wind and a crashing from above as the great sails filled. O'Barron paled and grabbed at the nearest rail for support. 'Wind,' he shrieked. 'Every man for himself.'

Trafalgar was looking with interest up at the masts where the sails were now billowing out. 'They've got a lot of washing,' he said. 'They must have *huge* beds to need sheets like that.'

Stilts ushered them all back on board the *Titanic* and O'Barron regained control of himself.

'Right,' he said, 'I'm doing it this time. Out of my way, Hurlock.' He sat down at the keyboard. 'I've been watching. I know exactly how to do it. No more nonsense. King Elvis, here we come, then we can get ourselves sorted out properly in nice surroundings. You'll see.'

Trafalgar, trying to control his anger, stalked off and looked out of the window. To his surprise, he noticed that the *Mary Celeste* was now moving, though he hadn't heard any engines start, and the crew had all turned round in the water and were trying to swim back to it.

'I expect they'll get back on board as soon as we've gone,' was all he had time to think before the air thickened and changed colour and the usual explosion inside his head told him, for better or worse, they were off into the unknown again.

To understand fully what happened next you would need to know a great deal about practical chrononavigational interface synthesiser mechanics. On one planet in a solar system roughly in Orion's groin, there was a magazine with that title – a title which unfortunately left very little room for any pictures on the cover. It came out every Thursday and always contained much the same articles, but as there were eighteen thousand days to each week, and only one of them was Thursday, the readers had invariably forgotten the previous issue by the time they got the next one.

The method by which the global positioning system in the chrononavigational device safely moved the machine from place to place depended entirely on a very accurate record contained in its memory of exactly where the surface of the earth had been at every point in its history. This was intended to avoid silly accidents, such as rematerialising underground through anticipating erosion that hadn't yet had time to happen and erosion, of course, does tend to take its time. In a device whose time base corrector is malfunctioning, however, the global positioning system can be fooled into thinking it is arriving at the right spot but at the wrong moment in geological history. This was, in fact, the subject of a very long reader's letter in the latest edition of *Practical Chrononavigational Interface Synthesiser Mechanics* but as that was only available at newsagents two hundred and thirteen light years away, it was of no immediate help.

The result of all this was that the machine gently deposited the *Titanic* on top of a grassy hillock that had last been there one thousand seven hundred years earlier. The *Titanic* therefore stopped in mid-air and gravity then – very ungently – deposited it into the grassy hollow that *was* there ten feet lower down. Woodwork splintered, glass shattered, crew members groaned and the computer gave a disturbing 'vweeep' and died. Trafalgar and Stilts looked at its blank screen where a little dot of colour was receding fast. They pressed buttons and flicked switches hopefully but it stayed dead.

'Oh dear,' said Stilts.

In its final seconds, the machine had made a pretty good stab at fulfilling the hopeless orders it had been given. It had failed to locate anything remotely akin to the Kingdom of Graceland, nor could it find any king in known history with the name of Elvis. It did, however, discover a sort of king, though perhaps chieftain would have been a more accurate description. He was called Olvis and when the machine couldn't make any closer match, that was where it decided to go. Olvis lived in unimaginative times. The land in which he lived was called Olvisland. Just before the computer died, it displayed the year to which it had brought them. The year was 3018 BC. As Trafalgar had no idea what BC stood for, this, by itself, was not as frightening as it should have been. Alongside, however, it said -5630 SEGS and *that* was.

'Whoops,' he said.

Stilts already had the back off the computer and was peering inside.

'Nothing I can't fix,' he said. 'Just a few spare parts.'

'Did we bring them?'

'Yes. I wrapped them up well for safety in the . . .'

His voice tailed off.

Trafalgar prompted him, 'In the . . . ?'

'In the box of green cloth,' Stilts whispered and his face was pale. 'Right in the middle of the material.'

'That's good,' said Trafalgar. 'They won't have come to any harm then. They'll be fine because the padding will . . .' He remembered what the old man had done to the green cloth and he turned equally pale.

Unwisely, the old man chose that moment to come over to them.

'I say,' he said, 'are we going home soon? I left a stew in the oven.'

'Don't worry,' said Trafalgar savagely. 'It won't start burning for quite a while yet.'

He explained the situation so succinctly that the old man looked about to burst into tears.

'It's very simple,' he said. 'Thanks to you, all we have to do is wait for the computer shops to open. Just a few millennia, that's all.'

Word of their predicament spread rapidly round the ship. Stilts was deep inside the bowels of the computer. O'Barron had disappeared into the cupboard again and most of the team were busy trying to repair the damage to the *Titanic*'s woodwork.

Sopwith Camel was gazing out of the window with intense interest.

'Fascinating foliage,' he said. 'Might as well start work, I think.'

'Take your time. I have a horrible feeling there's no hurry at all,' said Trafalgar. 'By the way, what exactly *is* your work? Nobody ever had a chance to tell us.'

'I'm a naturalist,' said Sopwith. 'Old Tinker there, he's ornithology and mammals. Belle's the geographer. Tinker's awfully excited about the whole thing, you know. He's made a life-long study of pre-Sleep mammals in the datastores. There's one in particular that he's dying to take a closer look at, so keep your eyes open.'

'What does it look like?'

'You can't miss it. Long trunk, pouch, stripes and a hump.'

'What's it called?'

'The gas-billed platypus.'

Stilts got up from the computer wearily and threw his screwdriver at the desk. 'Let's go and explore,' he said. 'I'm stuck. I think I need some exercise.'

The three of them climbed down the ladder and stood in grass that came up to their knees. The sides of the hollow rose steeply all around them. They scrambled to the top with some difficulty and gazed out on mile after mile of grassy downland. A gentle breeze was blowing.

'Look over there,' said Stilts, pointing. 'Isn't that smoke?'

It was at that moment that the wind changed. It changed to a series of hot gusts from behind them and the gusts carried with them a strong smell of raw meat. The hairs on the back of Trafalgar's neck stood on end and he turned round very slowly, aware that a great shadow had fallen over them. Standing right behind them, looking at them with interest, was a huge shaggy animal, with a lolling tongue and teeth which were each the length of his forearm.

'Sopwith,' he said quietly, 'is that a gas-billed platypus?'

Camel turned and gave it a glance, then snorted and turned away. 'Of course not. Nothing like it. That's a wolf,' he said.

TWELVE

By the time of the Sleep, due to a long series of accidents, there were no predatory animals. In a misguided attempt to preserve the balance of nature, scientists had tried to put this right by developing a series of mechanical replacements such as the cyber-stoat and the electro-fox but these hadn't been entirely successful. They tended to run out of battery power halfway through any chase and some of the more intelligent animals which they were designed to prey upon had learnt to short-circuit them by leading them through puddles. As a result of all this, the worst thing that could happen to you in 95 SEGS as the result of the actions of another species was to be squashed under a falling building but no one would seriously suggest that the housefly responsible for that actually meant you any personal harm. The events that led to this curious state of affairs were unfortunate and will be explained in due course.

All this meant that Trafalgar, Stilts and Sopwith – staring at the animal – were not immediately seized by the conviction that they were about to die. Instead they said things like 'Oh, what an amazing sight,' 'Gosh, what a horrible smell,' and 'Where did I put my camera?' respectively. For a very short time, this may have helped. Wolves such as this were used to seeing their intended victims trying to escape and all their carefully honed skills were geared up to deflection pouncing, aiming off, predicting evasive swerves and all that sort of thing. When the three curious-looking little snacks just stood there

157

pointing, this particular wolf gave all the appearance of being somewhat flummoxed. When Trafalgar began to move one leg, it tensed like a goalkeeper preparing to save a penalty. A wolf expert would have said it was carefully analysing which way its hors-d'oeuvre was about to leap.

At just this moment, Sopwith said, in a conversational tone, 'Interesting incisors.'

'Eh?'

'The wolf. Its teeth. Fascinating. Clearly a voracious carnivore.'

'What's a ferocious carnival?'

'Voracious carnivore, I said. That means it eats anything it can catch.'

'*Anything?*'

'Oh no, no, dear me, no. I use the term loosely, you understand. Not literally anything. Oh dear me, no, only organic matter.'

Stilts looked relieved. 'I don't play the organ,' he said.

Trafalgar wasn't so sure. 'Does that include . . . us?'

'Oh, I don't know, I suppose it does,' said Sopwith with the genial perplexity of one who has just been asked an interesting academic question. 'Fascinating problem. Quite probably. I'll get Tinker. He'll know. He's the mammals man.'

'How can you tell? He never finishes saying anything.'

'Doesn't he? Is *that* what it is? Known him for years. Always wondered.'

Trafalgar finished moving his leg. All he was in fact doing was lifting his foot so he could scratch a troublesome itch on his ankle but the wolf, guessing completely wrong, made a powerful lunge to the right. When Trafalgar suddenly put his foot back down exactly where it had been, the wolf, totally fooled, over-corrected wildly, lost control of its back legs at a crucial point and went cartwheeling through the air. Trafalgar, Sopwith and Stilts were quite surprised to see several hundredweight of fast-moving wolf soar over their heads. It injected a new urgency into the situation.

'No, don't bother,' said Trafalgar. 'I don't think it knows it's an academic question.'

The wolf tried to turn itself the right way up somewhere in mid-air but only succeeded in doing an athletic back-flip which took it sailing into the middle of a gorse bush. When it levered itself painfully out, it looked as though it had been through a hedge backwards, which it had. It was now panting hard and its teeth seemed to have grown more prominent. The old tale of *Little Red Riding Hood* no longer had any mention in it of wolves, thanks to the mice. It featured instead a hunchback who found a goose that laid golden cathedrals and tailed off into a knitting pattern for equestrian headgear, so suitable lines involving grandmas and what big teeth they had failed to come to mind.

'Logic would tend to suggest,' said Stilts, 'that we are about to die.'

'Maybe you are,' Trafalgar answered thoughtfully, 'but I can't be because I've still got all those things to do – like inventing the time machine.'

The wolf stood looking at them with an odd expression in its eyes.

'That's not as comforting as it might be,' said Sopwith. 'You couldn't possibly think of something which gets the rest of us out of this as well, I suppose?'

Trafalgar had a blinding flash of revelation.

There was a stone lying on the ground at his feet. The wolf was staring at him intently. He lifted his foot for the second time and the wolf tensed again, weaving from side to side, about to spring. He put his foot down and the wolf looked at him reproachfully.

Trafalgar smiled.

'I know what's going on here,' he said.

He kicked the stone as far as he could. The wolf pounced. Sopwith screamed. Stilts gasped. The wolf had indeed pounced, but what it had pounced *on* was the stone. It picked it up, wagging its tail, walked back to Trafalgar and carefully dropped it by his feet.

'Sit, Daisy,' said Trafalgar experimentally, picking the first name that came into his head.

The wolf sat.

'Er, Sopwith? Do wolves usually do that?' said Stilts.

'Not so far as I know,' said Sopwith. 'They're supposed to be more in the ripping and crunching line than fetching things. This may be a sub-species of course.'

Trafalgar was experimenting with other commands. The wolf knew sit, stay, lie down and roll over. He was trying to think of other possibilities.

Lettuce.

The word popped into his head. *This* was the wolf Trafalgar 2 had mentioned. It had to be. What had he said? Trafalgar liked lettuce. A bit of lettuce would go down quite well.

'Daisy,' he said.

The wolf gazed at him with what now looked more like slavish affection than murderous intent.

'Go and fetch some le —'

That was as far as he got. In an eruption of smoke and crackling, Trafalgar 2 appeared from nowhere, hurled him to the ground and sat astride him, pummelling him vigorously. He wasn't able to keep it up for long because the howl-round kept dislodging him and dragging him off to one side. Stilts and Sopwith looked on in frozen amazement for a second, then ran to pull them apart. Stilts was holding on to Trafalgar 2 as best he could but the two of them were hopping and dancing around together as Trafalgar 2 went on trying to land a blow on Trafalgar and a combination of howl-round and Stilts's tugging combined to keep him off-balance.

'I warned him,' Trafalgar 2 panted between blows. 'I told him. Don't mention bloody lettuce. Don't tell the bloody wolf to FETCH A LETTUCE.'

The wolf pricked up its ears at the words 'FETCH A LETTUCE' (probably because Trafalgar 2 said them in capital letters) and trotted off purposefully.

Trafalgar 2 screamed, 'NO. I DIDN'T SAY THAT. COME BACK HERE.'

It was too late. The wolf had gone.

'See what you've done?' Trafalgar 2 screamed almost incoherently. 'Have you any idea at all how much damage your foolish ideas do? Do you KNOW how long it's taken me to train that wolf just to stop you being eaten? Can you imagine the sort of headaches I've been getting lately? Have you any idea how long it'll take to train her to fetch lettuce when nobody GROWS lettuce? Have you? HAVE YOU?'

'I didn't say it, *you* did,' said Trafalgar, hurt.

'WHAT'S THE BLOODY DIFFERENCE,' howled Trafalgar 2 and vanished in an implosion that had a sharper edge to it than usual and left a large cloud of violet smoke hanging in the air for long after he had gone.

'Er, who, er . . . who was, er . . . who was, um . . . that?' said Sopwith faintly.

'Me,' said Trafalgar shortly, and he managed to inject so much venom into the two letters that Sopwith didn't dare ask anything else but stood there gaping at the smoke in mystified silence. When it finally dispersed, he wandered sadly away, talking to himself.

Stilts was nodding sagely as he thought it through. 'The juddering?' he said.

'Howl-round.'

'The smoke too?'

'I think so. That's what he said.'

'It only happened to him, not you.'

'He's the one doing the travelling, not me.'

'The headaches?'

'The same as we get but worse when there's howl-round. I think it's worse when there are illogicalities too.'

'You know what this means, don't you?' said Stilts.

'It means I just tried to inflict serious physical damage on myself and if the bastard was still here, I'd have a real go at me.'

'Ah, but he didn't really hurt you much, did he? And he would have known he wasn't going to because he, you, already lived through that bit. But if *you* hurt *him* that would be happening for the first time – except you'd have to live through it one day on the receiving end, so it wouldn't be a very good idea, right?'

'If you say so,' said Trafalgar with an uneasy feeling that he'd lost track of that somewhere in the middle and that Stilts was way ahead of him.

'Anyway, that's not the point. Before the wolf appeared, I *was* going to tell you some really bad news.'

'Which was?'

'That we're stuck here for ever on the grounds that I've worked out what the problem is with the machine and I can't see any possible way of solving it.'

'Stuck here?' Trafalgar looked around at the empty, rolling grassland and jumped as a spider a foot across scuttled past him. 'Oh bugger.'

'I said "was".'

'So what's changed? Have you thought of something?'

'Not really, but it's obvious, isn't it? Think. You come back from the future, your future – with a working time machine.'

'So?'

'So there has to *be* a future, doesn't there? A future with you and the time machine in it.'

'Oh, right,' said Trafalgar with a new surge of hope. 'How?'

'Well, maybe you simply decide to come back and give us a new machine.'

'Maybe,' said Trafalgar, doubtfully. He had a sudden uneasy feeling that this was yet another job he was loading on to his future self and it was obvious from Trafalgar 2's frantic demeanour that this was not altogether a good thing.

'Look,' said Stilts, 'it's exactly like the business with the wolf, isn't it? You just decide now that at some time in the future you're going to come back right now, right here and hand us another time machine.'

'I don't know.'

'Go on. Try it. Decide that in five seconds from when I say "Now" you'll reappear and hand us a spare machine.'

'I'll reappear?'

'Yes.'

'Without hitting me?'

'Yes, yes.'

'And without hitting you?'

'Why would it . . . er, he . . . well, you hit me?'

'Because this is your idea.'

'OK then, without hitting me.'

'I don't know if I can promise that.'

'Whatever, I'll take the risk. I'm going to say it, OK? Here it comes. NOW.'

Trafalgar noticed that Stilts had tensed up and was looking round him nervously and that he'd unconsciously clenched his fists.

'One,' he said, 'two, three,' then more slowly 'four,' then there was a long gap and he said 'four and a half.'

'You can't do that,' said Trafalgar. 'I'm not coming.'

'It's your fault,' said Stilts angrily. 'You weren't trying properly, were you?'

'Yes, I was.'

'Well, why hasn't he come?'

'How should I know?'

'Because it's you.'

'It's not me *yet* though, is it?'

'It wasn't much to ask.'

'How do you know? What about the headaches, eh?'

Stilts sat down dejectedly on the edge of the hollow looking down at the *Titanic*.

'If I didn't come,' Trafalgar said thoughtfully, 'then either I couldn't or I – the future I, that is – know it's not necessary. Now, because we know I do get out of this, either way that *must* mean we solve the problem ourselves. In other words, you're going to come up with something that fixes the computer.'

'Oh great,' said Stilts. 'Any idea what?'

'Er, no.'

'I couldn't try counting to five again, could I?'

Trafalgar didn't answer because he became aware that there was a new sound approaching, a loud snuffling, grunting, rootling sort of sound. They both looked up and from over the slope of the hill they saw Sopwith's portly figure come running for all he was worth, which in running terms at one-sixth scale speed was not a great deal. Catching him up rapidly was a truly horrid beast. It was all shoulders and bristles with two long tusks and a stubby snout and it was much taller than they were.

'Maybe *that's* a gas-billed platypus?' Stilts suggested.

'No, I don't think so. It looks more like a pig.'

'It's a bit ferocious for a pig, isn't it?'

'Maybe it's a war-hog. I suppose we'd better help him.'

'How?'

This was a good question – a question, indeed, that

went right to the heart of the matter. Three unarmed very small men against one very big wild boar was not likely to be a fair match. Trafalgar summed up the situation, realised it was hopeless, took a deep breath and charged on a head-on collision course towards the onrushing boar, hoping that Stilts would follow. He met Sopwith Camel coming the other way first and the naturalist rushed straight past him without hesitation. The boar came at him like a four-legged, foul-breathed mountain. Trafalgar gave up all hope of survival and started shouting at it for all he was worth. He was gratified and not a little surprised to see it skid to a sudden halt, look at him with horror in its bulging eyes, turn tail and race off as fast as it could go. A feeling of warm pride was just beginning to creep over him when he was overtaken from behind by the real reason for the boar's sudden loss of self-confidence: Daisy, who bowled him over in her slipstream and chased the boar safely into the middle distance, then circled round and came back to Trafalgar, wagging her tail. She dropped a soggy green bundle at his feet, licked him on the face with a huge, wet, sticky tongue and rolled over on her back to have her tummy scratched.

Stilts panted up behind Trafalgar, and looked at the thing the wolf had dropped.

'Well done,' he said. 'What's that?'

'I rather fear that's what passes for lettuce around these parts.'

'It doesn't look very appetising, does it?'

It had never been very big or juicy, being the far-off ancestor of modern lettuce, and it had suffered severely from Daisy's over-excitement during the chase. She'd carried it very carefully until then but now it was definitely on the slushy, wolf-saliva-soaked, torn end of the primitive wild lettuce spectrum.

'I'm not eating *that*,' said Trafalgar.

The wolf rolled over, got to her feet and looked at the lettuce, then at Trafalgar.

'Yuk,' said Trafalgar. 'Horrible. Not in a million years.'

'It'll be shrink-wrapped in plastic in a million years,' said Stilts.

The wolf gave them a hurt look. She got down on her front paws, her bottom sticking up in the air and wagged her tail. She pushed the lettuce closer to them with her nose.

'No. I mean it. I'm not touching that.'

The wolf gave them another look, a look which spoke volumes. Her eyes said, do you know how far I had to go for that? Do you care about the mountains I climbed, the ravines I leapt over, the rivers I swam all because of the deep love and devotion I bear for you, my master, just so your every wish could be fulfilled?

She was exaggerating like mad, but wolves do that. She stared at them with deep reproach in her eyes, then turned slowly and lay with her back to them, ears down, tail stationary, whimpering slightly to herself.

'Oh, for heaven's sake,' said Trafalgar.

She wouldn't get up again until he'd eaten every single leaf.

Halogen Tinker greeted them with what might well have been considerable excitement on their return to the *Titanic*.

'Good gracious,' he said. 'What an absolutely magnificent specimen of a . . . Didn't know there were . . . Goodness me, look at its . . . And quite remarkably large er . . . Very dangerous thingies, you know, these er . . . Shouldn't go too close if I were . . .'

The wolf licked his face so hard she knocked him over and he sat on the ground with wolf dribble running down his shirt. 'Quite,' he said.

Other members of the team came to the open hatchway and looked down at them.

' 'Bout time you were back,' said O'Barron bossily from behind a packing case. He seemed to prefer not to look directly at the wolf. 'Got jobs for you. Cheesemaker, you get back to sorting out the electronics. Hurlock, you're to pick a team – two people – and go and make contact with King Elvis. Tell him I'm here and he should start making arrangements for my state visit. Be dignified but firm with him. We don't want him to think we're just any old time travellers.'

Trafalgar thought it was highly unlikely that this primitive landscape would contain anyone remotely resembling the fabled monarch with his skin-tight silk clothing and the ornate helmet of greased hair which, according to legend, was lowered on to his head every morning before the ceremonial microphone which symbolised his power was put in his hand.

'We can't be entirely sure we're in King Elvis's land,' he said.

'SIR!' shouted O'Barron. The wolf gave a long, menacing growl and O'Barron flinched. 'Anyway,' he said in a suddenly quieter voice, 'we must be. That thing's probably one of the Hound Dogs. Now get on with it. And you'd better get rid of it.'

'I don't think I can ... sir. As for a team, I'll take, let's see . . .' He wondered who he should pick. 'Rumpole please.' He might be appallingly bad tempered but he was a good man to have around in a tight spot. He'd love to have Anya in a tight spot too, but would he ever be able to talk to her? I'll have to try, he thought. Surely one day soon I'll be able to tell her how I feel even if I have to do it in semaphore.

'I'll take Miss Ninety-Five,' he said, avoiding looking at her and feeling his cheeks redden.

167

'No, you won't,' said O'Barron. 'I need her here for consultation. I might as well tell everyone I have made Miss Ninety-Five my personal assistant with effect from now.'

This announcement clearly came as a surprise to Anya who didn't look entirely pleased. Trafalgar looked entirely displeased but in the end he had to settle for Halogen Tinker as the third member of his group.

They loaded backpacks with compasses and other emergency supplies and set off up the slope out of the hollow, the wolf trotting immediately at Trafalgar's heels, trying her best to take dainty little steps to avoid overtaking him. Trafalgar looked back and Anya lifted her hand to him in a clenched fist salute. His own hand flushed bright red and locked solid so he couldn't wave back and she turned away, disappointed, to follow O'Barron into the depths of the *Titanic*.

They took bearings carefully and decided to head north for want of any better idea. The rolling grass on the downland was short to the wolf, but knee-deep for the rest of them.

'Bloody stupid direction to go,' said Rumpole, 'right through all this.'

'It was your idea as much as mine,' Trafalgar objected.

'Didn't say it wasn't. Still bloody stupid.'

'But it's the same whichever way you go.'

'Exactly,' Rumpole said which didn't really help.

It was very hard going and after fifteen minutes they were getting fairly tired. When the idea of riding Daisy first struck him, Trafalgar flinched, half-expecting something else to strike him as well in the form of Trafalgar 2's suddenly materialising fists. He said nothing, figuring that if they tried and failed, then that wasn't imposing on anyone else's time and trouble in the future. If, on the other hand, he was to say something like, 'Allow

168

us to climb on your back, Daisy, then follow our every command to take us wherever we order you to,' then it was a fair assumption that he would be flat on his back with a bleeding nose before he got to the end of the sentence. So all he said was 'Sit', then 'Lie down,' which she did and they climbed carefully on her back. Whether she had been trained to or not, she set off as if there were nothing unusual in this whatsoever.

From this higher vantage point, the best part of fifteen feet above the ground, they could see much farther in all directions, which simply meant they could see even more rolling grassland plus a few little humpy mounds, some with white chalk showing through.

Then Halogen Tinker said, 'Oh, I say, there's er ... Um, do look at the jolly old ... I wonder if that's a ...' They followed his pointing finger and there, curling up from the far side of a gentle hill, was a thin column of smoke.

THIRTEEN

Trafalgar had only half his mind on the job when they saw the thread of smoke rising ahead. The other half was brooding darkly on O'Barron and the man's designs on Anya. There must be something he could do. Perhaps he could train the wolf to sit on O'Barron's lap because having Daisy on your lap would mean you stayed sat on for a very long time. Better still, perhaps he could train Daisy to talk, then she could speak to Anya for him. He took great care to wonder very silently indeed for fear of reprisals from Trafalgar 2.

'Oh no,' said Rumpole. 'Smoke! I hate bloody smoke. Makes you cough, smoke does. Bloody fire. I suppose I'll be expected to go and put it out.'

'What do you think it is?' Trafalgar asked.

'Stupid bloody question,' snarled Rumpole. 'It's the unburnt by-products of combustion rising on a convected column of hot air generated by the source of the heat, isn't it?'

'That wasn't exactly what I meant,' said Trafalgar. 'I meant what do you think is on fire?'

'Must be the grass,' Rumpole said sourly. 'There's nothing else, is there?'

They didn't associate fire with cooking. According to the datastores, the microwave oven had been one of primitive man's earliest inventions with the discovery of the wheel coming soon afterwards when it was found that you needed a flat circular plate in the middle of the microwave to turn the food round and round. The idea that smoke might mean cooking and cooking might mean people didn't occur to them at all. It had certainly occurred to the wolf because Daisy slowed right down and kept sniffing the air with an expression of long, wary experience on her face.

They came to the top of a gentle rise and could see the smoke coming from somewhere down in the valley ahead of them, hidden by trees. Between them and the trees the grass was studded with large white hummocks.

'What do you think those are?' said Trafalgar.

Halogen Tinker was staring at them. 'I know what those . . . They're er . . . You know, they're . . . I just need to have a . . . Won't be a . . .' Daisy had stopped and squatted down and Tinker slid off her back. They all got down to look at the peculiar view.

'White haystacks,' said Rumpole. 'Obviously.'

'How many are there?'

'Typical,' said Rumpole. 'Now you want me to count them. One, two, three, four, five, six, eight, seven, nine . . .'

He got to forty-eight, but before he could say forty-seven he began to yawn uncontrollably. Two things then happened. A head emerged at one end of the nearest haystack. Two yellow eyes turned to them and blinked and the entire haystack got to its feet and said 'Maaaaaah.' Immediately an enormous figure rose terrifyingly out of the long grass next to the sheep, took one look at the wolf, gave a great yell and hurled a boulder a yard across straight at them. They threw themselves headlong into the grass to get out of its way. Daisy sidestepped, looked at the rock, wagged her tail, picked it up and brought it to Trafalgar.

'No, Daisy!' he hissed. 'Drop!' Then he had to dive for his life for a second time as she obeyed him and let go of it just above his head.

He picked himself up, punched a disturbingly large ant that was trying to make friends with his leg and, parting the grass, stepped out into the open with Rumpole at his shoulder to confront the Gulliver. Tinker and Daisy followed.

They were extremely lucky. At the sudden appearance of a tame wolf and a number of foot-high people, most of the members of Olvis's tribe would have either fainted, screamed and run or – if made of tougher stuff – thrown a lot more stones. Cliff was different, which was why she spent much of her time tending the sheep instead of bothering other people with her peculiar ideas.

She was called Cliff because that was what she had fallen down as a baby. It was a choice of that or Rock which was what she'd landed on. The tribe considered it was the impact which had given her the various peculiar ways for which she was now well known. A fanciful child, she was apt to tell long stories about the strangers from the skies who came to talk to her in gleaming silver saucers, leaving their patterns in the grass. This didn't mean a great deal to her audience as they hadn't yet invented the cup, let alone the saucer, and they were inclined to think she'd made the patterns herself. She was, therefore, uniquely qualified to be the first of Olvis's people to greet the time team which she did by giving only a very small scream, then hiding her eyes for quite a long time. When she opened them again, Daisy was lying on her back with Trafalgar standing on her chest, scratching her tummy with one foot, while the others studied Cliff with interest.

'Me Trafalgar,' said Trafalgar, banging his chest with one hand and emphasising the 'Me'.

(Hello 'Me',) she said in the Olvis folk dialect of ancient Uguro-Finnish. (That's a nice name.)

She thought to herself, 'Trafalgar' obviously means 'my name is'. I'd better remember that.

'Cliff Trafalgar,' she said politely, banging her chest in turn and emphasising the 'Cliff'.

'"Cliff" must mean "Hello,"' said Trafalgar. 'Cliff, cliff,' he responded, smiling and waving at her. She seemed pleased. 'Introduce yourselves,' he said to the others.

Rumpole stepped forward, forgetting to be cross as he always did when faced by anything a bit dangerous. 'Me Rumpole,' he said.

Ah, thought Cliff, he's also called 'Me' so 'Rumpole' must mean something like 'by a very curious coincidence my name happens to be "Me" as well.'

The last was Halogen Tinker and he made a supreme effort.

'Er, let me see now. I er . . .' His attention drifted off.

(Thank goodness for that,) Cliff said. (Nice to meet you Erletmeseenow.)

Greatly daring, she knelt down and scratched the wolf's tummy. Daisy licked her hand.

'Elvis?' said Rumpole inquiringly. 'You take us to Elvis?'

(Olvis?) she replied, startled, not realising she didn't need the brackets round it. (You know Olvis? He's never mentioned he had any friends your size. Do you want to see him?)

'Have you any idea what she's saying?' Trafalgar asked the others.

'No.'

'Let's just nod and look friendly then.'

Cliff left her sheep, which was not at all sensible, but somehow it was hard to take wolves quite so seriously when one of them kept trying to lick your face, and slowly led them down the hill. They came through trees

173

to a shabby village of makeshift wooden huts and she motioned for them to stay back under cover.

They looked at the village in surprise and wonder.

'No igloos?' said Rumpole. 'I thought in old times they lived in igloos.'

'Maybe their fridges broke down,' said Trafalgar. 'Anyway this can't really be where they *live*, surely? This must be the place where they keep all their broken bits of rotten wood and their spare mud and things like that. No one could live in a place like this.'

They watched as Cliff went to the middle of the village to the biggest hut. It had a sheep's skull stuck on a pole outside the door, not because a sheep's skull was a particularly magnificent ornament but because there wasn't a lot else lying around in the way of decoration and they were a lazy tribe who were decidedly low on creativity. She knocked politely.

Olvis came to the door. He was a short, fat, bald man with black teeth.

'What do you want, Cliff?' he demanded angrily. 'I'm busy chiefing. Here, anyway, why aren't you off with the sheep?'

'Some very small people appeared,' she said. 'I think they want to see you.'

'How small?' he said, scratching his tummy button with a fingernail, ejecting a woodlouse in the process.

She put her hand down below knee level. 'That small,' she said.

'Nah,' he said. 'I don't know anyone that small.'

'They've got a tame wolf with them.'

'Oh yeah,' he said. 'Pull the other one. I've had enough of this. Get back on the job,' and he slammed the door which, in a ramshackle hut, was definitely a mistake because the front of the hut fell off. He sat down with his back to the gaping hole to preserve his dignity.

She knocked again a short time later, bending right down to do it because the door was lying on the ground and when he turned round, he was quite surprised to see three very small people sitting on the back of a large wolf standing next to her with the rest of the villagers crowding around in a ring. He could see the villagers' teeth because they all had their mouths wide open. This annoyed him on the grounds that most of them had better teeth than he did.

'You lot,' he shouted, waving his arms at the group on the left, 'get on with the hunting and gathering and as for the rest of you, there's slashing and burning to be done. Go on, get to it. We haven't got all day.'

In fact they had got all day so none of them paid him the slightest attention. They were all gazing, fixated.

Trafalgar and his companions couldn't understand a word he said.

'It's going to be a bit difficult arranging O'Barron's visit,' Trafalgar remarked, listening to the guttural grunts and whistles coming from the man.

'Chief,' said Cliff, 'this is Me, Me and Erletmeseenow. They seem to think they know you.'

Trafalgar stepped forward, performed a neat curtsey, learnt from the datastores, and said, 'Greetings, King Elvis. We bring you salutations from our own chief.'

Olvis heard something that sounded quite like his own name and it bothered him. He was fond of the odd drink, and the drink they drank in Olvisland was a very odd drink indeed. Schlop was fermented from cow dung and the liquid that appears if you keep a cabbage for a very, very long time in unhygienic surroundings. It was customarily served in a bowl made from an ass's skull because they were bigger than sheep's skulls. After a large number of bowls of schlop, he had seen something quite like these little people from time to time but he had never thought they might come to visit him when he was sober. It was disconcerting. Then there was the wolf to consider as well. Having a wolf on their side definitely seemed to give the balance of power to the little people.

'What did he say about me?' Olvis demanded of Cliff, hearing his name.

Cliff, wanting him to think the best of her new friends, had a worthy stab at it. 'I think it was something like, "It is a great honour to meet you King Olvis."'

He thought about that for a while. It seemed about right.

'Where did they come from then?' he said grudgingly. 'One of your flying things?'

Cliff hadn't a clue, but she wasn't prepared to lose her new credibility by saying so.

She hazarded a guess. 'From a deep tunnel leading to the nethermost depths of the earth, O King.' They had after all sprung up out of the grass.

Olvis regarded this as essentially uninteresting. 'Did they bring me a present?' he said. 'In the stories, people from the nethermost wotsits always bring the king a present.'

This was true though because of the limited experience and narrow imagination of the average Olvisland storyteller, the presents never got far beyond the fresh sheep's skull or interestingly twisted stick level.

Cliff turned to the team. She wasn't quite sure how to do this, not yet knowing enough of their language but not wanting to lose face with her tribe. She performed an elaborate mime involving taking something out of her pocket and presenting it to Olvis.

'What's that all about?' said Trafalgar, bemused.

'It's probably some bloody stupid form of ceremonial greeting,' said Rumpole. 'Just do what she did.'

176

They each put their hands in their pockets and then extended them, palm upwards to Olvis, bowing slightly – except Tinker that is, who got as far as putting his hand in his pocket, then forgot what was meant to be happening next and instead took out the compass which happened to be in the pocket in question and began taking bearings on the nearest sheep's skull. They hissed at him and, startled, he turned back and held his hand out too.

Olvis squinted down at the row of mostly empty hands.

'Are they taking the piss?' he grunted. ''Cos if they are, I might have to eat them. And you,' he added, looking at Cliff with a very unfriendly expression. Daisy opened her mouth to pant and showed off her teeth. 'I only said "might",' he added hastily.

'O King, these are special gifts of food from the finest cooks in the kitchens of the nethermost depths of the earth. They are of such fine quality that only a true king such as yourself can even see them,' Cliff improvised desperately.

'Oh yeah, course,' said Olvis quickly. 'I knew that.' He reached out a finger and thumb and pretending to take something from Trafalgar's palm, raised it to his mouth, 'Mmmmm, cor. Lovely stuff,' he said, making loud lip-smacking noises and belching appreciatively. 'Hits the spot, eh?'

He did that with Rumpole too, then came to Tinker and picked up the compass. It felt a bit hard. 'And this is . . . er, some more of it, is it?'

Cliff nodded hopefully and the King swallowed the compass. A thoughtful expression came over his face. 'Maybe I should have taken the shell off,' he said. 'Very good though,' he added hastily, 'but one of those goes quite a long way.'

Tinker was looking indignantly at his empty palm.

'Hey, hang on,' he said, 'I want that back,' forgetting to forget what he was saying.

Trafalgar looked up at the belching giant. 'No, I don't think you do,' he said.

'No? Well, maybe you're . . .'

Trafalgar picked up a small twig. 'I'd better try to show them what we have in mind.' He smoothed an area of dirt in front of Olvis with a sweep of his foot.

'This is our time ship,' he said and drew the shape of the *Titanic*.

'Here is our leader.' He drew a man next to it and, for luck, added a dramatic crown on top of his head.

'We . . .' He pointed at himself and each of the others. 'Go . . .' He did walking legs with his fingers. 'To . . .' He pointed at the ship. 'Bring our leader . . .' He pointed at the picture of O'Barron. 'Here.'

'What is he saying?' said Olvis to Cliff.

She had been studying the scratches in the dirt doubtfully. At first she had thought Trafalgar was trying to plough himself a very small field, though it seemed thoughtless to put it just in front of what would normally have been the doorway to Olvis's house, then it gradually dawned on her that the lines were meant to represent something. Art was a new concept in Olvisland where the only things hanging on walls usually had at least six legs.

She looked carefully at the shapes. She'd never seen a crown.

'They have hidden a man with an exploding head inside a hollow tree,' she improvised. 'They want you to heal him, great King.'

'Me?' said Olvis. 'How?'

'Using your great wisdom and royal powers of healing, O King.'

'Powers of healing?' he said blankly.

'*Royal* powers of healing,' she prompted hopefully.

'What's them then?'

'Well, you could try using that weed thing that grows round the back of the cow byre.'

'What, mangewort? How do you mean, use it?'

'Couldn't you just try rubbing it on them in a royal sort of way. That's what kings do in the stories.'

'All right then,' said Olvis uncertainly, then he brightened. 'Tell them it'll cost them eight sheep's skulls and a bucket of schlop and if they don't like it, they can take that wolf and bugger off.' He turned his back on them and stalked away.

'Time to go, I think,' said Trafalgar. 'I suspect we're in serious danger of outstaying our welcome.'

They did a lot of waving and smiling and backing away, then climbed on Daisy's back and beat a retreat. Cliff came with them, back to her sheep which seemed to number a few less than when they had last been there.

Trafalgar told her in sign language that they were going back to their chief but would come back within two days.

(I understand,) she said. (You will go to the man with the exploding head, take him out of the hollow tree and turn him round twice. I'm not going to hold my breath waiting for you.)

They waved until they were out of sight, which, because of the long grass, was about half a second. Up at the top of the hill they stared all around at the giant, empty landscape and shivered, then looked back at the single column of smoke.

'State visit, eh? The Blue Suede throne and all the golden discs. King Elvis!' Rumpole gave a chuckle so nasty that it thought of choking him on the way up his throat. 'I think that pillock O'Barron's in for a bit of a surprise and I can't say I mind too much.'

FOURTEEN

O'Barron simply didn't believe them. 'No, no, no,' he said. 'You've got it all wrong. I just can't trust you with the simplest things, can I? It's quite obvious you haven't found the *real* King Elvis. You've stumbled over some common bunch of ancient Gulliver peasants and you've been taken in. Dear, oh dear, do I have to do *everything* myself?'

'All he's done while you were gone is sit there telling Tits what a wonderful leader he is,' said Stilts sourly when they'd both gone back to the computer.

'Do you mean Anya?' said Trafalgar stiffly.

'Tits – Anya, whatever,' said Stilts carelessly, then did a double take. 'Oh, sorry. Do I detect a little flutter there by any chance?'

Trafalgar said nothing and Stilts raised his eyebrows. 'Aha.'

'Aha what?'

'Your feelings are showing.'

Trafalgar checked his clothing.

'No,' said Stilts, 'you blushed.'

Trafalgar knew he always turned bright blue like a stop sign, when he was embarrassed.

'So you're a little bit keen on Ti— Miss Ninety-Five, are you? Are you sure you're up to it?'

'What do you mean?'

'She's a tough cookie.'

'Anya? Tough? She's . . . well, she's as sweet as a daisy.'

'You mean the story's not true?'

180

'What story?'

'That she threw you through a window the first time you met.'

'Oh sure, but it was just a misunderstanding.'

'And then she hurled you into a pond?'

'She was only trying to say sorry for throwing me out of the window.'

'Hmm. Have you ever eaten a daisy?'

'No, why?'

'They're not sweet.'

'It's only a saying.'

'Anyway, if that's where your heart lies, you'd better move in there smartish. I think O'Barron's got more plans for her.'

'What sort of plans?' said Trafalgar in alarm. 'She's already his personal assistant.'

'*Very* personal assistant, I reckon. If he has his way she'll be the next Mrs O'Barron. Like I say, better get in there quick.'

'I can't,' said Trafalgar miserably. 'Every time I try to talk to her my brain short-circuits.'

'Oh dear,' said Stilts. 'Well, just to take your mind off it, let me tell you about the state of the time machine.'

'Yes?'

There were electronic bits and pieces all over the table.

'As far as I can tell,' he said, 'subject to the proviso that I haven't dared look inside it, there's probably nothing wrong with the time machine itself. It looks like it was designed to survive a direct hit by a fairly large asteroid.'

Here, those who regarded themselves as chrono-navigational technofreaks might have argued with him, pointing out that in fact the machine had a bust time-base corrector. They would in fact have been (as technofreaks usually are) completely wrong, having failed to notice that the machine had now passed back well before the time when the damage to its time-base corrector happened and was, therefore, in working order again until such time as it passed once more into the future and broke again. Stilts, who had no way of knowing any of this, went on.

'The problem seems to be in the computer we hooked up to drive it through. Bust central processing unit interface.'

'Can you fix it?'

'It was dead simple. I *have* fixed it,' he said but he didn't look as though the thought gave him much pleasure.

'So can we go?'

'Not exactly.'

'Why?'

'We need to reboot the computer.'

'And?'

'That bloody old man threw out the boot disk with all the rest of the stuff.'

'Oh.'

'"Oh" doesn't quite cover the situation. In fact "Oh" tends towards serious understatement.'

'Isn't there anything else we can do?'

'Oh, yes. I could boot it from another computer. All we need is another computer. I don't suppose you came across anything resembling a computer shop on your travels?'

Trafalgar thought of Olvis's village.

'I'm not sure we came across anything resembling intelligent life,' he said.

'Maybe I could try counting up to five again?' suggested Stilts hopefully. 'I mean if it's not going to be too much trouble for you one day.'

Trafalgar thought about it. The situation seemed desperate enough to justify it and, anyway, he could always choose to ignore it later on.

'All right. If you like.'

'Are you concentrating?'

'Yes.'

'*Really* concentrating?'

'Yes,' said Trafalgar, slightly tetchily. He was trying hard. This is where I have to remember to reappear with spare parts if we really can't fix this thing ourselves, he said firmly to himself.

'One,' said Stilts, then there was a long silence.

'Get on with it.'

'Two . . . three . . . four . . . er, five.'

There was a crackling noise, wisps of smoke strengthening then a double 'whomp'. For the tiniest fraction of a second, the shape of a man appeared and disappeared and the smoke went with him, leaving behind only a burning smell. On the ground where he had been lay a small, slightly singed envelope.

'Yippee,' shouted Stilts. 'Wow, great, look at that!'

Trafalgar looked at it cautiously. 'It's not very big, is it?'

'Big enough for a disk or maybe some new chips or something. Gotta be, hasn't it?'

'I don't know.'

Stilts opened the envelope and took out a plasti-sheet. He shook the envelope but nothing else came out. 'Oh well, it must be instructions or something.'

He unfolded it and read it at a glance. A strange expression came over his face.

'Is it instructions?' Trafalgar asked.

'Sort of,' said Stilts and passed it over.

It was a small, clean, white sheet. Right in the middle, written in clear block letters were two words: SOD OFF.

'Oh dear,' said Trafalgar.

'I think you've got a pretty bloody awful sense of humour,' said Stilts angrily.

'Me?' said Trafalgar, hurt.

'Yes, you. Well, anyway, you're going to have.'

'Look, it proves the point. There is an answer. You've just got to work out what it is.'

'It wasn't much to ask for. If you were going to take the trouble to come back, you could have fixed it.'

Trafalgar was still searching for a suitable reply when O'Barron's voice boomed through the *Titanic*'s public address system.

'All time team members to cargo bay immediately.'

O'Barron was standing on a box waiting for them, Anya at his side, looking as though she didn't much want to be there. They gathered around.

'Following the ignominious failure of the first expedition to establish contact with King Elvis,' O'Barron said with a withering glance in Trafalgar's direction, 'I have decided to proceed with the state visit regardless. To that end, a new expedition will go out in two parts. Hurlock, you will take that creature of yours and carry a fresh advance party straight back to the outpost you found last time. That will consist of all members of the team except myself and my personal assistant here.' He patted Anya's head in a repulsively familiar manner which brought a burst of rage to Trafalgar's heart. It also brought a suppressed twitch to her hands as if she were weighing up the consequences of throwing her commander out of the door.

'On its way there, that party will also start work on the first of our assignments. It will keep a sharp lookout for houseflies.'

There was a nervous murmur among the group, a slight shuffling of feet and a general mutter of 'After you,' 'No, no, old chap, after you.'

'There is no cause for alarm,' said O'Barron firmly. 'I shouldn't have to remind you that the housefly in this

184

time is a far, far less terrifying prospect than it is in our own time. Our scientists estimate that a full-grown specimen here will be no more than a yard or two long, so you are in no danger at all of being crushed. What we need to do is find their lair so that we can plan a raid to extract some DNA, so please keep a good lookout.'

He turned to Trafalgar.

'Hurlock, when all is prepared for us, you will come straight back here to collect me and my assistant. The rest of you, while you wait for our arrival, will choose a suitable member of the group of Gulliver peasants at the outpost to learn our language so that they can act as interpreter. By the time I arrive there, that will give us the ability to communicate with the group, thereby discovering the exact location of Graceland and King Elvis's court. Is that understood?'

Belle Tower raised a hand. 'Exactly how do we teach this creature to speak, sir?'

Trafalgar had been wondering the same thing.

O'Barron looked very pleased with himself. 'I am, of course, fully prepared for that,' he smirked. 'I had the foresight to bring with us a pre-Sleep artefact of great rarity and importance, from a hoard discovered only a month before we left. It will do the job for us.'

He turned to a packing case behind him and, with a great effort, lifted out a giant pair of metal disks linked by curly leads to a black plastic box. Trafalgar read what was on the box. It said, 'Hypnolingo. Overnight language programme. Speak perfectly in just two hours' hypnotic teaching. Plus FREE stud poker tutor at no extra cost.'

'Our scientists have investigated it thoroughly and recharged its power packs. It has enough power for one use only so choose the subject well. Now, get going.'

185

Trafalgar realised with some alarm that O'Barron had arranged this carefully so that he and Anya would be alone together in the *Titanic*. From the doubtful look on Anya's face, she had come to the same conclusion.

'Sir?' he said. 'Shouldn't one of the team be staying behind to guard the *Titanic* after you've gone?'

'Good idea,' said Anya, which earned her a harsh glare from O'Barron. 'I mean, security must come first, sir, don't you think?'

'I suppose you're right,' said O'Barron. He looked around. The former Hereward Richthofen was studying the writing on the Hypnolingo. 'You,' he said.

The old man looked behind him in surprise, then back at O'Barron.

'Me?'

'Yes. What's your name?'

The old man drew himself up to his full height. 'Bluto O'Barron,' he said proudly.

'No, it's not,' said O'Barron indignantly.

'Not what?'

'Not your name.'

'What's not my name?'

'Bluto O'Barron.'

'Of course it's not,' said the old man as if humouring a child. 'It's *your* name.'

'So what's your ... Oh, never mind. You're staying behind to guard the time ship, right?'

'What time ship?'

'*This* time ship.'

'Is this a time ship?' said the old man in a tone of great surprise and seemed to drift away into some far-off realm of deep thought.

'Right then. First party outside on the double. Ration packs for two days. Just take what you ...'

'GOT IT!' yelled the old man.

'Got what?' asked O'Barron, annoyed.

'The name, man, the name of course. I remember it now.'

Even O'Barron was interested despite himself.

'Go on then, tell us,' he said.

'The *Titanic*. That's it, isn't it?'

Seven people only just fitted on one wolf and if Daisy had had any proper say in the matter she would have said she was a four-seater, absolute maximum, and no way was there space for the other three, especially when one of them was Sopwith Camel who would have made an ideal recruit for the Windguard.

Daisy was very relieved when the field of giant sheep came in sight and Cliff loomed up, high above, to greet them.

(Where's the man with the exploding head?) she asked, puzzled. (Did he die?)

Trafalgar mimed the shape of the crown on his head and pointed back the way he'd come. He held up two fingers.

'Our chief will come with another,' he shouted up at her and pointed at the sun. He swung his arm right round once. 'In one day's time from now.'

(Oh right,) she said, (You've got *two* people with exploding heads now and their arms are whirling round. Sounds like an epidemic.)

She was quite used to epidemics. Being a shepherd off alone in the fields meant you missed most of the good ones, which was often just as well.

Belle slid down off the wolf and untied the lashings of the Hypnolingo.

(Hello, Me, Me and Erletmeseenow,) said Cliff. (What are all your friends called?)

'We would like you to put these on,' said Belle.

187

(Can I call you 'Wewould' for short?) said Cliff. (Just to save time.)

Belle gazed up at her.

'We'll never stick these on her head,' she said doubtfully. 'Not unless you can get her to bend down.'

'Stick them on her foot,' said Puckeridge. 'I don't suppose it really matters.'

It seemed the only answer so with four of them tugging hard, they peeled the backing material off the sticky pads on the two metal plates and stuck one of them on each of Cliff's feet.

(That's nice,) she said, looking down and wiggling her toes. (Are they presents?)

'All right,' said Belle. 'Turn on and let's see what happens.'

Stilts kicked the ON button until it clicked down. A light glowed on the front of the machine. The effect was dramatic and instantaneous. Cliff gave a single loud snore and toppled into the grass like a falling tree.

'Blimey,' said Puckeridge. 'Was that supposed to happen?'

'Is she dead?' asked Belle.

'Dead people don't snore like that,' said Trafalgar, walking up to her head and bending down to take a closer look. 'It's just hypnosis, that's all. If the thing works, she should stay like that for a couple of hours and wake up speaking like we do.'

'If's the word,' said Stilts sourly. 'If it works properly, it'll be the first thing that has.'

'Hang on,' Trafalgar objected. 'My time machine would be working perfectly if O'Barron hadn't messed it up.'

The journey back seemed to Trafalgar to take absolutely ages though Daisy, relishing being a single-seater, went much faster. He spent the time miserably wondering what O'Barron might have been up to during his absence and whether the former Hereward Richthofen would have been any use as a chaperon. He wished the former Hereward Richthofen had settled on a shorter name not to have.

He was nearly back at the hollow when a small figure rose out of a clump of grass and said in a tremulous voice, 'Halt! Who goes there? Advance stranger and give the password.'

It was the former Hereward Richthofen, looking somewhat the worse for wear with his hair full of bits of vegetation, his clothes torn and one eye swollen and half-closed.

Trafalgar stopped Daisy.

'What on earth are you doing?'

'Orders,' said the old man, looking as if he might burst into tears at any moment. 'You have to give me the password.'

'Whose orders?'

'O'Barron's. He told me I had to stand here and challenge anything that came near.'

'And has anything?'

'Three ants, but I stopped them. Oh yes. They didn't know the password, you see.'

'Was it difficult?'

'Not as difficult as the rabbit.'

'Did he know the password?'

'I don't know. He might have done but he had his mouth full.'

'What of?'

'Me.'

'I don't know the password either.'

'Why not?'

'There wasn't a password when we left.'

'There's one now,' said the old man defiantly, 'and

you'd better know it or I shall have to stop you coming past.'

'But O'Barron told me to come back and get him.'

'And he told me to challenge anything that came along.'

Trafalgar looked towards the *Titanic* and fretted. He knew perfectly well that this was just a trick of O'Barron's to get the old man out of the way and he dreaded to think what might be going on inside the *Titanic* with O'Barron and the lovely, sweet, defenceless Anya. Well, maybe not defenceless so much as hampered by the requirements of discipline.

He could have just ridden Daisy straight past the old man but it didn't seem quite fair so he tried a new tack.

'Well, what *is* the password then?'

'You can't ask me that,' said the old man, affronted.

'Why not? Did O'Barron *say* you couldn't tell people the password?'

'Well, no, but . . .'

'There you are then. What's the password?'

The old man was very silent and looked a little sheepish.

'You've forgotten, haven't you?'

He stayed silent.

'You have.' Trafalgar scratched his head. 'Oh, hang on a minute. I remember now,' he said. 'It was "cucumber".'

'I thought you said he gave it to me after you went off,' said the old man suspiciously.

'Can you definitely tell me it's *not* "cucumber"?'

'No-o,' admitted the old man.

'Well, that's okay then,' said Trafalgar triumphantly and urged Daisy into motion. The old man was tougher than he thought.

'What about that thing then?' he said, pointing at Daisy. 'It's got to give the password too.'

'Cucumber,' growled Trafalgar in the lowest voice he could manage, through closed lips.

The old man stepped back, impressed.

They trotted down the slope to where the *Titanic* sat at the bottom of the hollow. Trafalgar was craning his head apprehensively trying to see Anya. As soon as he came round the corner of the ship to the open cargo bay door, he saw her. He saw O'Barron too. The Minister, purple in the face, was lumbering around the packing cases which were stacked in the middle of the cargo bay floor. Anya was nimbly racing along in front of him, though every now and then she had to slow down for fear of lapping him. O'Barron's face was a picture of lust. Anya looked very annoyed.

'I'm back,' called Trafalgar loudly.

O'Barron stopped abruptly and Anya almost ran into him from behind.

'What do you think you're doing, creeping up on me like that?' he spluttered with what little breath he had left. 'Just when I was catching up, damn you.'

Trafalgar tried to suppress his fury. 'Catching up?' he exclaimed indignantly.

'A race,' said O'Barron rapidly. 'Just exercise, that's all. Just exercise. We were just keeping fit with a little exercise.'

Anya raised her eyebrows.

'Right then, no time for discussions,' said O'Barron hastily. 'Better crack on. Everything's ready for our visit, I hope?'

Daisy looked hard at him and growled as he climbed down from the cargo bay. O'Barron blanched.

'Is that thing safe?' he asked.

'It's a ferocious carnival,' said Trafalgar. 'That means it eats anything it wants to. It doesn't seem to like you very much so I'm not completely sure but, on balance, I'd say that "safe" wasn't the most suitable word to use for it . . . sir.'

He could see O'Barron's mind working, counting up the words before the final 'sir'. He could see O'Barron's mouth opening, preparing to reprimand him. Daisy saw it too and gave a longer growl. O'Barron's mouth closed sharply. He looked at the wolf for a long time, then shuddered and climbed on. Anya followed, sitting as near the tail as possible to stay away from him.

'Hold on tight,' said Trafalgar, more for Anya's sake than O'Barron's. That's good, he thought. I can say things sort of generally in her direction as long as I can pretend I'm talking to someone else. Well, it's better than nothing, anyway. A bit better than nothing.

They got to the top of the slope where the old man was wrestling with a small slug. He threw it into the bush and wiped his hands, looking pleased with himself.

'That showed him,' he said. 'Now then. Friend or foe? Stand and deliver. Password if you please.'

'Minister,' said O'Barron.

'No, that's not it,' said the old man. 'Back you go.'

'Of course that's it, you idiot,' O'Barron shouted. 'I made it up myself. I was the one that told it to you, all right?'

'No, it's not right,' said the old man firmly.

'I know,' said Trafalgar, holding up a hand for silence. 'It's "cucumber".'

'No, that's not it either,' said the old man with a pleased smile.

'It was five minutes ago,' objected Trafalgar.

'It may have been, but I kept forgetting it, see? So I changed it.'

'You changed it?' howled O'Barron. 'What's the point of a password nobody knows but you?'

'All right,' said Trafalgar to save time. 'What is it?'

The old man looked suddenly sad. 'I don't know,' he said, 'I've forgotten it again.'

FIFTEEN

They went *almost* directly back to the flock of giant sheep. Trafalgar was rather pleased with the way he had taken to wolf driving. He had no trouble at all steering Daisy with the lightest of pressure from his knees, or at least that was the way it seemed until the wolf proved she hadn't been taking much notice. Towards the end of the journey, she veered off left despite his attempts to keep her on course and stopped abruptly next to a clump of vegetation. She sat down, looked expectant, made a self-satisfied little whining noise and seemed to be waiting for a round of applause. Anya and Trafalgar jumped off to investigate and as O'Barron slid down the creature's back on to the ground, Daisy picked that moment to wag her tail violently, sending him flying head over heels into a patch of brambles. He pulled himself out, cursing, and Daisy opened her mouth in what looked suspiciously like a laugh but might just have been a pant.

O'Barron stared at her hard and the wolf narrowed her eyes and licked her lips. O'Barron suddenly found the plants in front of them very interesting instead.

'Why have we stopped, Hurlock?' he demanded.

'Lettuce,' said Trafalgar, grimly.

'Let us what?'

'Lettuce leaves.'

'Leave, Hurlock. You say "let us leave" not "let us leaves". Anyway that doesn't explain why we've stopped.'

'These are lettuces,' explained Trafalgar carefully.

'Primitive, giant lettuces. The wolf thinks we like them. It probably doesn't pay to disappoint the wolf so I suggest you eat one.'

Daisy bent her head, uprooted one of the plants and dropped it, only slightly saliva-coated, into the dust at Trafalgar's feet.

'What about the "sir", Hurlock?' O'Barron roared, enraged. 'I've had enough of this insolence. I . . .'

The wolf turned abruptly, stuck her huge nose into O'Barron's face and pushed gently. O'Barron fell backwards into some more brambles. Trafalgar heard a muffled chuckle from Anya.

'No,' he said, emboldened, 'I've had enough of it too. I'll call you "sir" when you deserve it. You're the commander so I'll obey you but let's have a bit less of the bullshit.'

O'Barron extricated himself for the second time. His face flushed purple.

'I'll have you . . .'

The wolf took a step towards him.

'. . . pass me a bit of that delicious lettuce.'

The wolf wagged her tail and watched carefully while O'Barron chewed his way through the entire, stringy, dusty, sticky, unpalatable plant.

They climbed up on Daisy's back and this time Anya jumped up and sat right behind Trafalgar.

'You were marvellous,' she whispered into his ear, putting her hands lightly on his hips. 'I've been dying for someone to stand up to him.'

'I er . . . I er . . .' The hands were just too much. 'I habblefugableeuch,' said Trafalgar.

'Oh, bloody hell,' Anya mumbled and moved back, taking her hands with her. Trafalgar regretted their departure from the depths of his soul.

* * *

They arrived at the place of the giant sheep to find the rest of the team sitting disconsolately in a circle, looking up, while Cliff strode round and round, waving her arms and shouting.

'This is the interpreter, I suppose. Has the machine worked?' demanded O'Barron, anxious to reimpose his authority on the nearest person, who happened to be Belle.

'Depends what you mean, sir,' said Belle, sourly. 'She'll talk all right. It's what she wants to talk *about* that's the problem.'

Cliff saw them and came over. She looked very excited.

'Gotta deck of cards?' she thundered down at them. 'Wanna play? Deal me in, bud. Any game you like. Ante up. Three-card blind brag, Wild Widow, Klondike Bob. Wanna try a hand of Omaha?'

'No, no,' said O'Barron quickly. 'We've been there. We want you to take us to King Elvis. Where does he live?'

'Olvis, you mean. No Elvis round here. These guys already been there, seen Olvis. Now how about you get the cards out. Cliff's my name, poker's my game. Aces wild, deuces wild, whatever, I don't care. Just deal 'em as they fall. Sky's the limit.'

'What's she talking about?' O'Barron hissed to Belle.

'This game called poker. Free gift with the hypno-thingy. She got the whole lot, sir. It's all she can think about. She calms down a bit from time to time. You just have to be patient, sir.'

O'Barron tried patience for six and a half seconds, then decided to try impatience instead.

'Cliff!' he bellowed and she turned to him eagerly.

'You found the cards?' she said.

'We don't have any cards.'

'No cards?'

'No.'

196

'None?'

'No.'

'Not one?'

'No, not one.'

'Waaaaah.'

Tears began to fall like water bombs, each one large enough to soak the team. They hurried away into the shelter of a bush, where they wrestled briefly for possession with an unpleasantly large lizard, and watched as she went on crying.

'We'd better go and see this king of theirs, I suppose. What about the rest of the assignment?' said O'Barron to Belle. 'Have you carried out my instructions?'

'The houseflies, you mean, sir?'

'Yes, of course I mean the houseflies.'

'Yes, we have.'

'You've seen one? Where?' O'Barron looked nervously up in the air.

'You said there was nothing to be afraid of,' Belle reminded him. 'You said they were likely to be much smaller here than they are in our time.'

'Yes,' said O'Barron, but he still had the look of someone who hadn't quite convinced himself and had no particular wish to meet a fly even if it was only his own size.

'The good news is you were right, sir. In fact there's one just about to land on your head.'

They had to bring him round by splashing his face with cold water and he went on whimpering until Belle persuaded him to sit up and open his eyes.

'You're quite safe,' she said. 'We caught it.'

'Did you tie it up?' he said, looking wildly around him. 'Are the knots tight? Don't let it get free. Where is it?'

Belle held out a matchbox. 'It's in here.'

He looked at the box, then at her. 'All of it,' he said, 'or just a bit of it?'

'All of it. They're tiny.'

'Maybe this one's just a baby,' he said fearfully. 'I expect its mother will be coming to find it and she'll be really cross.'

'Now calm down, sir,' said Belle. 'They're all like this, I promise. It's just another thing we've got wrong. Anyway, the important thing is we've got original fly DNA to work from.'

O'Barron saw that Cliff, interested by the spectacle of his panic, had stopped crying and was staring at him curiously. He was anxious to change the subject.

'Now then, Cliff,' he said, 'will you take us to your king so we can talk to him?'

'Not allowed to leave the sheep,' she said sulkily.

'I'll tell Daisy to stand guard,' Trafalgar said.

'A wolf guarding sheep? You can shove that one up . . .'

'Yes, yes, yes,' O'Barron broke in. 'I don't know what period that machine came from but in a few thousand years I'm going to be writing to the makers to voice a really strong complaint.'

In the end they all went – the wolf, the sheep, Cliff and the entire team, except, of course, the old man, who was still on sentry duty back at the *Titanic* if nothing had eaten him.

Olvis had put the front of his house back up again since they'd last seen him but this time Cliff contented herself by shouting in her own language. (Chief! Come on out. The little people are back.)

(How many?) came a bad-tempered bellow from inside.

'Eight.'

(What do you mean 'eight'?)

(That's their language. I can't count in our language. Two handfuls less a small accident with an axe.)

The door began to open, then the makeshift lashings

198

holding the front on gave way and the whole front crashed to the ground again. Olvis stood in the doorway, dirty, fat and ugly.

'*That's* King Elvis?' said O'Barron.

'No,' said Cliff, crossly, 'that's King Olvis. That's what I've been trying to tell you. He's never heard of anyone called Elvis – says it's a silly name.'

O'Barron felt a further loss of face approaching rapidly. 'The machine brought us here,' he insisted. 'It must have been right.' A cunning expression came over his face. 'It's just a front, I bet. I expect he keeps all the good stuff out of sight. There's probably gold discs and blue suede as far as the eye can see stashed away inside this lot somewhere. I'm right, you'll see.'

(Bloody hell,) said Olvis looking at them all. (Where's the one with the exploding head, then?)

Her mind racing with full houses, straight flushes and the mathematical chances of drawing a third ace to a pair, Cliff had forgotten all about exploding heads.

'Er, are any of your lot not very well?' she said to Trafalgar.

'Not that I know of,' he said. 'Why?'

'What did you mean when you did that thing with your hands then?' She mimed a crown.

'Oh, that. I just meant I was going back to fetch our leader.'

'Nothing to do with exploding heads?'

'No. It was meant to be a crown.'

'What's a crown?'

'A thing a king has on his head. Doesn't Olvis have something like that?'

Cliff looked at Olvis. 'Oh, right. Those things. We call them lice.'

'No, not those. A gold thing.' He had a sudden inspiration. 'Like the kings wear on a deck of cards.'

He regretted it instantly.

'Cards?' she bellowed. 'Now you're talking. Cut those babies. Deal me a hand. I'll raise you ten. Four of a kind. Royal straight flush. Full house, queens on the roof and I ain't bluffing.'

'Cliff,' Trafalgar said firmly. 'There are no cards. We didn't bring any cards with us. STOP TALKING ABOUT CARDS.'

'We can't play poker?'

'NO.'

'And you haven't got exploding heads?'

'NO.'

Cliff turned back to the chief. Now that she really could understand the little folk, she wasn't about to give up her new status by admitting she'd made a mistake.

(It was this one,) she said, pointing to O'Barron. (He's better.)

(Better? You don't get better from an exploding head.)

(He did,) she said firmly. (They're funny like that, little people. Heads flying all over the place one minute. Back together again the next.)

(Well, he'd better have the medicine anyway,) said Olvis crossly. (I spent all afternoon making it and if he doesn't get the medicine, I don't get paid, do I?)

If he had spent all the afternoon making it then he'd moved very slowly indeed. All he seemed to have done was tossed a couple of handfuls of mangewort weed into a bowl of schlop. They were still floating on the surface, roots, dirt and all.

'Um, Chief,' Cliff said to O'Barron, thinking hard, 'this is a tradition round here. You have to drink a bit of this, then you have to give Olvis a present, like, say, a few sheep's skulls and a bucket of this stuff.'

'How do I get those?' said O'Barron.

'You haven't got any sheep's skulls?'

'No.'

'Or a pack of cards?' she put in slyly.

'NO.'

'Well, make sure Olvis drinks most of it, then he'll probably forget all about skulls and things. He usually just falls over and snores a lot.'

'I don't want to drink that. It looks disgusting.'

'Oh no,' she said, 'it's not. It's much worse than that. You've got to drink it though.'

'Why?'

She improvised desperately.

'Because you don't count as a king here unless you drink it.'

Olvis filled a cup that had once been the top of the head of a particularly big-headed ass and passed it over. O'Barron could barely hold it with both hands. He drank and put it down. A strange look crossed his face and left by way of his ear. He waved a hand at the liquid. 'Please,' he said, 'ask King Elvis to have some of it with me so we can . . .' His knees buckled and he toppled head first into the cup.

Olvis picked him out, shook the drops off him irritably and put him on the ground where he collapsed in a heap.

(Bloody awful table manners they've got where they come from,) he said. (Look, he's made the schlop all dirty.)

He drained the cup, then had another for luck and a third just in case. Then his knees slowly buckled too.

'It's the mangewort,' he said, 'always gets me like this.' Then he slid to the ground alongside O'Barron and was out for the count.

Left to themselves and the large crowd of villagers gathered around them, the team looked morosely at their sleeping leader.

'Bloody typical,' said Puckeridge. 'He gets the cushy bits.'

Trafalgar looked at the bowl of schlop.

'There's some left if you want it.'

'No thanks,' Puckeridge said hastily.

Cliff had found a sharp stick and was scratching away at a mangewort leaf.

'Look,' she said, 'I've done an ace of spades. Fifty-one more leaves and we can start playing.'

'Cliff,' said Trafalgar sternly, 'I want you to concentrate.'

'Right.' She put the stick down reluctantly.

'Is there a computer shop anywhere near here?'

'No,' she said definitely.

'Do you know what a computer is?'

'No.'

'Do you know what a shop is?'

'No.'

'Then how do you know there isn't one?'

'Because I know everything that there is around here, and there isn't one of those.'

Trafalgar sighed. Stilts stepped in.

'What is there then?' he asked.

'There's you. There's us. There's the Uglies three hills away towards the sunrise but they don't like us. There's Big Bottom and his lot down by the river but we don't like them. There's the sheep. There's wolves and things.' She stopped then brightened up. 'Oh yes, there's trees and grass and stuff.'

'Nothing else at all?'

'Just the temple.'

'What temple?'

'We haven't put it up yet,' she said sadly and waved an arm. 'It's over there.'

It was obvious that the two chiefs were going to be out

of communication for some considerable time. Trafalgar was getting bored with being stared at by the rest of the tribe and they'd taken to poking the team with their enormous fingers and giggling moronically if they could make them fall over.

'Let's go and see the temple,' he suggested. 'We might as well. There's no point in staying here.'

'All right,' said Cliff, 'the sheep need a walk. It's back towards where you came from.'

The wolf lowered her ears, whined and looked absolutely miserable at the prospect of carrying eight people but Cliff put Sopwith, Halogen Tinker and Belle on the back of a large sheep where they disappeared up to their heads in the wool.

'There's things in here,' said Belle nervously.

'What sort of things?' Trafalgar asked.

'Moving things. One just ran past my leg.'

She disappeared completely into the wool and they could hear her wrestling with something.

It was quite slow travelling by sheep and Daisy's attempts to speed things up by rushing behind them and growling ferociously tended to make the flock scatter in panic, so it was an hour and a half before they got back to an area very close to where the *Titanic* had landed. There, on top of a gentle hill, they stopped and Cliff pointed. Lying near the rounded summit in the long grass were lines of great grey blocks. They climbed down and investigated. The things were colossal rectangles, each of them a hundred feet long. They had been hacked from hard, grey rock and there were many of them, lying flat in neat rows in the grass.

'*This* is a temple?' said Trafalgar, puzzled.

Cliff shrugged. 'That's what Olvis says. He got it cheap.'

'Who's it a temple to?'

'What do you mean "to"?'

203

'Well, what god?'

'What's a god?'

'You know, gods. Great powerful things up in the sky who hurl thunderbolts at you and things like that.'

Cliff looked up at the sky, puzzled. 'We call those clouds.'

'No, no. Gods. Things you believe in. Things that are really important to you, things you worship, things that control everything about your life.'

'Like poker?' Cliff's face brightened. 'Hey, this could be a poker temple. We could build it and play inside. How about that?'

'No, temples aren't for poker, they're for gods. What did Olvis buy it for?'

'He was drunk. Come to think of it, they said it was a something or other temple.'

'A sun temple?'

'No.'

'A moon temple? A temple to the god of thunder?' Trafalgar ran through all the known gods he could remember from the databases until he was scraping the barrel. 'Vishnu? Shiva? Bobby Charlton? Lincoln Continental?'

Cliff just went on shaking her head, then she smiled.

'I remember. It's a flatpack temple. That's what they called it. Is Flatpack a god?'

'Not really. Anyway why hasn't Olvis got round to putting it up yet?'

'It came with the wrong instructions. Either that or there's some bits missing. There's meant to be some curvy bits with funny ends and we couldn't find them.'

'Yes,' said Trafalgar. 'It's always like that.'

On the way back, Stilts, who was sitting right behind Trafalgar, seemed distracted, taking no interest in the journey and mumbling when Trafalgar tried to speak to him. They were almost back at Olvis's camp when he suddenly hammered Trafalgar on the back and shouted in his ear, 'STOP! Stop the wolf, I want to get off.'

He slid down to the ground and sought around for a stick. Trafalgar and the others joined him as he scratched feverish diagrams in the dirt.

'YES!' he said. 'It might work.'

'What might?'

'My idea. If we can't go micro, let's go macro!'

'What do you mean?'

'We can't get bits, right? No silicon chip shops round here, are there?'

'No.'

'So forget microchips. We'll go macro. We've got bloody great lumps of silicon sitting right there. Let's build Olvis his temple. We'll build it into the biggest motherboard you've ever seen then we can boot up and go home.'

'Is it possible?'

'I think I can see a way to do it. Depends whether it's the right sort of stone.'

Trafalgar turned to Cliff who was whiling away the time scratching the nine of clubs on another leaf.

'Where did those rocks come from, Cliff?'

'Long way off.'

'Who were they? The people that sold them to Olvis, I mean?'

'Foreigners.'

'What were they like?'

'Shiny.'

'Where did they come from?'

'They just turned up one day, like you did. I was the first one to see them,' she said proudly. 'Well, no, actually, one of the sheep saw them first, but I was the first human.'

'How did they move all that stone?'

'Easy. They brought it with the round things.'

'Wheels?'

'Wheels? What are wheels?'

They tried to explain the concept of the wheel but it seemed beyond her.

'No,' she said. 'They brought them in their flying saucers. 'Course they stored them in compacted form in their dimensional distorters, then they moved them around with anti-gravity sledges. Now tell me about these wheels one more time, I can't quite get the hang of them.'

They were still discussing Stilts's plan when they arrived at the village and there they saw a sight so extraordinary that it drove all thoughts of temples, macrochips and flying saucers clean out of their minds.

SIXTEEN

Olvis's hair was the first thing Trafalgar noticed. When they had last seen him, lying in the dirt in a stupor of schlop and mangewort, it had hung around his ears like a very old squid which had been dropped on his head from a great height. Now it had been liberally coated with some greasy substance and heaped up in a great ridge which projected forward over his forehead like a wave about to break on a particularly polluted beach.

Cliff's nostrils wrinkled. 'Mutton fat,' she muttered. 'Must have used up our whole year's supply.'

O'Barron was standing looking at him admiringly. 'There you are,' he said. 'That's the first step. What do you think? Is that a helluva quiff or is it not?'

'What *are* you doing?' said Trafalgar.

'It came to me in a vision,' said O'Barron. 'It's my destiny, you see. The databases aren't wrong. They're absolutely right and they *have* brought us to the right place. This *is* Elvis. He just doesn't know it yet. It's my destiny to help turn this into the great empire of the blue suede throne, you see, so that he and I can both go down in history. I'm glad the interpreter's back. Now I'll show you I haven't been wasting *my* time.'

He turned to Cliff. 'Please ask King Elvis to sing the song I've taught him.' He looked at the time team with pride and suppressed excitement. 'Watch this.'

Olvis was smoothing his hairstyle into shape with hands from which great gobbets of rancid mutton fat ran down on to the ground.

'Show them, King Elvis. Hit them with a little burst of the anthem.'

Cliff translated as best she could.

(Really?) said Olvis, preening. (Oh, I couldn't. I'm not ready.)

'He says he needs more practice,' said Cliff. 'I think he's right. I've heard him sing.'

'Tell him he sounds marvellous. Just a couple of bars.'

Olvis was only too willing to be persuaded. He struck up a stance, head turned to one side, staring moodily at his shoulder blade, legs wide apart, bouncing slightly at the knees, shoulders hunched, arms turned outward.

He took a deep breath and then exploded into a monotonous howl that sent every insect in the area – and there were quite a lot of those – scudding for cover. 'It's a wurn fer the mummy, twooo fer the show, three to get ready, now go, cat go.'

The wolf howled, dropped to the ground and covered her ears with her paws. The last of the discordant soundwaves sped outwards across the countryside, creating sensations of violent nauseous panic in the assorted sensory organs of every animal, reptile and insect they passed.

'See,' said Cliff, 'he was right. I told you.'

'Very good,' shouted O'Barron. 'Very good indeed.' He turned to the rest of the team. 'Come on,' he urged. 'Give the King some encouragement.'

There was a scattering of unenthusiastic applause.

'By the way,' said O'Barron quietly to Cliff, 'can you tell him that's "money" not "mummy" and just a little bit more pelvic rotation next time if he can manage it. I think we'll have to get those tummy muscles in trim.'

Cliff looked doubtful. 'I'd rather you told him stuff

like that yourself. He's liable to bite my head off.'

'Oh, come on, surely you're not afraid of a few harsh words?'

'Who's talking about harsh words?' said Cliff in amazement. 'I'm talking about decapitation by chief-bite. You don't get over having nothing left above the shoulders except tooth marks.'

'Tell him if he gets it right it's the first step on the way to a life of luxury, palaces, white suits and gold discs all over the place.'

Cliff translated. It was quite clear that she and Olvis were a bit hazy on most of the concepts involved but some of it seemed to get through.

She came back to O'Barron.

'He says when does he get the clothes and the gold things?'

O'Barron turned to Olvis. 'Patience, King Elvis, patience. Glory will follow. It's written in your stars.'

(He says 'not yet', Chief,) said Cliff.

O'Barron turned to the nearest member of the ELV who happened to be Stilts. 'We need to make him some dark glasses. That's the next step. Can you form a working party and come up with some designs?'

Stilts objected. 'Sir,' he said politely, 'I think we've got some more important things to do here. I've got a plan which just might get us back to . . .'

'Cheesemaker,' said O'Barron in tones of withering scorn, 'there can be no more important task than helping establish the greatest dynasty the earth has ever known. Whatever small plans you may have pale into insignificance beside that noble task, and I, Bluto O'Barron, will have been responsible for setting the empire of Graceland on the path to its destiny.'

Stilts looked helplessly at Trafalgar who felt bound to intervene.

'When did this vision come to you?' he asked O'Barron.

'While you were away. I was prostrated by a blinding light, rendered insensible by a great flash.'

'It was that drink, wasn't it?' said Trafalgar. 'You got pissed on schlop, that's all. This is complete madness. This bloke's a primitive peasant called Olvis. The history in the datastores is all wrong and there's no way you're going to change that.'

O'Barron pulled Trafalgar off to one side by the arm. Daisy sat up and began to pay attention.

'You're quite mistaken, Hurlock,' he said. 'It's just your blinkered thinking. That's why I'm a minister and you're just a nobody. You *will* do as I say.'

Daisy growled, got to her feet and padded towards them.

'Just because you've got that animal on your side, it does *not* mean you can ignore me. Do you understand?'

'*I* do,' said Trafalgar, 'but I don't think *she* does.'

As the shadow of the wolf blotted out the sun, O'Barron changed tack. 'Look, Hurlock. We have an opportunity to start making history here. It's quite obvious to me that if there is anything wrong with the databases, then it's our job to put that right and this is where we have to start. It's probably just a very simple little tweak. We'll probably find that all it needs is for us to make Elvis some dark glasses and then all the rest will follow. He'll become a style guru and get written up in the magazines and all that. That way he'll get a bit more self-esteem, then he'll suddenly become really wise and powerful and he'll get his empire going in no time flat, gold discs and all. After that, who knows what else will follow? I mean, you'll probably find that good King Adolf is a descendant of his, then Omaha Beach will turn out to be a really nice place and not full of those horrible guns and stuff. All it needs

210

is a little tweak in history at the right moment and I, Bluto O'Barron, intend to be the one to make that tweak and change the entire destiny of the planet.'

Daisy was now taking a close interest, bending her head down so that her nose was almost in O'Barron's face. O'Barron was trying, unsuccessfully, to ignore it.

'I'm starting to think it doesn't work like that,' said Trafalgar. 'You can't use the time machine to change history. Someone has to keep fixing things when we mess up. Quite frankly I'm getting fed up with piling up more and more work for myself for the future.'

'I don't care what you think. I'm in charge and I *order* you to do what I say,' shouted O'Barron, temporarily forgetting the wolf. It was a mistake. Daisy reminded him of her presence by picking him up very gently in her mouth and dropping him from a moderate height. He sprawled, saliva-soaked in the dust.

'That's no answer,' he bawled.

'Tell the wolf,' Trafalgar suggested. 'Stilts has a plan to get the computer working properly again. We're going to need Olvis's help to get some manpower together to do it. There's a lot of huge rocks we have to move. Maybe you could use your new influence to persuade Olvis.'

'Use your own damned influence,' said O'Barron with a wary eye on the wolf. 'You go and play with your stones. I'm staying here to get a dynasty up and running.'

Trafalgar tried asking nicely.

'King Olvis,' he said, through Cliff, 'I wonder if you can help us. We want to help you build the flatpack temple and it means moving all the stones around a bit and sort of standing them up in a special way. You're much bigger and stronger than we are.'

(Tell him he must be bloody joking if he thinks we're

going to move that lot,) said Olvis. (That's a specialist job. Anyway I've got a bad back.)

It was Anya who solved the problem and, like most things in the brief career of the ELV, it was a complete accident. It had dawned on the time team that so far their day had included near destruction by a giant housefly, a narrow escape from death on an invasion beach, an encounter with a giant musician followed by a rapid return to the dawn of time but, significantly, what it had *not* included was any lunch. They sat down to set this right.

In their backpacks they had each brought various condensed, dried or powdered food supplies but it was quite clear that one thing Olvis's village lacked was any reliable and hygienic supply of water. It did have what might have been a pond but it also might have been a giant test centre for the incubation of interesting new bacteriological cultures. It buzzed and pulsated with nauseous life, and even the locals, when they ambled over to scoop up a cup of it, would gaze gloomily into the container, stabbing at things inside it with a sharp knife for several minutes before drinking from it. Even then, they would often stop halfway and plunge their fingers down their throat to pull out some tiny creature on which they would stamp repeatedly with wild shrieks.

Anya brought out a pack of powder. 'Cliff,' she said politely, 'I don't suppose there's any milk, is there?'

Cliff had a pile of leaves next to her and was putting the finishing touches to the jokers. 'Sheep's milk,' she said. 'Come with me.'

The milk was kept in a large bowl inside a hut. Trafalgar climbed on a stool to look in. As hygiene goes, it was more a question of lowgiene, but the grey, fatty liquid swimming inside the bowl looked a lot better than the water. Something big and athletic was doing the crawl across the surface with several of its legs but Cliff scooped it out with her hand, inspected it closely for a second then ate it.

Half the village had followed them and they were crowding round waiting to see what the tiny strangers did next.

'Cliff,' said Anya, 'can you pass me a cupful?'

'What are you going to make?' asked Belle.

Anya looked at the label on the packet. 'It's instant yoghurt culture – fruit flavour. There should be enough to go round.'

'Stop shoving,' Rumpole shouted at one particularly insistent villager who was pushing him in the small of the back with a filthy fingernail.

(He says stop pushing him around,) Cliff translated.

The villager gave the sort of inane giggle that often precedes mindless violence.

(Ask him what he's going to do if I don't.)

'He wants to know what you're going to do if he doesn't,' Cliff said.

Rumpole was a bit short of answers. 'Get very cross,' he said. 'You'll see.'

(He says he'll get very cross,) Cliff said, and, deciding this definitely lacked something in the line of a definite and awe-inspiring threat, she added, (then he'll do a magic trick to punish you.)

(He can't do magic, can he?) said the pushy villager. (Naah, 'course he can't.) But he drew his finger back a little.

(Oh, yes, he can,) said Cliff. (I'm warning you.)

(I don't believe you,) the villager said.

Others in the crowd joined in. (Go on then, Mudhole. Give him another shove. We want to see the magic.)

Mudhole seemed disinclined to take the risk so they started catcalling and chanting.

213

(Mudhole's a softie. Mudhole's a big girl's blouse.) At least that was what they meant. What they said was, (Mudhole's a big girl's rough, scratchy tunic) which, because men and women in Olvisland wore exactly the same clothes, lacked some of the power of its later, more refined version.

Mudhole wasn't having this. He gave Rumpole a mighty shove and sent him flying into Anya. Anya was bowled bodily over. Her arms flew up as she fell and the packet of instant yoghurt culture arced up through the air and dropped, unnoticed in the general hubbub, into the pot of milk.

Rumpole lost his temper. He got to his feet, jumping up and down with sheer fury and, both arms windmilling, advanced on the one who'd pushed him, shouting at the top of his voice.

(Is this a magic spell?) asked Mudhole, chortling in an unpleasantly mindless way and working himself up for a bit of violence. ('Cos if it is, I don't think much of it.)

(Yes, it is,) said Cliff quickly, (and you'd better flee for your lives.)

(From that?) the villager jeered. (I can squash it with one hand.)

The rest of the villagers, not sure who to believe, were watching closely, poised either to run or join in the carnage.

(That is a mighty wizard,) said Cliff, going for broke. (That is Rumpole and next to him is his valiant cousin Stilts, who will support his kin to the death.)

(Death,) said Mudhole, dribbling with excitement. (Sounds fun. I'd like to see that.)

Two things happened at once. The wolf, apparently sensing something was amiss, came flying over the heads of the crowd, hit Mudhole in the middle of the chest and sat firmly on him as the villager crashed flat on his back

214

on the ground. That would have been impressive enough but at the same moment a cry of terror went up from an old woman who was standing nearer the milk pot than anybody else.

(Aieee,) she shrieked. (They've cast a spell on our milk. It's gone solid. We should never have doubted them. They have unearthly powers. They will ruin all our food if we disobey them. Woe is upon us. Kneel and beg their forgiveness or we shall starve.)

A hundred pairs of eyes turned on the pot to take in the unusual sight of a cockroach walking across the surface of the milk without even getting its feet wet. A moment later, the time team found themselves gazing out across a village full of prostrate people all moaning and keeping as close to the earth as they could – all except Mudhole who was having his face and upper body licked very hard by the sticky tongue of an extremely large wolf.

'What happened?' asked Rumpole in surprise. 'What did you say to them, Cliff?'

'Oh, I just told them how it was,' said Cliff airily. 'Used my powers of persuasion on them.'

'What do we do now?'

'Whatever you like, really. They think you're those cloud things. What did you call them? Gods?'

'That could be quite useful,' said Rumpole thoughtfully.

'Well, while we've got a bit of peace and quiet, who wants some yoghurt?' Anya asked, looking into what had been the milk pot. 'Salami's my favourite flavour. It's really good and fruity.'

After that, it was childishly easy to persuade the villagers to do exactly what they wanted them to do. O'Barron left them very much to their own devices while he tried to teach Olvis the finer points of being a monarch, preferring to do it without Cliff because he always had a suspicion she was laughing at him. When Cliff wasn't there, Olvis couldn't keep demanding instant payment in silk suits and lumps of gold, which was a definite advantage, though he also couldn't understand a word O'Barron said, which was a definite disadvantage.

The story of the solid milk spread like wildfire to the nearby villages. The reputation of the little people who could tame wolves preceded them, so when they went recruiting with Daisy for transport and Cliff along as interpreter, both the Uglies and the Big Bottoms were keen to join up.

In no time flat, the first of the great stones was being heaved upright and slid into the hole that Stilts had marked out.

'I don't know the conductivity of the earth here,' he said with a worried expression. 'I'm having to guess. They've got to be far enough apart to be insulated from each other.'

'Just try it,' said Trafalgar. 'Remember, you *do* find a way. We know that.'

'We think we know that. That's all.'

At one stone a day, it was sixteen days before Stilts decided he had enough macrochips in place. The *Titanic* was conveniently close for their cooking and their nightly sleep. The only inconvenience was the old man who insisted on staying on sentry duty until O'Barron told him otherwise. He forgot every password they gave him so in the end, to avoid wasting time, they decided the password should be 'password' and painted it in large letters on a sign next to his sentry-bush.

The next problem was what to use as connectors between the chips. There wasn't nearly enough cable in the *Titanic* to connect up two of them, let alone sixteen, but this time it was Rumpole who had the bright idea. He was in a really positive frame of mind since the yoghurt incident. He seemed to thrive on the hostile environment and he'd hardly been angry more than fifteen or twenty times a day lately.

'This stuff's like straw,' he said, climbing up a large weed and swaying violently backwards and forwards until the stem tore in two and brought him crashing to the ground. 'We could spin this into rope.'

'Rope doesn't conduct electricity,' objected Stilts.

'No,' admitted Rumpole. 'Anyway we'd need a spinning wheel.' He sat down dejectedly.

Stilts cocked his head at Trafalgar. 'Come on,' he said quietly, 'I want a quick word.'

They sat down behind one of the stones.

'It's not going to work,' said Stilts sadly. 'Not without cable. I think I'm just wasting our time, I . . .'

There was a series of increasingly loud crackles and a smell of scorching, then curling wisps of smoke and a double 'whomp'. They saw a figure for the briefest of moments then it disappeared back into smoke. Where it had been there stood a large wooden gadget and a metal pot. 'Gold paint,' said the label on the side of the pot. 'Highly conductive to electrical current.'

'Which means that must be a spinning wheel,' said Trafalgar. 'I think we must be on the right track.'

'WHY can't you do things the easy way,' said Stilts. 'Surely it would have been just as simple to bring me a new computer?'

'There must be a reason,' said Trafalgar slowly, 'and I think maybe I'm starting to understand what it might be.'

SEVENTEEN

The temple site set a new record for that particular part of the world at that particular time in history. It had more people in one place who weren't killing each other than ever before. Normally the only reason three tribes would come together would be to beat the living daylights out of each other with large clubs. This event would undoubtedly have appeared in the *Schlop Book of Records* had there been such a thing as books. Now, though, the site was a hive of peaceful cooperation. Two hundred giant villagers were working away as hard as they could, united by a common fear.

Yoghurt.

Though Anya had stumbled by accident on this new management tool, Puckeridge had taken wholeheartedly to the underlying principle, delighted to have such a large, unsuspecting and completely impressionable target audience for his practical jokes. He carved some especially realistic wooden turnips to drop in the stewpot when no one was looking. This wasn't entirely successful as some of the villagers ate them with evident enjoyment and said flattering things about the flavour.

His *pièce de résistance* was created by injecting some ferociously strong epoxy glue from the *Titanic*'s tool kit into a pile of lamb chops waiting to be cooked, giving them all the succulent juicy tenderness of stainless steel.

The net result of all this, apart from Mudhole breaking his teeth and losing his remaining cynicism all in one bite, was that the entire group of assembled tribes, Big

Bottoms, Uglies and Olvis's, were now hacking away at the macrochips with unrelenting effort, for fear that their entire food supply would be magicked into inedibility if they slowed down. Meanwhile Stilts paced among them with a furrowed brow, measuring and calculating to get each macrochip into just the right configuration of size and thickness. To start with, all they had to do the chipping with were other lumps of the same stone so it was a question of luck whether the chips came off the chip or the chipper. The technical breakthrough came from Mudhole, who had become one of the most enthusiastic workers since his encounter with the lamb chop. He often failed to notice when his chipper was completely worn away and could then be found hacking at the stones with his bare hands or sometimes his head. It may have been an accident, though he insisted it was deliberate, but one day he tried hitting the rock with a lump of Puckeridge's joke meat and it worked so well that after that they all wanted one. The bronze age was still a long way off but the resin-impregnated lamb chop age had arrived.

Next to the growing macrochip motherboard, Rumpole had been working hard with the spinning wheel from dawn to last thing at night, toiling his way through a great pile of straw so that he was now surrounded by vast coils of spun straw rope, glistening with conductive gold paint as they dried in the sun. Loops of the rope were suspended between selected stones, crisscrossing the spaces between them.

When the motherboard was nearly complete, they persuaded ten of the villagers to drag the *Titanic* out of its hollow over the hill so that it now stood next to the temple, ready to be connected up. The old man had come with it and was now zealously guarding it from nothing in particular over on the far side of the temple site. In the shelter of one of the stones, Cliff had a poker school in full swing. She'd taught Puckeridge, Sopwith Camel and Halogen Tinker the rudiments of the game though they hadn't yet found a satisfactory way of shuffling mangewort leaves. There was mangewort growing all around them so every time they dropped a card, which was often, they had to hunt around among the heaps of leaves to find the right one. It was a slow business, made slower because they were playing with Tinker and he would go trailing off halfway through every bet.

'I'll see you and I'll raise . . . Oh, I say, is that a . . . ? It reminds me of . . .' he was saying as Trafalgar walked past, deep in thought.

'. . . you a hundred,' Cliff finished for him.

'No, I meant, er . . .'

'You meant two hundred.' Cliff laid her leaves out in front of them. 'Four aces,' she said triumphantly. 'I win, I think.'

'That's not an ace,' objected Sopwith, picking up one of the leaves and inspecting it. 'It's a beetle of some sort. Look, it's moving. Anyway I'm not even sure this is a card. I think you just picked it up off the ground.'

Cliff squashed the beetle on to the middle of the leaf. 'It is an ace,' she insisted. 'See? It's not moving any more. That means you owe me eight thousand five hundred.'

'Eight thousand five hundred what?'

They hadn't really found anything suitable to bet with which was just as well as Cliff won every single game.

'You've added up wrong. I can't owe that much.'

An argument seemed about to develop but at that moment Trafalgar saw something quite remarkable coming slowly into view over the brow of the hill and his exclamation nipped it in the bud. Nothing had been heard from O'Barron and Olvis back at the village for three whole weeks. This suited all of them but, on a personal level, Trafalgar had been unable to turn it to his own advantage. Besotted as he was by Anya, he was still completely unable to keep his brain in gear for long enough to say anything to her that made sense. It had got so bad that he had more or less given up trying and now stayed as far away from her as he could, suffering in silence whenever he caught a glimpse of her or heard her voice. He kept busy connecting up rocks to Stilts's instructions, but he was an unhappy man.

The sight that now stopped them all in mid-movement, time team and villagers alike, was Olvis looming unsteadily into view with O'Barron trotting as fast as he could to keep up. This wasn't as hard as it might have been because Olvis was weaving backwards and forwards across the grass, completely unable to see where he was going because of the contraption balanced on his nose. It was a ramshackle structure made out of sticks lashed together more or less in the shape of primitive spectacles. Stretched across the holes where the lenses should have been were sheets of the villagers' rough cloth material. Quite a lot of adjectives could be applied to this material but 'transparent' wouldn't be one of them, which made it far from ideal for lenses. It was also dyed a deeply unpleasant shade of dark brown and there was a large cloud of flies swirling around Olvis's head, which confirmed Trafalgar's suspicion that he didn't really want to know what substance had been used for the dye. Whatever it was, it seemed to have been used in a very unwise concentration.

That wasn't all. The cloth from which the villagers normally made their clothes was a paler version of that same stuff, the sort of cloth that gave you a skin rash just to look at it. They only knew how to make one sort of garment from it – a crude tunic with a hole for their heads, stitched roughly together down the sides. Now, as Olvis came zigzagging across the hill top, stumbling through bushes and brambles, he was dressed in something startlingly different, though quite what it was meant to be was hard to say. As whites go, it had the disgusting hue of a week-old corpse, and as Olvis lurched along, clouds of white dust flew up from it, allowing patches of the original pale dung tones to show through.

'Chalk,' shouted O'Barron as they got near. 'I rubbed chalk into it. Pretty good as silk suits go, eh?'

He was wrong on three separate counts, good, silk and suit. It was nothing like any of them but O'Barron now had a slightly mad look about him and it was clear that what he saw when he looked at Olvis was not at all what they were seeing.

'Great clothes, don't you think?' he yelled. 'Just like the old pictures. All my own work.'

Instead of a tunic, Olvis now wore what might have been trousers, or might equally have been the outer covering for a small, v-shaped airship. The top half of them tightly gripped his enormous belly and the pudgy thighs of his fat legs, while lower down they billowed out around his ankles into wide flares. His torso was squeezed into a tight tube with a high open collar, heavily padded shoulders and long sleeves. O'Barron had found a lot of small bits of sheep's backbones in the village rubbish heap and polished them carefully until they shone. He had then sewn these on to the shirt in rows for the sort of decorative effect which inspires instant nausea in passers-by. Olvis's quiff had set solid with yellowing mutton fat but you could only see the fat from time to time because of the cloud of flies which had settled on it, bringing a temporary illusion of shiny blackness.

'I told you,' said O'Barron to his astounded audience. 'I was right all along. Here he is, King Elvis just as the

222

datastores describe him. All it took was a bit of effort. You didn't believe me, did you? Well, I've done it, all by myself. I've set the glorious history of the world back on track. Me, Bluto O'Barron, the power behind the blue suede crown.'

Olvis struck his pose again, took a deep breath, gyrated his pelvis so enthusiastically that the stitches burst right down one side of his trousers and let fly in an unknown key somewhere beyond G.

'THE WODDA FROO A PARDY ATTA COWDY JELL . . .'

The wolf began to howl and Olvis stopped, looking pleased with himself. He took off the wooden spectacles and blinked in amazement at the motherboard.

(Cliff,) he said, (what the hell's this?)

(It's the temple, Chief,) she said. (They're just finishing it.)

(I don't like it. Where's the roof? What use is a temple without a roof?)

(They say we can put the roof on later when they've finished with it.)

(It's square. I didn't want it to be square. I want a round temple.)

'He wants it round, not square,' Cliff said.

Stilts clenched his teeth. 'Tough,' he said. 'He can whistle for it. Motherboards are always square.'

(It is more of their magic, Chief,) she translated diplomatically. (After they have used it for their mystical purposes, they will turn it into any shape you desire.)

(Oh good,) said Olvis. (Do you want to hear another song?)

'Tell him we're ready to test the motherboard,' said Stilts quickly as Olvis drew in his breath.

They got the villagers to stand back at a safe distance and coupled up the last of the straw cables.

'Will this work, Cheesemaker?' O'Barron demanded bossily.

'I don't know,' said Stilts. 'I've never done it before. Nor has anyone else come to that. It's all very marginal. I hope so.'

He looked at the dead computer screen.

'Here goes,' he said and pressed the power switch.

They all looked out at the motherboard. The results were both spectacular and disappointing at the same time. Bright grey sparks erupted, arcing from the rope cables. A glow that seemed to come from within the stones spread from the nearest stone to the next and on round the outer edge of the motherboard. The watching villagers prostrated themselves on the ground. More sparks flashed across the surface of the stones. A deep hum began, breaking into a buzzing crackle as the sparks arced across. The screen in front of Stilts flickered once, then twice, then faded to black again.

'Blast,' he said and turned up the power. The hum grew louder. More sparks flashed and the screen came to life, lines of figures scrolling across it.

The team cheered but it was short-lived. There was a sudden puff of smoke from one of the straw ropes. Flames burst out of it and smoking fragments dropped to the ground. The hum softened and faded, the glow around the stones dwindled. The screen went black and stayed that way.

They all went outside and looked moodily at the smoking remains of the straw.

'Another great mess,' said O'Barron. 'You just can't be left alone, you lot. I knew you were wasting your time but you wouldn't listen. When will you realise that I'm right and you're wrong. There's nothing whatsoever wrong with the datastores.' He pointed at Olvis who was scratching his groin moodily with one hand while he picked his nose with the other. 'This is our mission – to be instrumental in the setting up of the greatest kingdom the world has ever known.'

Something in Trafalgar snapped. 'You're off your head,' he said. 'He's not King Elvis and he never will be.'

'Have you heard him do "Lonesome Tonight"?' demanded O'Barron. 'Born to it, I tell you. It brings tears to your eyes.'

'I'll agree with you there,' said Trafalgar.

'The databases bear me out,' said O'Barron. 'You've got to abandon this absurd belief that they're wrong. A little adjustment, that's all it needs.'

The villagers were still prostrate but Cliff, who by virtue of her instant education was less prone to panic than the others, walked over and joined them.

'Was that what it was meant to do?' she said politely. 'All those yellow sparks and stuff?'

O'Barron laughed. 'Foolish girl,' he said. 'You haven't got the language quite right yet.'

'What are you talking about?' said Cliff, affronted.

'Well, how on earth can you have *yellow* sparks? There's no such thing as a yellow spark. You wouldn't be able to see it. Those sparks were bright grey.'

It was Cliff's turn to laugh. 'Bright grey? Grey's never bright. You can't have bright grey sparks.'

'Oh yes, you can.'

'Oh no, you can't.'

'Oh yes, you can.'

'Wait a minute,' said Trafalgar. 'Cliff, is that what you learnt from the Hypnolingo?'

'Of course,' said Cliff politely. 'It showed me all the colours in my head, so I knew their names.'

Trafalgar looked around him and pointed at a magnificent grey flower, the colour of the sun. 'What colour's that?'

225

'Yellow.'

He pointed at O'Barron's shoes. 'How about those?'

'Grey.'

'Don't be ridiculous,' said O'Barron. 'I wouldn't wear anything so vulgar.'

'And our tunics?'

'Green,' said Cliff.

'Well, at least we agree on that.'

'What's all this about, Hurlock?' said O'Barron huffily.

'Can't you see? This proves it. It's the mice. They've even changed some of the colours. You've got to accept it. The *only* true record was the one that came with the time machine and you wiped that.'

'Nonsense,' said O'Barron, but even he didn't sound as if he thought that was much of an answer.

'We've got to get on with the rest of the mission. Forget all this nonsense about Elvis and rewriting history,' said Trafalgar. 'It can't be done. We've got housefly DNA.' He looked across at Olvis's hair-do and its accompanying cloud of insects. 'In fact, thanks to you, we're got more of that around than we could ever need. Now we need to sort out the mice but we can't do that if we're stuck here.'

Stilts had been sitting nearby, head cradled in both hands, thinking hard. Now he looked up at them with a grim expression.

'More power,' he said. 'It needs more power. The processor's not powerful enough.'

'What do you mean?' said O'Barron.

'What we've got here,' said Stilts, looking up at the tops of the macrochips towering above him, 'is a sixteen-megalith computer. It's not enough. We need to go to twenty-four megaliths.'

Trafalgar shuddered. 'More stones? We've got to put up more of these?'

'Worse than that,' said Stilts. 'We'll have to move all the others to make space.'

'That will take weeks.'

'There's no choice.'

They called a meeting of the time team in the cargo hold of the *Titanic*. O'Barron had flounced off with Olvis back towards the village saying he had better things to do. They pulled out boxes stencilled with the expedition's initials and sat on them in a circle. Cliff squatted on the grass outside, looking in through the open doors at them.

'We'll never keep this lot working here for all that time,' said Anya gloomily. 'There's not enough instant yoghurt left.'

Trafalgar was dying to say something incisive, brilliant and leaderish to her, something that would make her love and admire him, something that would finally break down the barrier between them.

'Whibble,' he said.

'I'm sorry,' she said in a startled voice. 'What was that?'

'Er . . . I . . .'

'I'VE GOT IT!' bawled Stilts from where he had been scribbling furiously on a plasti-pad. He sprang to his feet. 'WE WON'T HAVE TO MOVE THEM!'

'Go on, tell us.'

'Jumpers. We'll put the new ones on top then we can leave the old ones where they are. One new chip across the top of two of the others. Simple. Why didn't I think of it before? Dead easy.'

Trafalgar thought about it.

'You mean we have to get them to *lift* those bloody great stones up on top of the other ones?'

Stilts sat down heavily.

'We'll do it somehow,' said Puckeridge. 'I'll make some rubber porridge. That should scare them enough.'

They did their best. Puckeridge had the entire work-

227

force scared stiff of stopping to draw breath with his interesting variations on what they used to regard as their staple diet. His best effort was the high-speed lettuce, powered by a miniature gas turbine engine, which came to life just as Mudhole's hand was closing round it and howled off over the horizon at well over a hundred miles an hour with Daisy in futile pursuit. It was the distant ancestor of fast food.

However hard they worked, however many ramps they built, whatever scaffolding they lashed together from tree trunks and woven rope, there seemed to be no way to get the massive stones up and into place.

'It's no good,' said Belle on the third evening. 'We just can't do it.'

They went right round the circle of time team members and nobody could come up with a single new idea which stood any chance of lifting the remaining stones into place.

'That's it then,' said Trafalgar. 'Back to square one.'

'You didn't ask me,' said Cliff from her usual position outside the cargo hold. She'd been grumpy of late because, under pressure of work, no one had the time to play cards with her. 'You never ask me.'

Trafalgar took a deep breath. 'I'm very sorry, Cliff,' he said. 'I should have asked you.'

'Yes, you should.'

'Do you know any way we can move those stones?'

'Yes,' she said with her nose in the air.

'How?'

'Not telling.'

'Oh, come on.'

'No.'

'Why not?'

'Because.'

'I don't believe you,' said Trafalgar cunningly. 'You're

just making it up. I don't think you know how at all.'

'I do too.'

'No, you don't.'

'Yes, I do. I know where the anti-gravity sledge is.'

There was a moment of silence while they all looked at her, then pandemonium broke out.

Trafalgar calmed them all down with difficulty.

'There really is an anti-gravity sledge?' he said.

'I told you. That's how the shiny people moved the stones.'

'That wasn't just a story?'

'No.' Cliff looked hurt.

'And there's one still here?'

'Yes.'

'Where is it?'

A sly look came over her face.

'Not saying,' she said.

'You've got to tell us.'

'No, I haven't.'

She reached in her pouch and produced a bundle of manky-looking leaves.

'There's only one way you'll get that sledge,' she said.

'How?'

'You've got to play me at poker.'

'Just one game of poker and then you'll tell us?'

'No, no,' she said, 'you've got to play me until you win.'

EIGHTEEN

Three hours later, as night fell, Cliff had won fifty-eight hands of poker and was thoroughly enjoying herself. The stakes were the *Titanic*'s entire stock of vitamin tablets. They'd started with two hundred each and now there were just five left on the ELV side of the table.

'You're nearly wiped out,' she said. 'When you are, we stop. Then if you still want, we try again tomorrow, okay?'

The time team were taking it in turns to play against her and it was Sopwith who was now sitting opposite, staring gloomily at his hand. They had all been doing their best but none of them, not even the three she had taught, had a very clear idea how the game ought to be played. As their opponent had been hypnotically elevated to world championship level, their best was a very long way short of being anything like good enough. They had so far won a total of seven hands, six by the blind luck of the deal and one when Daisy, who was keeping a jaundiced eye on proceedings, grabbed two aces from Cliff's hand and presented them to Trafalgar, growling menacingly at Cliff when she tried to protest. They told Daisy not to do it again and she sulked but after that she contented herself with snaffling the odd vitamin tablet from Cliff's winnings when she thought Cliff wasn't looking.

They were also finding that mangewort leaves didn't stand up too well to repeated dealing.

'This isn't going to bloody well work, is it?' said Rumpole, watching Sopwith as the fat naturalist peered at the ragged, frayed remains of his fifth card, trying to see what it was the eight of. 'We're going to be playing poker for the rest of our lives.'

Trafalgar was sniffing the air. Dozing off a minute or two earlier he had been almost certain on waking that he'd noticed a familiar scorching smell lingering in the air.

'Three sixes,' said Cliff, laying down her leaves face up.

'Hey! Wow! Got you!' said Sopwith triumphantly, spreading out his hand. 'Straight flush.'

A caterpillar crawled off, carrying with it a large chunk of the top card. The rest of the team stirred sleepily as an expectant buzz spread.

'Has he won another hand?' asked Puckeridge.

'Five, six, eight, seven, nine of clubs,' said Sopwith.

'Yes!' screamed Belle.

'Jolly well er . . .' shouted Halogen Tinker.

Cliff shook her head, reached out a giant finger and thumb to pick up the caterpillar and pulled the other piece of leaf out of its mouth.

'Thought so,' she said, holding it up.

There was a little club scratched on it.

'That was the ten, not the nine,' she said. 'Caterpillar damage doesn't count. I win.'

'This is ridiculous,' said Sopwith despondently. 'We're going to need to make some new cards now. Anyway, what's the point? What chance have we got?'

Sniffing the air again, Trafalgar reached for his hand-kerchief, but his hand touched something hard and unfamiliar filling his pocket. He pulled it out with diffi-culty and looked at it. 'I wouldn't give up quite yet,' he said slowly. 'I think it must be my turn to play.'

Cliff was delighted to have real cards to play with at last, although she simply couldn't think how Trafalgar could have been walking around with them in his pocket for so long without realising they were there. They were a good compromise size, about the same length as a mangewort leaf which made them inconveniently large for Trafalgar and inconveniently small for Cliff.

On the first hand, Trafalgar beat Cliff's two pairs with a full house and doubled his stake. On the next, he knew she was bluffing and doubled it again. After eight more hands, he was back to where they'd started with equal piles of tablets in front of them and Cliff was starting to wear a haunted expression.

She dealt him another hand. He picked it up and looked at it. A good hand, three jacks, a nine and an ace – definitely worth a big bet, even before he changed any cards. Then he looked across at the back of Cliff's cards where she held them, fanned out, opposite him. He read the words printed clearly on the back of them. King of spades, king of diamonds, king of hearts, king of clubs, queen of clubs. He changed his mind.

Definitely not a hand to bet against. He chucked his cards in, losing only one vitamin tablet. She looked as though she was going to burst into tears. It had only occurred to him when the cards arrived that although the Hypnolingo had taught her to speak, it hadn't taught her to read. He'd heard of marked cards but this pack carried marking to a new extreme. He might have felt guilty if there hadn't been so much at stake but he knew the safety of the entire expedition and maybe even the entire future world hung on the outcome of this card game.

Cliff gave in with, judged by the behaviour standards of the other villagers, fairly good grace. That's to say that though she kicked over the crate they were using for a table, screamed until she was sick over Daisy, threw the pile of vitamin tablets into the nearest bush and hurled a large rock at Trafalgar, she was careful to miss him by a narrow margin.

'Okay,' he said. 'Calm down. I've won.'

'How did you do it?'

'I could read your cards like an open book.'

'It's not fair.'

'I didn't say it was.'

'What about double or quits?'

'No. Where's the anti-gravity sledge?'

'Back at the village,' she said unwillingly. 'It's under Olvis. He sleeps on it.'

They sneaked into Olvis's hut without being seen. Olvis and O'Barron were on the other side of the village, making a very approximate copy of a Fender Stratocaster out of badly split logs from the firewood pile. Olvis's sleeping chamber had a floor of deep, glutinous mud kept well stirred up by all the rats. Olvis's bed was hovering above the floor at about the height of Trafalgar's head. It had a nicely padded grass mattress neatly arranged on the flat upper surface of a shiny silver oblong. A lever on the side was marked with two arrows for up and down. He grasped the lever and pulled it down and the sledge silently sank to the level of his knees.

They got it back to the *Titanic* with no trouble at all. It glided easily along at the slightest push. Trafalgar spent a little time worrying what Olvis's reaction would be if he found out but he hoped they'd have it back before that.

The sledge did the job in no time flat. It took no more than ten minutes for the villagers to load each new macrochip on to it, and then a press of the lever would set it gently rising to the desired height just like that. Stilts had put small slabs of wood as insulators on top of the other stones and in less than three hours they had a twenty-four-megalith motherboard all cabled up and very nearly ready to go. About one minute later, they became aware of a far-off roaring and saw Olvis coming towards them over the hill looking considerably upset.

'Hide it,' said Cliff, turning white. 'Quick.'

This seemed a very good idea except that it was too big to fit inside the *Titanic* and there wasn't anywhere else for it to go.

'Cover it with grass,' Puckeridge suggested and they all set to, tearing out great clumps of the stuff and spreading it over the sledge. After some frenzied work they stopped to look at it. It looked almost exactly like an anti-gravity sledge covered in grass.

'Tell the wolf to lie on it,' said Puckeridge, 'then we can say it's a dog bed. He'll never dare look.'

Daisy obediently curled up on the heap of grass.

'Nice one, Puck,' Stilts said gratefully, looking across to the looming shape of Olvis who was still two or three minutes away. A small dot in the distance, trailing far behind him, was gradually turning into O'Barron.

'Let's get busy. We could be ready to test by the time he gets here.'

There was just one more cable to fit and it had to be connected to the tallest of all the macrochips. They had lashed together a simple ladder and Halogen Tinker was at the top of it, straining to reach.

'I can't quite . . .' he called down. 'I wonder could . . . Perhaps if someone . . . I could try standing on . . . The view's wonderful if you . . .'

Belle cut him short by climbing up after him.

'Stand on my shoulders,' she said, 'then you can reach.'

Stilts drew Trafalgar to one side for an urgent discussion. 'Even if this works,' he said, 'we're not out of the woods. It needs calibrating. We don't know the date, you see.'

234

'Cliff?' Trafalgar called. 'You don't happen to know what date it is, do you?'

'What's a date?' said Cliff.

'It's sort of . . . well, it's a way of saying what day and year this is.'

'Yeah,' she said, 'of course I do. It's now.'

'It's probably the stone age,' said Stilts, looking round. 'It could be the megalithic age. It's definitely not the iron age because their clothes are really wrinkled.'

'That's not quite precise enough, is it?' asked Trafalgar. 'I mean, is calibrating the machine to within a couple of thousand years going to get us back?'

'Not quite,' said Stilts. 'For a really pinpoint return it's got to be a bit closer than that.'

'How much closer?'

'Errors get magnified, you see, so the starting point's got to be pretty good. Let's say roughly, er . . .'

'Yes?'

'A thousandth of a second ought to do it.'

'Oh, right.'

A loud noise behind them announced that Olvis had arrived and was greeting the villagers in his normal way, grabbing them by the throats in pairs and knocking their heads together.

(Where's my bed?) he yelled.

'It's all right,' whispered Stilts. 'He'll never spot it.'

(What's my bed doing covered with straw under that wolf?) Olvis bellowed.

'He's spotted it,' warned Cliff.

'Well, goodness gracious me, you naughty wolf,' said Puckeridge in a tone of vast surprise. 'Where *did* you get that from?'

Olvis, transported by rage, lunged at Daisy. Daisy lunged back at Olvis. A scuffle developed in which Olvis and Daisy turned into a ball of fur and flying, shredded bits of fake silk suit. Wrestling for possession of the sledge, some part of this whirling mixture caught the sledge's control lever a passing blow and it began to rise slowly into the air.

Throughout all of this, Tinker, perched on Belle's shoulders, had been working frantically away to connect up the last cable. Distracted by the unfamiliar sight of a wolf fighting a stone-age chieftain on an anti-gravity sledge, Tinker unwisely lost concentration for a moment, waving the end of the cable around in mid-air. A large spark leapt from the end of the cable to the nearest earth which was, inconveniently for Tinker, his head. There was a scream from Tinker, a flash of flame as his hair ignited and then complete pandemonium as Tinker, his legs still locked around Belle's neck, went flying off the top of the ladder, bounced off the rising sledge and caroomed through the air, leaving a trail of smoke behind him. They both landed on the ground where Tinker disentangled himself and raced over to the food supply where he stuck his entire head into the nearest container of liquid. This was an ass's skull full of milk which put out the fire but then stayed stuck firmly on the top of his head when he stood up again.

'Help,' shouted Tinker in a muffled way. 'Get this er . . . I've got a . . . Can someone please . . . ?'

No one had time to do anything about him. They were watching a terrible tableau unfold above the motherboard.

When Tinker had crashed into the sledge, he had brought the fight to an end as Olvis lost his grip and plunged off the edge. The chief fell to the ground, landing on his head and taking no further notice of anything much. That left Daisy on the sledge which was still rising gently and had just passed the fifty-foot level.

'Here, Daisy,' yelled Trafalgar. 'Jump!' But the animal

236

with the happy yip and alert stance of a wolf that was somehow about to fulfil her destiny stayed on board, soon reaching a level where the strengthening wind began to waft the sledge away across the countryside.

Trafalgar felt a lump in his throat as he watched it go, dwindling to a dot.

'Just as well, isn't it?' said Stilts. 'I mean you could hardly take her back with you, could you?'

'I wonder if I'll ever see her again,' said Trafalgar, brokenly.

'No,' said Stilts, 'I shouldn't think so. Come on. We're ready to test.'

O'Barron refused to play any part in the test. He was fussing over the insensible chief.

'You might have killed him,' he yelled. 'You might have been single-handedly responsible for completely obliterating the most significant king in the entire early history of the world.'

'Leave him,' Trafalgar said. 'We're going to test the motherboard,' but O'Barron, fanning Olvis's brow, took no notice.

They pulled the ass's skull off Tinker's head and stood, once more, round the control desk in the *Titanic*. This time the villagers, deeply impressed by Tinker's pyrotechnics, stood so far back that only the tops of their heads could be seen protruding above the next hill. Stilts counted solemnly down and pressed the button. The same glow spread around the stones, with little sparks leaping between the jumpers across the tops of the macrochips. There was a tense silence while their eyes were all fixed on the blank screen then it flickered once, then twice and filled with scrolling figures. For the merest fraction of a second it displayed a message: 'Shareware. For registration please send eight million dollars to Ephraim Carbox' but before they could write down the address it was replaced by the familiar coloured picture of a cobweb-encrusted vault and a tinny fanfare of trumpets. Trafalgar had never been so glad to see second-rate computer graphics in his life.

Cheers rang out round the *Titanic*.

'OKAY,' said Stilts. 'You little beauty! We're up and running.'

'We still don't know the date,' said Trafalgar, wondering where Daisy had got to.

'Right. What we have to do is perform a little test run. We'll set it to go forward, let's say one day and we'll leave someone here with a stopwatch then we can compare the two and recalibrate. It can't be that far out.'

He called out of the window, 'Mr O'Barron, sir. Can you come on board now. We're ready to go.' He turned away. 'Who are we going to leave behind?' he said.

'I don't know,' said Trafalgar, reluctant to leave anyone who'd be there when Olvis woke up. 'I suppose I'd better do it myself.'

'I'm not coming back with you,' O'Barron yelled from outside. 'Furthermore, I forbid any of you to go. Our work is here. I must nurse King Elvis back to health. He's the future.'

Olvis, snoring face down on the ground, looked more like the immediate past.

Trafalgar and Stilts glanced at one another and a plan was born.

'We'll be straight back, sir,' said Stilts. 'We've just got to do a quick calibration trip. If you're staying here, would you mind taking the stopwatch? We'll be back tomorrow.'

'Oh, give it to me then,' said O'Barron crossly, 'but when you get back I expect you to keep your mind on the job in hand, all right?'

They disconnected the ship from the motherboard,

watching as the glow faded from the stones. They gave O'Barron the stopwatch, synchronised with the counter on the time machine and waved goodbye to the villagers. Cliff was trying to teach Mudhole the basics of five-card stud but this was clearly going to take a long time. They settled themselves in the seats, swallowing painkillers, while Stilts set the machine to jump twenty-four hours ahead. Then he seemed to hesitate before pressing the button.

'What's the matter?'

'What happens tomorrow when he still doesn't want to come? Do we just ignore him?'

'We'll take that as it comes,' Trafalgar said. 'I think twenty-four hours tending Olvis's sore head might just refocus his mind a bit.'

'That's another thing. I hope it will be twenty-four hours. I have no way of knowing how far out the calibration is. It could be two days or even three.'

'All the better. That's more time for him to come to his senses.'

'Here goes then.'

Stilts pressed the button. It was the usual horrible experience but at least this time they knew they only had to move in time and not in space. When the thumping in their heads eased, they looked out of the window to see the same vista of grassland stretching away.

Then they looked out of the other window.

NINETEEN

The motherboard was still there, after a fashion. When they'd left, it had been rectangular – macrochips laid out in neat rows with the jumpers across the top of them. It wasn't like that any more. It was a circle now, but still with the jumpers laid around the top. There was no sign of the straw ropes.

They opened the cargo door and climbed cautiously out.

'Someone's been very busy,' observed Belle, looking at the rearranged stones. The circle was almost complete. There was just one stone left to go on top to fill the remaining gap. A long earth ramp stretched nearly to the top of the final pair of stones.

Sopwith bent down and picked something up off the ground. 'Look at this,' he said.

They gathered round. It was an ancient, withered section of plaited straw rope with one or two tiny flakes of dull gold paint still clinging to it. As they looked, it crumbled in his hand.

Rumpole gazed at it. 'I think we've been a bit longer than twenty-four hours,' he said.

A wild cackle rang out from behind them. An unfamiliar man of their own size stepped out from behind one of the macrochips. They could hardly see his face for filthy matted hair and a ragged beard hung down to his knees. He swept the hair to one side to reveal wildly rolling eyes

'A bit longer?' he said. 'A bit longer! Ten years longer,

that's all, just ten years. I've been waiting for you for ten years. Do you know what that madman's made me do? Do you?' He seemed about to cry. 'He made me move ALL THE STONES, that's what he made me do. Said he'd been promised they were magic stones and we'd move them where he wanted them. Well, WE didn't, did WE? Oh no. I HAD TO MOVE THEM. ALL BY MYSELF. Have you TRIED moving one of these stones? Have you? Go on, have a go.'

He started cackling again then swung round. 'I do it with sheep, you know. Takes a hundred sheep to move one stone. They don't like it, not one little bit but they have to do it because I'm their king. I'm the king of the sheep, oh yes, I am. There's one more stone, just one more and if I don't get it done in time they're going to sacrifice me.'

He swung round on Anya who backed away hurriedly. He gazed at her and began to pant in a particularly horrid way with his tongue hanging out. 'And do you know what's worse?' he said. 'He still CAN'T SING IN TUNE. In fact he doesn't even TRY.'

He got down on his knees and wrung his hands together. 'You've got to help me,' he said. 'If you all help, we could get that stone up on top and then my life will be spared. I'm begging you.'

'There's an easier way,' said Trafalgar. 'Just come with us, that's all you have to do.'

'YES,' shouted O'Barron. 'That's it! Quick, before HE comes back. Let's go.'

'Just before we do,' said Stilts, 'I don't suppose you've still got the stopwatch, have you?'

A shudder crossed O'Barron's face. 'No,' he said, 'he made me eat it.'

'Well, then I don't suppose you know exactly how long we've been gone, do you?'

'Yes, yes. Look.' He led them over to one of the stones. There was a long line of scratches on it. 'There's one for every day.'

'You're sure?'

'Of course I'm sure.' Some of his old authoritarian nature reasserted itself. 'How dare you question my word!'

They counted, then they counted again to make sure. There were three thousand six hundred and twenty-eight scratches. Stilts dialled it into the machine.

'Do you think we ought to make a quick trip to the village?' Trafalgar asked as they prepared for the next leg of their trip. 'I never really said goodbye to Cliff.' Mostly he was thinking of Daisy, thinking perhaps she might have found her way back.

'NO,' screamed O'Barron, 'DON'T GO ANYWHERE NEAR THAT PLACE. The man's mad, I tell you.'

'So you've given up trying to turn him into King Elvis?'

A cunning look came over O'Barron's face.

'I've sown the seed, Hurlock,' he said. 'I've given him the basic grounding he needs. There's only so much a man can do. Now it's up to him. If he'll just practise that guitar, he could make it but you can't tell them, you know – you just can't tell them.'

'Okay, now listen,' said Stilts. 'We have a calibration. We can go forward a thousand years and be pretty much spot on IF that really was the right number of notches. The trouble is we still don't know what date it is now so we're going to be flying blind. We have to head for a time period where they have accurate clocks and they know the date. Anyone want to make a guess?'

No one did. In the end they drew lots and settled on five thousand years. It seemed as good as any other guess so they dialled it into the machine, crossed their fingers, took three more painkillers each and got ready to press the button.

'Hang on a minute. We also don't have any idea *where* we are. We need to recalibrate the geographical coordinates too,' Stilts pointed out.

'One thing at a time. Let's leave it where it is now so we can see what's happened to this place,' suggested Trafalgar.

Stilts's finger was on the button when O'Barron lunged forward. 'NO,' he screamed. 'Get me away from here. I never want to see this place again.'

He stabbed at the control panel, flailing away at random just as Stilts launched them on their time jump.

'Get back!' yelled Stilts. 'What are you doing? Haven't you caused enough trouble?'

'Stop him, Stilts,' shouted Trafalgar.

'Too late.'

Damn, thought Trafalgar, what now?

Just as the *Titanic* creaked off into the unknown future, his last thought was, I really would have liked to talk to Cliff again, in case she found Daisy.

If he had seen Cliff, he would have been quite surprised by the changes that had come about since he had seen her last. Her shepherdessing days were over and she now had much higher status. The village was a lot bigger than it had been. It really had turned out to be the start of a new civilisation but it was all down to her, rather than Olvis. The Uglies and Big Bottoms had moved to Olvis's village because of Cliff's renown as a storyteller. In the evenings, they would cluster round the fire to listen to her. She always sat on the ceremonial box, the only arte-fact the time team had left behind. She lived to a great age and in the end she learnt the secret of the marked cards. From deciphering the letters on the back of them, she also learnt never to play cards for high stakes with little men in long floppy hats. She also learnt the true identity of the tiny green-clad people.

'Come gather round,' she would say, 'and I will tell you of the ELVs. I will tell you the tale of the little people who came from nowhere, the little people who could charm the wild animals. You had to obey them and do what they wanted or they would use their magic to turn your milk sour.'

'Tell us, Cliff,' they would chorus.

'There was the wizard Stilts and the ferocious Rumpole, Stilts' kin, who spun straw into gold. Then there was Puck, naughty Puck who would play most terrible tricks and, oh, there was the extraordinary Tinker and Belle, who together flew through the air like a bright burning light.'

'Did Tinkerbelle wear green too, Cliff?' the little ones would ask.

'Why no,' Cliff would say. 'It was two of them, not one, Tinker and Belle and *they* wore blue and red.'

'Weren't they elves then, Cliff?'

Here Cliff would look at the stencilled initials on the box which belonged to the other part of the expedition, the GEOGRAPHERS, NATURALISTS, ORNITHOLOGISTS AND MAMMALIAN EXPLORATION SPECIALISTS.

'No,' she would say. 'Those other three weren't ELVS, they were GNOMES.'

Cliff's stories spread across the length and breadth of the country that would later be England and became the basis of folklore for thousands of years to come. Starting from the limited alphabet provided by the marked cards and the stencilled crate, she insisted on teaching the villagers to spell. This counteracted the baleful influence of Olvis who was only interested in getting a backing group together and trying to tune his guitar, which was hard

244

with woollen strings. The village did indeed become a significant influence on the future of the country but that was as a centre of literacy and storytelling, not rock music.

As for Daisy, she drifted far to the south-east across Europe and over the Alps before a short-sighted eagle bumped into the sledge and nudged the lever towards DOWN. The villagers there were very impressed by the flying wolf who would keep forcing them all to eat lettuce. Daisy lived a long, happy and pampered life, troubled only by a particularly persistent pair of human babies who would keep insisting she was their mother. The anti-gravity sledge had an important long-term effect on the political balance of power in the region. With its help in moving blocks of stone, the local people rapidly built their village of Rome into a great fortified city. Daisy had many more adventures and when she eventually died at a ripe old age, the local people laid her reverently on the sledge, set the lever to the full UP position and watched as she rose gradually out of their sight into a clear blue sky, displaying the strange writing on the underside of the sledge that, had they known it, spelt out the words, 'If found, please return to Planet 118, Horsehead Nebula.'

On fine days, when they weren't doing their spelling lessons, Cliff's villagers would go to look at the rearranged motherboard. It was never much use as a temple because of not having a roof but it made them feel good. Olvis, tone deaf to the end, had himself buried near it after trying unsuccessfully to start a new cult of himself. For many years they called the temple the twenty-four-megalith motherboard, but times changed and new gods came on the scene. Looking for a more catchy name with a view to setting up a franchise, they finally settled on Stonehenge.

*   *   *

The *Titanic* flew onwards through the ripples of the newly literate world and rematerialised in dense woodland.

Trafalgar massaged his forehead and groaned. He looked out of the window at giant trees.

'Where are we?' he said.

Stilts opened his eyes with difficulty and tried to focus on the dials. 'Somewhere further north,' he said after a bit. 'He moved the setting.'

'Five thousand years on?'

'If the calibration was right.'

It was, more or less. They didn't know it but they were four thousand six hundred years on and almost exactly one hundred old miles north of the site of Olvisland. It didn't look as though it was going to be easy to find a clock. In fact, peering outside, it didn't look as though it was going to be easy to find anything that didn't involve twigs, leaves and branches. They sat around groaning for a while until the headaches cleared. O'Barron insisted that Anya should shave him and cut his hair and Trafalgar watched in suppressed fury. As the familiar face resurfaced through the grime, so did the familiar arrogance, now overlaid with a disturbing new touch of mad dictatorship which was probably the rebound from ten years in Olvis's company.

'I'm changing a few things around here,' he announced. 'From now on, I expect to be addressed as Most Excellent Majesty King Elvis Bluto O'Barron or Celestial Highness for short. You may only approach me on your knees. Furthermore, the mission of the TS *Titanic* will now be redirected to establishing *my* kingdom in a suitable location, which I will be deciding shortly. It has become clear to me that you were all mistaken in believing that primitive Olvis to be the holder of the Blue Suede Crown. It is me, me, I tell you.'

There was a stunned silence while they all gaped at him.

'We will stay here for one day,' he said. 'That will give you time to prepare for the royal wedding.'

'What wedding?' asked Trafalgar with a sense of horrible foreboding.

'MY wedding of course. My wedding to the royal consort.'

'The . . . the royal consort?'

'My future wife.' He waved a hand behind him. 'Tits Anya.'

She dropped the towel and turned white.

'Future wife? You have to be bloody joking,' she said and looked wildly around. 'Trafalgar, you're not going to let this happen, are you? Go on, say something.'

He steeled himself for a decisive intervention as her beautiful, pleading eyes locked on to his.

'Fweeeep,' he said.

Later, utterly miserable and furious with himself, Trafalgar went into a huddle with Stilts.

'We can't let him do this,' he said.

'I know but officially he's in charge.'

'He's mad.'

'It's still mutiny.'

'What do we do?'

'I don't know.'

Unable to bear it for a moment longer, Trafalgar looked out of the window. 'I'm going outside for a walk,' he said. 'I may be a little while.'

'Be careful,' said Stilts. 'Do you want me to come too?'

'No. I need to be alone.'

'Don't get eaten by anything. Oh, and if you happen to come across a clock and a good map . . .'

Trafalgar took a compass with him but found, once

he'd pushed through the dense leaves for a minute or two, that he'd got past the worst of it. He was still in a wood but it was more open and he could see around him. Big birds flew off when they saw him but there was the usual mixture of ants and other significantly large bugs to watch out for. After a few minutes meandering along the side of a small stream, he found a grassy bank and stretched himself out under an overhanging dock leaf to think. No thoughts came except profoundly depressing ones so instead he went to sleep.

He woke, annoyed to find someone thundering in his ear.

'I know a bank whereon the wild cow parsley
    blows,'

said the voice.

'Where oxlips and the nodding violet grows,
quite over-canopied with luscious woodbine
with sweet musk roses and with eglantine:
There sleeps Agnes some time of . . .'

'Oh pestilential poxes,' it said and broke off. 'Blasted syllables. Oh, how I hate syllables.'

'Thyme,' said Trafalgar crossly, 'the whole bloody bank's covered in wild thyme. That's not cow parsley.'

There was a short silence, then the dock leaf was swept back by a huge hand and he found himself looking up at a bearded giant.

'How now, spirit!' said the giant in an astonished tone. 'What art thou? Art thou that shrewd and knavish sprite called Puck who is otherwise Robin Goodfellow?'

'No, no,' said Trafalgar, still confused by sleep and rather startled to be addressed in this way. 'I'm Trafalgar.

Puck's back in the *Titanic* and he's never robbed anybody.'

'I am delighted to make thy better acquaintance though never before have I believed the ancient tales of the little people. What sayest thou regarding thyme?'

'Oh sorry, I didn't mean to interrupt. I was just saying that's wild thyme, not cow parsley.'

'I know a bank whereon the wild thyme blows . . .'

said the other.

'Yes, yes. That worketh so much better though "Agnes" still doth grate upon the tongue.' He seemed to take in Trafalgar's mournful face for the first time.

'Do I divine by thy sad countenance that fell trouble lieth heavy on thy breast, small friend?'

'No, I'm just feeling a bit pissed off,' said Trafalgar.

'I too have troubles,' said the other. 'Speak to me not of troubles. I have a sea of troubles. I suffer the sticks and axes of outrageous fortune but I must take arms and by opposing up-end them, as must thou. What ails thee?'

'Well, there's this girl . . .'

'Oh, tell me not of fair maidens. Of that poisoned goblet I have quaffed my fill. Never satisfied are they, wanting always more than I can give, more fine silks to wear, more sweetmeats, more fripperies, complaining always of my lack of silver coin to purchase for them what they will. But enough of me, what is it that bothers thee?'

'There's this total moron called O'Barron who . . .'

'If I could just make my fortune with my pen, then would I be truly happy. But the muse doth sit fretfully at my shoulder and my miserable scratchings come to nought. Full five years have I tried to make my mark upon the world as a writer of fine dramatic entertainments for the stage and yet it seemeth I cannot devise a

249

tale full fine enough to impress itself upon my fellow men.'

'You're a writer?'

'That is my dearest wish.'

'You want to write plays?'

'Indeed, dear sir.'

'Then just shut up and listen and I'll tell you a story,' said Trafalgar and for the next hour he poured out his heart to the bearded man. He told him the entire story of the trip from beginning to end while the man scratched furiously away with his quill pen on sheaves of parchment, in an unsuccessful attempt to keep up.

At the end, feeling slightly better, Trafalgar stopped to draw breath. The man's face was alive with delight as he leafed through his notes.

'By Thucydides,' he swore, 'this makes fine reading, small sir. I think there are more tales than one in this. The mad king, oh yes, that's meat for a fine yarn. But this is best I think, this business of the man Oberon, his servant Puck and the fair Titania.'

'No, that's O'Barron,' said Trafalgar impatiently, 'and I'd really rather you called her just plain Anya.'

'The magic with the ass's head is a pretty touch.'

'It was an ass's *skull*, and it wasn't magic – it was just the quickest way Tinker could find to put the fire out.'

The man was off in a world of his own, barely listening, jotting further notes. 'This identical twin of thine who came in his disguise, oh yes indeed, wolves, Sopwith Camel, motherboards. Oh yes, I can indeed perform wonders with all of this.'

A sudden realisation dawned on him. 'If thou comest from our far-off future, small sir, then thou willst know if I do indeed achieve my lofty ambition. In the history of our race recorded in thy time, who is the most celebrated scribe of plays?'

'Schwarzenegger,' said Trafalgar absently, realising the time was fast approaching when he would have to return to the *Titanic* and the O'Barron problem. 'Is that you?'

The man's crestfallen look could have told him the answer.

'Alas no.'

'By the way,' said Trafalgar, belatedly remembering Stilts's instructions, 'can you tell me the date today?'

'It is the first of July in the year of our lord fifteen hundred and eighty-two.'

'And where are we?'

'In the fair forest of Arden, close to Stratford on the river Avon.'

'You don't happen to know the grid reference, do you? No? Never mind.'

'I wish thee fortune with thine endeavour to overcome the travails of thy heart, small sir, and will always cherish the private memory of our meeting.'

'Oh good,' said Trafalgar who was starting to feel he'd had enough of the long-winded would-be writer. 'I'd best be off.'

'Before thou goest,' said the other, who had the grace to look just a tiny bit embarrassed, 'may I ask, have they heard of me at all in thy time?'

'I don't know. What's your name?'

'Breakspear,' said the other. 'William Breakspear.'

'No, sorry,' said Trafalgar.

He went off, leaving the bearded man muttering over his quill pen.

'I know a bank whereon the wild thyme blows . . .

'Yes, that's much better, and let me see . . .

'. . . there sleeps Titania some time of the night.'

251

He chortled to himself then fell back into gloom.

'Little this doth avail me,' he mused aloud, 'if my name is not to be remembered. But wait!' A thought dawned on him. 'I have but to change mine own name to match that given me by the little man then I shall truly be the very same playwright of whom he spoke! True success and glory shall then be mine, echoing down the far ages. Now what was that name he spoke again? Bugger me, I know it started with "Sh".'

TWENTY

It was perhaps a shame that Shakespeare's greatest play, *All's Well That Ends Smaller*, subtitled 'the engaging tragedy of Sopwith and the flying wolf' was to be lost to the world, devoured by a freak lightning strike within minutes of the final words being written but then it might have been a little too advanced for a late-sixteenth-century audience. It had changed a lot by the time he got round to rewriting it in the early sixteen hundreds. By that time the whole encounter in the forest seemed like a midsummer daydream to him. Indeed, the only line which survived from the original into the final version, under the amended title of *All's Well That Ends Well*, was 'your date is better in your pie and your porridge than in your cheek,' which was so completely nonsensical that it gave away very little to his audience about advanced datastore design techniques.

Trafalgar, retracing his steps to the *Titanic* with some difficulty, had too much on his mind to bother for long with his recent conversation. Unless he did something dramatic, O'Barron would have his appalling way and Anya would be lost to him for ever. A rebellion seemed the only way out but he wasn't at all sure he could persuade the others to rise up against their mad leader and lock him safely away. They were used to obeying the rules and the fact remained that O'Barron was not only their commander but was also a powerful political figure in the time to which they were trying to return.

He found Stilts sitting outside the *Titanic*.

'He's got them all sewing in there,' said Stilts, 'making a bloody great wedding dress. They're using up all the other signal flags. He insists it's got to be the whole lot, veil, long skirt, train, everything.'

'How sickening. He'll look absolutely absurd in a veil.'

'Of course he will but he's not in a mood to listen to anyone.' Stilts gave Trafalgar an appraising glance. 'Don't you think it's time you did something to stop the wedding?'

'If only I knew how.'

'I've got an idea,' said Stilts. 'Remember, he's a real coward. If you rushed in pretending we were under attack, he'd order another time jump. That would hold things up a bit at least.'

It wasn't a great plan but it was the best they could think of. Trafalgar told Stilts what he'd found out from the would-be playwright about the present date and time.

'Fine, let's programme in a destination so we're all ready. Where and when?' said Stilts.

'Maybe if we get on with the mission, it will force O'Barron back to reality. Supposing we head for the final days before the Sleep.'

'Sounds good to me. Where?'

'There must have been some central pre-Sleep head-quarters, where they controlled all the downsizing and stuff. See what the computer makes of that. Mind you, with the state it's in, we could wind up almost anywhere. We'll just have to risk it.'

Stilts went inside and got quietly to work while O'Barron fussed in the middle of an unwilling crowd of crew members who were busy with pins, needles and thread. Anya was sitting angrily on the fringe of the crowd, already dressed in a pair of overalls roughly cut up and retailored to look like a morning suit and tie.

The computer came up with a location straight away

when he tapped in the outline of where they wanted to go, Grand Central Fortress, New York City. That was a thrilling thought. If it worked, they would actually see the fabled lost city of New York. The year, they already knew, had to be 2112. The rest of the date? Stilts hadn't a clue so he put in 1 January. It wouldn't do to get there after everyone else had gone. When he was ready he signalled out of the window.

Trafalgar put on a good show. He burst in through the door screaming at the top of his voice, 'Quick, they're coming, they're after us! Let's get out of here. Hurry. There's no time. Press the button!'

'What are?' quavered O'Barron.

'Huge, horrible things.'

'What sort of things?'

'Nasty, foul, flesh-ripping things that tear your heads off and pull out your . . .'

There was a thud and O'Barron slid to the floor in a dead faint, eyes rolling upwards. The others were mostly screaming, running round in circles and looking, panic-stricken, out of the window to see what Trafalgar was talking about.

'Okay,' he said, 'settle down. I might have been wrong about the flesh-eating thingies. The wedding's postponed. Press the button, Stilts.'

It was sheer bad luck that Trafalgar had happened to ask the date in the year 1582. It wasn't that Shakespeare had given him the wrong answer, it was just that 1582 was a slightly odd year in which to do the asking. It was the year that Pope Gregory came to a decision over in the great city of Rome – the city founded according to a very defective legend by twins who were suckled by a she-wolf, thereby giving far too little credit to the wolf herself, let alone her anti-gravity sledge.

255

Pope Gregory had spent a sleepless night, after a particularly rich meal of cream fried in butter, worrying about the calendar. By dawn he had decided that there were too many days creeping into the year and what the world needed was a one-off reduction in their number. It seemed to him that chopping out eleven days would bring everything neatly into line.

The Gregorian Calender, as it was known, was introduced into England, with a great sense of urgency, one hundred and seventy years later in 1752. The announcement that eleven days were to be lopped off the calendar in that year caused riots in the streets as the people of the time, with typical intelligence, leapt to the conclusion that someone was stealing eleven days of their life and, making the obvious response, decided to burn their own houses down.

None of this really mattered to the time team except that in putting their reckoning out by eleven days, the magnified effect of that took them not nearly as far forward as they wanted to go. The time machine did get the address right, but Grand Central Fortress was still ten years away from being built and so the place where the *Titanic* came to rest was right in the middle of the most violent and decaying part of the city of New York, at a moment in its overcrowded history when anyone who moved and wasn't protected by carbon fibre body armour and a 20,000-volt personal protection stun field was likely to be eaten by someone who was.

This didn't particularly surprise Trafalgar who had long ago given up expecting anything much to go right on this trip, nor did it surprise O'Barron who, having passed out on being told that flesh-eating monsters were approaching, more or less took it in his stride on coming round to find that the monsters had arrived. They looked out of the window to see a scene of utter urban devastation – vast decrepit buildings, separated by streets running with chemical slime through which armoured figures splashed, flailing at each other with vicious weapons.

It didn't seem a good moment to open the door, which was why they were somewhat aghast to hear someone down below in the cargo hold doing exactly that.

Halogen Tinker, who had been down in the hold throughout, trying to find something that would pass as lace for O'Barron's marital underwear, had no idea what was going on outside. First he'd been through an entirely unexpected time jump without the benefit of painkillers, then he'd heard loud hammering noises on the outside of the cargo hold door, coupled with bangs, screams and violent jolts. In addition he was, for an extremely clever scientist, very stupid in that way that only extremely clever people can be, so, naturally, he opened the cargo hold door.

A small giant pitched in through it head first, shouting, 'Hide me,' at the top of its voice.

Tinker said, 'Who are . . . ? Why are you . . . ? Where do you . . . ?' then looked out of the door and said, 'What's that man pointing that gun at me for?'

'To kill you,' said the small giant. 'Duck.'

'Don't be silly, I'm not a du — I'm a . . . Why's he . . . ?'

The small giant lunged across and banged the cargo door shut as the top quarter of it disintegrated into splinters. Then the ship shimmered away out of that scene of berserk violence and into new surroundings that were just as alien but not quite so immediately likely to cause your body to explode into little quivering damp slices.

On the upper deck, Stilts had lunged for the control panel as soon as he had seen the danger they were in. All he'd had time to do was reset the lateral coordinates to jump a hundred miles west before the mounting clamour

257

outside and the appearance of what seemed to be a small personal tank in fetching pink metalflake colours with a nice garland of plastic sunflowers woven round its laser cannon persuaded him it was again time to leave.

They landed in a place so barren that the word 'desert' would have had entirely unsuitable connotations of cosy homeliness. It was bare rock, across which a thick cloud of dust was blowing. This stopped them seeing very far in any direction but from what they could see, this was probably no great loss. Halogen Tinker was even less coherent than usual when he appeared from the hold with something urgent to say.

'Perhaps you'd better . . . I think it would be a good idea to . . . If anyone has the time . . . He's only a small . . . Didn't expect . . . When I openèd the er . . . Just sort of fell in to . . . Means no harm, but . . . Probably knows what's . . .'

It no longer seemed so unusual to find an unexpected passenger in the hold. This one was a relatively good fit for once, being no more than three times their size, and seemed to be about ten years old. He was also extremely pleased to see them and not very surprised.

'Wow, zoomy!' he said when they came down the ladder to look at him. 'Saved by a UFO. Are you guys from another planet?'

'No, don't be silly,' said Rumpole crossly. 'We're Neptunians from the future and this isn't a yoofo, it's a time machine.'

'Oh brillo.' The boy looked around at the planked insides of the *Titanic*. 'Is this *real* wood? You must be awful rich in the future if you have this much real wood. Can you take me there?'

'Don't you have wood?' said Belle in surprise.

'We don't have anything except rock and synthetic food and that's like, you know, real cacky.' He screwed up his face in distaste. 'There's trees on some of the fortress islands but even my dad's not rich enough to go there.'

'Your dad's rich?'

'He's the Godfather President of the United States of America and Europe,' said the boy proudly.

'Don't know what it means but it sounds rich,' said Puckeridge. 'What's his name?'

'Enrico Gates the Fourth. Haven't you heard of him? I'm his son, Groucho. Hey, how come you came boobling into Hellfire Alley without armour?'

'That was where we found you? Hellfire Alley?'

The boy nodded.

'Well, come to that, what were *you* doing there?'

He looked slightly abashed. 'Forgot to charge my scooter battery. I'm not allowed outside the fence by myself but sometimes I slip away. Normally I never fly below a hundred feet but then the motor stopped. I just had time to set off the locator beacon before the cannies found me.'

'Cannies?'

'Yeah, the flesh-eaters. You know they rip off your head and pull out the . . .'

There was a thud and O'Barron hit the floor again.

'What's with him?' said Groucho, interested. 'Malnutrition?'

He looked around at all of them. 'Anyway, feed my brain, guys. Input. How far off do you guys come from and how come you're so little?'

'I think we're probably the solution to your problem,' said Trafalgar slowly. 'Do you want to hear about it?'

'Just before you get started,' said Stilts with one eye out of the window, wondering whether there might be any cannies lurking in the stripped wasteland outside, 'what year *is* this? You don't happen to know the exact time and date, do you?'

'It's 2089. Are you gribbles flying blind or what?'

'Not 2112?'

'Definitely not. 2112? I mean like I'd be really old if it was 2112, like I'd be thirty-three. That's halfway dead.'

'You wouldn't happen to know the exact time as well?'

'Does cyber-pork taste bad? Is water solid? 'Course I do.' He showed them a tiny band on his wrist which projected a three dimensional hologram clock at the touch of a button. 'Accurate to one millionth of a second,' he said proudly, 'and it's got a full GPS location system built in.'

'Could I borrow that?' asked Stilts. 'I'll be right back.'

While Stilts was gone, Groucho – who was clearly a very bright boy – bombarded them with questions. Trafalgar answered a little evasively, feeling it might be dangerous to pass on too much information but in any case their conversation was cut short dramatically just as Stilts handed back the watch.

An amplified electronic voice boomed at them through the blowing dust.

'Attention, attention. This is Enrico Gates the Fourth speaking. We have you surrounded. Let my son go or you will be blasted into oblivion. I will count to twenty.' There was a short pause as if a logical problem had just struck the speaker. 'If you don't let him go, I'll blast him anyway. I've got three more sons and . . .'

They heard a muffled voice interrupt. 'Er . . . two more sons. I'm starting counting. Twenty . . .'

Stilts went back upstairs.

Trafalgar turned to the boy. 'How did he follow us?'

'I told you. Locator beacon. Anyway, *he's* not out there. That's just the rescue robots. He's probably back home by the pool.'

'Nineteen . . . eighteen . . .'

'Does he mean it?'

' 'Course he does. That's why he's Godfather President. I better go. You better go too. He'll blast you anyway when they've got me.'

'Seventeen . . . sixteen . . . fifteen . . . fourteen . . .'

They opened the cargo bay door and the boy slipped out into the swirling dust towards a dim flashing light, turning to give them a final wave as he disappeared.

'Get going, Stilts,' Trafalgar shouted up the ladder, 'or we'll be in real trouble.'

'What's new,' grunted Stilts. 'Hold tight.'

'Thirteen . . . twelve . . . eleven . . . ten . . . nine . . . eight . . . seven . . .'

'Did you hear that?' said Rumpole. 'This lot can't count either.' He was interrupted by a brain-splitting thump, a wild lurch and sudden dead silence.

TWENTY-ONE

It was a violent arrival because the *Titanic* was well over-due for its ten-thousand-year service and the solid object detection and avoidance system wasn't working. It therefore rematerialised halfway through a dividing wall inside Grand Central Fortress, bringing the rest of the wall crashing down around it. When the pain in their heads eased, they looked out into a vast, empty, windowless hall, lit by stark flickering tubes. Rows of bright yellow painted machines were lined up along its walls. They were fitted with crawler tracks and complicated hydraulic arms.

A giant was standing watching them with a cool, con-sidering expression on his face and pointing something very weapon-like in their direction. It looked as if it could do them serious damage.

They peered out through the window.

'Whoops,' said Stilts, 'bad choice. This is where we get fried. Better move on.'

He reached for the control panel but then the giant said something very unexpected.

What he said was, 'Hi, guys. Long time no see.'

There was something just vaguely familiar about his face and Trafalgar knew exactly who he was, although this was mostly because he had his name stencilled in large letters on his overalls. The label said GROUCHO GATES. GODFATHER PRESIDENT OF THE WORLD. They'd seen him two minutes before but twenty-three years had gone by in that time.

'The world, huh?' said Trafalgar, climbing out of the cargo bay door and looking up at the man towering over him. 'That's quite a jump.'

The others followed him out. Groucho gave a hollow laugh. 'Some world. You want to know exactly how many citizens I have control over?'

'Okay.'

'Three. Bill, John and Robert. Come to that, I don't have that much control over John.'

'What happened to all the others?'

Groucho sat down on a box.

'They're asleep,' he said, 'for five hundred years, starting now. It got worse and worse out there, you know. People everywhere. All we had left was people. Another year or two and they'd all have been eating each other. There wasn't anything else left.'

He looked around at them and gave a weary smile. 'You guys gave me the clue. I suddenly thought, hey, if everyone gets smaller there won't be a problem any more, so when I got to be President I decided I'd do something about it.'

'What happened to your father?'

'Oh, he got taken hostage and he had to call in an air strike on himself to prove he wasn't bluffing. Anyway I got all the best brains together and kind of forced everyone to accept the downsizing. Even the people on the fortress islands knew it made sense. They're all in the sleep pods now.'

'And these?' asked Stilts, pointing at the machines.

'We've got them all over the place, ready to go. They're the regeneration robots. As soon as we go into the pods they'll get started taking everything that's left apart and rebuilding it, sowing the new mini-seeds and all that.' He gave them a strange look. 'I guess I already know it works because I've seen you. I don't suppose

I'd ever have gone through with it if you hadn't appeared.'

Trafalgar remembered a far-off time a long way ahead in an underground tomb and he knew that only two of Groucho's three subjects were destined to go into the pods.

'What have you got left to do?' he asked and he thought he had already guessed the answer.

'Bill's just got the wasps and the flies to do. Robert's finishing off the mice and John's messing around as usual.'

'Bill's doing the *flies*?'

'Yup.'

'Right now?'

'He certainly is.'

'We need to talk to Bill, then we need to talk to Robert.'

Their conversation with Bill and Robert might have got off to a better start if O'Barron, who had just come to his senses again, hadn't finally succumbed to complete insanity as they were about to enter the laboratory. Groucho turned to look down at them all at the doorway, put his finger to his lips and said, 'Wait here quietly for a minute and let me handle this.'

At that precise moment, O'Barron rushed into the room between his legs and bawled out, 'Kneel dogs! It is I, the Celestial Emperor, who calls on you to make obeisance to me. Kneel or die!'

Two men in white coats were working away at tables covered in equipment. They both turned round with startled faces. There was a muffled oath and a crash of breaking glass.

Groucho stepped quickly into the room, picked up O'Barron and shut him in a desk drawer where he could still be heard calling for his imperial guard to come and decapitate everyone in sight.

'Sorry about that,' Groucho said. 'Let me explain. Where's Robert?'

'Gone off somewhere, Grouch,' said the nearer man in a shaky voice. 'Said not to expect him for a bit. Er, was that really a foot-high bossy midget or is this place finally getting to me?'

The other man, who was playing around with a circuit board, giggled.

Groucho ran through a quick explanation of what was going on. It did very little to calm them.

'Trafalgar here needs to talk to you – says there's some sort of problem with the flies.'

They were staring at him, goggle-eyed, and Trafalgar hesitated, embarrassed. 'It's not much of a problem. Well, I suppose it is really. Well, yes, it definitely is.'

'What is?' said the one called Bill.

'You see, I'm not suggesting there's anything wrong with your work, not for a moment, but I think something's about to go a bit wrong with the downsizing so I wonder if you'd mind taking a bit of extra care when it comes to the finer points of it. Not of course that you haven't been.'

Bill was looking, if anything, even more uncomprehending.

'Oh sod it,' said Trafalgar, throwing caution and politeness to the winds. 'What I mean is, you're about to screw up the entire future by making the houseflies get bigger, not smaller, so pull yourself together, take a bit of extra care and get it right.'

'I ALWAYS take care,' said the scientist, rather huffily.

'Yes,' said the other one, still giggling. 'We're affronted, taken aback and knocked sideways by that accusation.'

'Shut up, John,' said Groucho. 'This is serious. The fact is there is ... was ... er ... has been a mistake made and we've got to unmake it.'

'Well, it is true that there are two possible ways of altering the growth genes in the DNA helix,' admitted Bill. 'I'm happy with the wasps but the flies have been proving a bit tricky.' He sighed. 'It's been worrying me and I had just chosen the one I thought was the best bet but I suppose in that case I'd better change it to the other one.'

'Oh please do,' said Trafalgar. 'We'll be very grateful in the future.'

'Okay, that one's sorted out,' said Groucho. 'Now, what about these mice? I'm sorry Robert's not here.'

'Doesn't matter,' said Bill. 'I can show you. He left us the last ones to go in the pods all ready.' He took them over to where ten white rodents with long tails were scampering around inside a cage. 'What's the problem with them?'

'Those aren't mice,' said Sopwith Camel, surprised. 'They're elephants.'

Bill and Groucho stifled a burst of laughter. John didn't bother and when their ears recovered, Trafalgar stepped in quickly.

'Some of the names got changed,' he said. 'That's the point. I don't mean that sort. I mean the kind with plastic bodies and wire tails that rush round the place giggling.' He heard just such a giggle coming from John. 'That's it,' he said. 'Exactly like that.'

Groucho looked startled.

'Well, hold on now,' he said. 'That's what John's messing about with. He showed them to me this morning. He's made two of them. I don't suppose there's much harm in it.'

'What? My joker mice?' said John. 'Oh, come on. There's nothing wrong with those, surely?'

'Oh yes there is,' said Trafalgar. 'They're going to cause a lot of trouble.'

266

'No, come on. They've got artificial intelligence. They're terrific.'

'Do they reproduce themselves?' demanded Trafalgar sternly.

'Well . . . yes.'

'And do they have a terrible sense of humour?'

'No, it's brilliant. It's the first ever artificial humour.'

Everyone was looking at him in a way that clearly suggested his view of what made a sense of humour good might be open to question. 'Oh, come on, guys,' he said. 'They're really funny.'

'Can we have them please?' said Groucho. 'Now.'

John surrendered them with very bad grace. There were two of them and they were quite crude by later standards. They both wore bowler hats and you could hardly hear them giggling at all. Puckeridge, who was in many ways rather similar to John, looked at them with deep interest.

'How do I switch them off?' Groucho asked.

'I'll do it,' said John sulkily. 'If I really must. I can't see the point though. You're just a spoilsport.'

He slid open an access panel in the base and fiddled around. 'All right,' he said, 'I've done it. I've disconnected the power. They're as dead as dormice.' He looked as if he were about to cry.

'Into the sleep pod you go,' said Groucho sternly. 'Right now. You've done quite enough. I'm not having you wandering around.' He picked up the two mice by their tails, inspected them and slung them into a bin marked, WASTE MATERIALS. RECYCLING.

He looked around the laboratory. 'Are you done, Bill?'

'Yes, I think so,' said Bill, picking up one of the test tubes of fly DNA and looking at it with a lingering doubt in his mind. He would have bet almost anything that he'd made the right choice first time, but if the little guys said it was wrong, it had to be wrong. He put it in the hibernation hatchery and switched on. Bill felt his grip on reality had slipped quite a long way just lately, what with the World President on first-name terms, just about everyone he knew fast asleep and slowly shrinking and now the appearance of tiny little people. He wasn't at all sure he wasn't dreaming the whole thing so he was quite prepared to give way to their argument.

This was a real shame, because he'd been right first time round.

'What about Robert?' said Groucho.

'Oh, I wouldn't wait for him,' said Trafalgar hastily. 'I expect he'll make his own way.'

Groucho looked down at the time team. 'Listen, future people, we had a plan to programme a robot to press the final button once we were in the sleep pods, but if you don't mind hanging around for a few more minutes, you could close us up and send us off yourself. That seems kind of fitting somehow, don't you think?'

They all nodded.

'Hey, maybe you could meet us the other end, in the year 0 SEGS? That would be fun.'

'Maybe,' said Trafalgar. 'By the way, what does SEGS stand for? I've always wondered.'

'You don't know? I dreamed it up myself. I thought you'd all know. Since Everything Got Smaller of course.'

In the silence after the lids of the pods had been sealed in place and the buttons had been pressed, someone remembered O'Barron.

'Maybe we should just leave him here,' suggested Stilts.

'We can't do that,' said Belle. 'He *is* our commander. We'll get into terrible trouble when we get back.'

'We'll be heroes,' said Stilts. 'Just think, there'll be no

fly problem and no mouse problem. The datastores won't be corrupted. It'll be a different world.'

'I'm not so sure,' said Trafalgar, seized by a new doubt. 'If it *is*, they won't know why we went in the first place, because there never will have been a problem, will there?'

They all stared at him in silence.

'What I mean is, if there wasn't a problem, then they wouldn't have had to send an expedition, would they? And if they didn't send an expedition then we would still be there, wouldn't we? And there wouldn't even *be* an ELV or a Ministry, would there? There'd be no need for the *Titanic* or us.'

Halogen Tinker spoke first. 'Ah!' he said. 'But that means that . . . If I understand correctly then . . . The only logical conclusion is . . . We must take care to . . . Don't you see that . . . ? Isn't it obvious that if . . . ? Have we had lunch yet because I'm . . . ?'

They went on staring. Nothing else came out.

'Thank you for sharing that with us, Tinker,' said Stilts. 'Personally I think this is all far too complicated to even try to understand so I vote we go on to where we started and see what's happened.'

'Taking O'Barron?'

'I suppose we have to.'

When they let O'Barron out of the drawer, he seemed to have calmed down and was almost rational.

'Have they all gone?' he asked. 'All the big people?'

'Yes.'

'A shame. I was going to demand an apology.'

'There's no one left to apologise,' said Trafalgar. 'Now, we think it's time to get going. We seem to have sorted out the flies and the mice.'

'But there's one more thing, Hurlock, and let me remind you I still expect proper respect from you. There's one more thing, I say. Do you not know what that is?'

'No,' he said.

'My wedding to Miss Ninety-Five. It must be performed at once, without delay. This is very fitting. There is now nobody left but us. I am therefore the supreme ruler on this planet at the present and what I command must be obeyed.'

'Do I get a say in this?' said Anya.

'No,' said O'Barron.

'Well, it won't count then,' she said.

'Oh yes, it will, under section 1 of the Marriage Act of whatever year this is, which I have just invented, passed and made law this minute. So there.'

'There's no one to perform the ceremony,' Trafalgar objected, horrified.

'I shall nominate someone.' O'Barron looked around him. Anya, face twisted in a mask of furious misery, was staring at Trafalgar, hoping for him to say or do something. Driven to desperation, he tried his best.

'O'Barron,' he started, 'I've got a word to say about this . . .'

Anya whispered, 'Oh yes, Trafalgar!' and her voice had its usual dreadful effect.

'. . . rubberwuck,' he ended somewhat lamely.

'And a very interesting word it is too, Hurlock, but not, I think, of great relevance to the present situation.' In his disturbed state of mind, O'Barron seemed to have forgotten the individual foibles of his team. He pointed at Halogen Tinker.

'You shall perform the ceremony,' he said. 'I nominate you as a minister of the First Church of the Blessed Bluto O'Barron.'

'That should make it a long service,' whispered Stilts.

'Five minutes,' said O'Barron. 'The service will begin

270

in five minutes. You must all be ready. You, you, you and you, come and help me dress.'

His pointing finger didn't include Puckeridge or Trafalgar who both used the next three hundred seconds for different purposes. Puckeridge crept away to the laboratory bench where it had dawned on him that he could find the materials for the best practical joke he had ever dreamt of. He took the two disabled mice out of the recycling bin and hid them in a storage chamber in the *Titanic*. Trafalgar used the first two hundred and seventy of the three hundred seconds to good effect by crumpling up into a small ball of misery and wishing the whole thing had never started. He used the next five seconds to sniff apprehensively as a scorching smell began to grow in strength and the following ten to be shaken violently by Trafalgar 2 who had appeared from the wisps of smoke and was shouting at him.

'GET UNDRESSED!' he yelled. 'NOW!'

'Why?'

'Don't argue. It's the only thing to do. Just believe me.'

Trafalgar stripped down to his pants and Trafalgar 2 put on his clothes with difficulty, hopping sideways as he did. He produced a roll of some very thin cable.

'Clip this on,' he said. 'I've improved it.'

Connected together, the howl-round stopped and Trafalgar had to admit that his older twin looked very convincing, except decidedly tougher and more experienced.

'All you have to do is stay out of sight,' said Trafalgar 2. 'Just stay hidden inside the box. You can watch through the holes. Don't move and don't say anything.'

'What box?'

'The box I'm going to put you in.'

*   *   *

It was the strangest setting for a wedding in the history of the world up to that point. The roof of Grand Central Fortress gave them a view out over the city. It was a view that made them wonder.

'I thought this was meant to be New York,' said Sopwith.

'It is. The computer said so. Groucho said so too,' answered Stilts.

'Well, what's that then, over there?'

'It's Big Ben,' said Stilts, looking at the far-off giant green figure of the woman holding up her torch on her island in the bay.

'And there's the River Thames and look . . . there's the Other River. It must be London. Look, there's where the Ministry will be. It *is* London.'

Trafalgar, listening from inside one of the many boxes scattered around the rooftop, knew the answer but Trafalgar 2, standing with the others, spoke for him.

'It's what we call London,' he said. 'They called it New York before the mice got to the databases. That's not really Big Ben, it's the Statue of Liberty.'

'Nonsense,' said O'Barron testily, standing there in his multi-coloured wedding gown and deep red veil. 'It's London and it's always been London. Now let's get on with it.'

Whatever the city's real name, it was an awesome sight. Mostly it was wreckage – derelict, fire-ravaged hulks of giant buildings reaching blackened fingers into the sky, but here and there in the ruins, a thousand small yellow robots were already hard at work, tearing down, sorting, cleaning and recycling for the day when they would start to rebuild it all on a one-sixth scale.

'Hurry up,' said O'Barron to Halogen Tinker, grabbing Anya's arm and pulling her towards him, despite her resistance.

'Right you ... I'll just er ... Let me see now, I ...'

'GET ON WITH IT.'

'Dearly ... er ... dearly beloved, we ... er ...'

'I'LL DO IT!' roared O'Barron.

'You ... er ... you can't marry yourself ... er ...'

'I'm the captain of the ship, I'm the Emperor of the World. I'M THE KING OF THE SHEEP. I CAN DO WHAT I LIKE!'

He turned to face his cowering audience. Trafalgar, peeping through the holes at his future twin, standing there silently, felt his heart lurch.

'Dearly beloved,' said O'Barron, 'I'm marrying this woman, okay? That's me, marrying her, right? If anyone objects let them say so right now if they dare so I can have them shot.'

'I object,' said Trafalgar 2 in a calm voice.

'WHAT? YOU DARE? GUARDS, SEIZE THAT MAN!'

Everyone else looked at each other. There was a chorus of 'I'm not a guard, am I?' and 'No, I'm not either. No one said I was. Maybe he is.'

Trafalgar 2 sorted out the confusion by walking up to O'Barron, punching him accurately on the chin and folding his unconscious body into the nearest empty box. Then he turned to Anya.

'I've loved you for a very long time,' he said. 'I just couldn't say so because my voice would never work. Will you marry me?'

TWENTY-TWO

They carried O'Barron back to the *Titanic* but he began to stir as they laid him on the floor of the hold. Stilts went up to the control deck to set the coordinates for their final return with enormous care. Trafalgar was gazing into Anya's eyes in a somewhat soppy way and enjoying the experience of not really needing to try to say anything to her.

Puckeridge was feeling rather worried.

It had been a simple and delightful plan.

He had been thinking how very funny it would be to get back home, to a mouse-free London and scare the hell out of the others at some suitable moment by casually leaving the two deactivated mice somewhere where they would be sure to find them. He was so pleased with himself for thinking of it that he went and looked in the storage cupboard while everyone was busy getting ready to leave, just to have a quick gloat over them.

The cupboard was bare.

At first he thought someone else must have found the mice and moved them, so he went round casually saying things like, 'I hope those mice are safe in that recycling bin,' to see what reaction he would get, but everyone just agreed with him.

It was when he went back for a closer look that he found the small, splintered hole in the bottom corner of the cupboard and a terrible doubt grew in his mind.

In a sense it wasn't entirely Puckeridge's fault. John had been deeply attached to his joker mouse project.

When the President told him to switch the mice off, he hadn't fully obeyed. It was true that he had turned off the power but only on the half-hour delay circuit. He'd figured there was every chance they would find a way out of the recycling bin when the power came back on and he didn't know they were going to get a bit of outside help from Puckeridge. John was firmly of the opinion that the world had been taking itself far too seriously for far too long and that was one of the reasons it had got itself into this mess. He believed he had a mission to confuse and amuse and the world would be a better place for it.

All that Puckeridge believed was that he was going to be in deep trouble if anyone ever found out what he'd done. He went out into the great hall of Grand Central Fortress and searched around just in case he could see the mice but there was nothing. Standing in the silence, all he heard or thought he heard was the faintest of electronic giggles fading down a far-off corridor so he returned sadly to the ship.

'Okay, everybody,' said Stilts, 'take plenty of tablets. I think we're ready to go.'

'Nooo,' moaned O'Barron, sitting up. 'Nobody goes anywhere.'

'We can go home now, sir,' Stilts explained patiently. 'I've got everything ready.'

'This is home,' said O'Barron in a firmer voice. 'You are my subjects. This is my empire. We will stay. We will create the Empire of Graceland *here*. I was led astray before by you fools. Wasting my time with that pretender, the idiot Olvis. It is obvious to me now. I AM ELVIS. I am destined to be the greatest Emperor in the world. I SHALL RULE ON THE BLUE SUEDE THRONE and it shall be HERE.'

'Oh blimey,' said Rumpole. 'Not again.'

'It's all perfectly clear,' said O'Barron. 'WE are our ancestors. The future population of the world will come from US, from me and the Empress.'

'Do you feel like hitting him again?' Stilts whispered to Trafalgar. 'Because if you do, this would be a very good moment.'

Before anyone could do anything, O'Barron rushed at the control panel and began attacking it with his fists.

'We don't need this any more,' he panted. 'We don't need time travel because we are staying here for ever.'

Trafalgar and Stilts jumped on him to try to restrain him but he fought with insane strength against them, flailing around at the time machine. His fist connected with an unlabelled button they'd never dared try and a croaky synthesised voice came from within the machine.

'Thank you for setting the countdown timer. This machine will depart in thirty seconds from now. Please make sure you have all your baggage with you at this time.'

They stopped fighting and looked at it in surprise.

'The countdown timer is now operating. This machine will depart in twenty-five seconds.'

O'Barron pulled himself away from them and rushed to the ladder. They raced after him down to the cargo bay but he was out of the doors before they could catch him.

They leapt out after him but the countdown was still going on.

'This machine will depart in twenty seconds.'

'There's nothing we can do,' said Stilts, slowing to stop. 'We can't get left behind. Leave him. We can always come back for him.'

O'Barron looked perfectly happy, finally the monarch of all he surveyed. He climbed on to a box, gyrated his pelvis in the tattered remains of his wedding gown and launched into 'Lonesome Tonight' in such an appallingly flat monotone that Trafalgar finally decided he deserved to be exactly that and followed Stilts back into the *Titanic*.

'This machine will depart in ten seconds,' said the voice.

Trafalgar felt a hard shape digging in to his hip and pulled an envelope out of his pocket. Trafalgar 2 must have put it there before he gave him back his clothes. He was about to open it when a horrible thought struck him.

'Did you programme it for exactly the place and time we left?' he asked Stilts.

'Yes, of course,' said Stilts. 'Why?'

'Because if we didn't sort out the fly problem . . .'

'. . . we're going to be under a collapsing building,' finished Stilts as they both raced for the ladder up to the control deck. They got to the top to see all the others sitting ready for the time jump and three things happened.

The first was the voice saying, 'Zero. This machine is departing now.'

The second was the usual cranial explosion of a time jump.

The third was a building collapsing on them.

In the chaos of falling masonry and splintering wood, Trafalgar just had time to think, hey ho, so much for the fly solution, when everything went very black and dusty. When the noise stopped and he painfully levered himself out from under something heavy, he couldn't see a thing.

'Anya?' he called fearfully.

'I'm over here.'

'Wherbbbl?'

'Next to me,' said Belle. 'I think I'm on top of Tinker.'

'And I'm underneath Sopwith,' said another voice.

'Who's that?'

'Ah! You've got me there, I'm afraid.'

A new voice chimed in. 'I . . . er . . . I'm over . . . This is . . . Have we . . . ?'

The rest announced themselves one by one.

'So it didn't work,' said Belle. 'There are still flies.'

A light glowed, revealing a jumble of dusty faces. Stilts had found an unbroken torch in the wreckage.

Puckeridge looked particularly miserable. 'Er, guys,' he said, 'I have a horrible feeling there are still mice too.'

Trafalgar found he was still clutching the envelope. On the outside it said, 'To be read when you find you're still clutching this envelope.' He opened it and held it to the light.

'To myself,' it said. 'About now, you will finally realise that although it is possible to travel through time, it is impossible to do anything at all to change what is going to happen.'

Hang on, he thought to himself, what about all the things I *did* change, right from the very start – bringing myself clothes in the shower, rescuing myself with a boat, training Daisy, hitting O'Barron, telling Anya what I felt. He read on.

'No,' the letter said, 'you didn't *change* those things. They each only happened once and that's the way they happened.'

This is annoying, thought Trafalgar, it's like having someone reading over my shoulder.

'Yes, it is annoying, isn't it?' he read. 'But the point I'm trying to make is you can't go and change things that have already been seen to happen in the future. However much you try, history will always find a way to turn it back again, hence the flies, hence the mice. When you got yourself out of trouble by deciding Daisy was a *trained* wolf all you did was dump the job of training her on me, right? I mean *someone* was going to have to go back and do it. It always happened like that. Speaking of which, I can tell you, you're going to have a very busy time in the future. By the way, while we're on that subject, I'm afraid I've just lost the time machine in a poker game in the year 485 SEGS so I've had to come back while you lot were crashing and get it from you.'

Surely that's logically impossible, thought Trafalgar.

'Yes, it probably is,' said the letter, 'but quite frankly, I'm beyond caring. That's how I got the damned thing in the first place after all.'

You won it in a poker game? You mean after all *that* I didn't invent it? thought Trafalgar.

'No, of course you didn't,' said the letter. 'What on earth do you know about time machines? Anyway time travel gives you a terrible headache and gets you absolutely nowhere in the long run. By the way, you'll find the way out behind the control panel.'

Is that all? thought Trafalgar. I wonder if there's anything on the back? He turned it over. 'Yes, there is,' the letter said. 'Just remember, the idea you get when you're going up the tunnel is a very good one. Stick to it.'

What idea?

When they heaved the broken control panel to one side, Stilts noticed the hole where the time machine had been and Trafalgar had to explain the contents of the letter.

'Yes . . .' said Tinker excitedly. 'That's exactly what . . . I was trying to say . . . before . . .'

'Hey, that made up a sentence,' said Stilts.

'Oh, so it did,' said Tinker, pleased.

Dim daylight shone through a jagged hole. They pulled rocks out of the way and the daylight grew stronger.

'We'd better face the music,' said Trafalgar.

'Yes,' said Stilts, 'total ignominious failure on both parts of the mission, plus the fact that we've managed to strand

279

an important government minister several hundred years in the past. We are not going to be popular.'

There was a glum silence.

'I'll go first,' said Trafalgar and he began to crawl up the tunnel with Anya behind, hanging on to his ankle for comfort.

He could hear anxious voices calling. He recognised Anonymous McWhirter's raucous tones.

'It's a tragedy,' the PR man was yelling. 'All those wonderful, talented people squashed flat. The Minister too. Get the cameras in closer.'

A sudden wonderful idea came to Trafalgar out of nowhere. He stopped and heard a chain reaction of grunts as the rest of the team piled up behind him.

'Listen everyone,' he said, 'I think I know what to do. After all, nobody out there knows we've actually gone . . .'

The memorial service for Bluto O'Barron was held the following week. Saccharine Fernandez gave a speech and the time team were star guests, along with the new Minister of Knowledge, Genghis Lemmon. Trafalgar had his fingers firmly crossed that his future self wasn't going to deliver the minister back at some embarrassing moment, like halfway through the ceremony, but it all went smoothly.

'It is a tragedy,' said Saccharine Fernandez, 'that this epic voyage failed to achieve its objectives – this voyage so brilliantly conceived and prepared by the genius who now lies entombed for ever with the remains of his time ship under the building. We shall leave the rubble undisturbed as his memorial, his very own burial mound, and perhaps one day we shall build another time ship to replace the one we have lost. Then, in his memory, we shall sally forth again to push back the frontiers of time.'

She shook her head, squeezed an onion inside her handkerchief and a little tear trickled prettily down her face.

'Just another few seconds,' she said. 'It was a cruel fate. Another few seconds and the expedition would have had time to start their machine before the building collapsed. As it is they never had the chance to even try.'

Here she turned to smile at the time team, lined up beside her and they all nodded in solemn agreement.

Only Forward
Michael Marshall Smith

A truly stunning debut from a young author. Extremely original, satyrical and poignant, a marriage of numerous genres brilliantly executed to produce something entirely new.

Stark is a troubleshooter. He lives in The City - a massive conglomeration of self-governing Neighbourhoods, each with their own peculiarity. Stark lives in Colour, where computers co-ordinate the tone of the street lights to match the clothes that people wear. Close by is Sound where noise is strictly forbidden, and Ffnaph where people spend their whole lives leaping on trampolines and trying to touch the sky. Then there is Red, where anything goes, and all too often does.

At the heart of them all is the Centre - a back-stabbing community of 'Actioneers' intent only on achieving - divided into areas like 'The Results are what Counts sub-section' which boasts 43 grades of monorail attendant. Fell Alkland, Actioneer extraordinaire has been kidapped. It is up to Stark to find him. But in doing so he is forced to confront the terrible secrets of his past. A life he has blocked out for too long.

'Michael Marshall Smith's *Only Forward* is a dark labyrinth of a book: shocking, moving and surreal. Violent, outrageous and witty - sometimes simultaneously - it offers us a journey from which we return both shaken and exhilarated. An extraordinary debut.'
Clive Barker

ISBN 0 586 21774 6

Neuromancer
William Gibson

'A masterpiece that moves faster than the speed of thought and is chilling in its implications'   *New York Times*

The Matrix: a graphic representation of data abstracted from the banks of every computer in the human system; a consensual hallucination experienced daily by billions of legitimate users in the Sprawl alone. And by Case, computer cowboy, until his nervous system is grievously maimed by a client he double crossed. Japanese experts in nerve splicing and microbionics have left him broke and close to dead. But at last Case has found a cure. He's going back into the system. Not for the bliss of cyberspace but to steal again, this time from the big boys, the almighty megacorps. In return, should he survive, he will stay cured.

Cyberspace and virtual reality were invented in this book. It stands alongside *1984* and *Brave New World* as one of the twentieth century's most potent novels of the future.

'Case is the Marlowe of the mainframe age'   *Vox*

'The pessimistic vision of *Neuromancer* has inspired technologists from Silicon Valley to Wall Street and a global network of computer hackers who have committed countless nefarious deeds in the book's honour . . . *Neuromancer* was a literary Big Bang'   *The Sunday Times*

'Set for brainstun . . . one of the most unusual and involving narratives to be read in many an artificially blue moon'   *The Times*

'A mindbender of a read . . . fully realized in its technological and psychosexual dimensions'   *Village Voice*

ISBN 0 00 648041-1

Mona Lisa
Overdrive

William Gibson

'Brilliant . . . a delight to read. No one can ever hope to out-Gibson Gibson . . . A true original'   *Sunday Times*

'Gibson's most accomplished book to date, a futurist hybrid of Fleming and Deighton and Bester'   *Time Out*

Mona's pimp sells her to a plastic surgeon in New York and she's turned overnight into someone else. The pimp winds up dead. Mona weeps for him. She's a sweet, dumb girl . . . so far.

Angie the famous Hollywood stim-star has started remembering things. Despite the efforts of studio bosses to keep her in ignorance, Angie will discover who she really is . . . and why she doesn't need to jack into the Matrix in order to enter cyberspace.

In the depths of the rustbelt, the ring of steel garbage and toxic waste surrounding the Sprawl, Gentry obsessively seeks the darkest secrets of the Matrix. Seeking rapture.

When an impossibly tall and powerful skyscraper of data appears suddenly in the landscape of the Matrix, Gentry is ready for it, Angie is part of it, and Mona is set for overdrive. Rapture is on the agenda for all three, but others greedy for money and power will fight them to the death, whatever *death* means.

'Gibson can spin a gripping yarn. He builds up a great head of steam within the first few pages and doesn't relax until the end'   *Times Literary Supplement*

ISBN 0 00 648044 6

Philip K. Dick

The Game-Players of Titan

'The most brilliant sci-fi mind on any planet' *Rolling Stone*

Roaming the pristine landscape of Earth, cared for by machines and aliens, the few remaining humans alive since the war with Titan play Bluff to maximise the remote chance some pairings will produce a child. When Pete Garden, a particularly suicidal member of the Pretty Blue Fox game-playing group, loses his current wife and his deed to Berkeley, he stumbles upon a far bigger, more sinister version of the game. The telepathic Vugs of Titan are the players and at stake is the Earth itself.

'One of the most original practitioners writing any kind of fiction'
Sunday Times

Philip K. Dick

Clans of the Alphane Moon

'My favourite author'   FAY WELDON

Chuck Rittersdorf, a 21st century CIA robot programmer, decides to kill his wife by remote control. He enlists the aid of a telepathic Ganymedean slime mould called Lord Running Clam, an attractive female police officer, and various others – witting or unwitting. But when Chuck finds himself in the midst of an interplanetary spy ring on an Alphane moon inhabited entirely by certified maniacs, his personal revenge plans begin to go awry in this brilliantly inventive tale of interstellar madness, murder and violence.

'If it is ideas that you want, then Philip K. Dick is the author to read'   *Vector*

The Plenty Principle

Colin Greenland

'The Verdi of Space Opera' BRIAN ALDISS

Tabitha Jute is back, in a revealing excursion to the Galaxy's weirdest backwater. Umbriel, where daytime is night, where dreams rise gasping in boiling wells – where Tabitha must courier the most bizarre cargo she has ever encountered.

Here, under one cover for the first time, are Colin Greenland's finest short stories. The brand new Tabitha Jute novella, *The Well Wishers*, forms the centrepiece around which many other gems revolve. They include the author's curve on Neil Gaiman's Sandman, Michael Moorcock's Elric and Brian Talbot's Rose Wylde, alongside his own equally unsettling creations such as Grandma who really must not be let downstairs; obstinate, canine policemen; and the long-dead ticket collector in the station with no name.

Greenland's characters range from the merely colourful to the incandescent. They populate worlds that shift when you blink. Some of these worlds are our own. But some of them may not be.

Praise for the Tabitha Jute series:

'A heroine so real she keeps tampons in her handbag' *The Face*

'Tabitha Jute . . . a cussed, cantankerous, self-centred Han Solo - who saves the world regularly, pulls all the sexy guys, and still ends up all alone in the launderette of life, watching her socks go round' GWYNETH JONES, *New York Review of Science Fiction*

'Space-opera of the grungy, dirty-realist variety . . . *Seasons of Plenty* is a superior example of distressed-leather, high-octane interstellar swashbuckling' *Time Out*